# Bel Amour

~ .~ .~. ~

## Caroline Muntjewerf

Coinyard Publishing®

The right of Caroline Muntjewerf to be identified as the author of this work has been asserted by her in accordance with the Copyright, Designs and Patents Act 1988.

ISBN/EAN: 978-90-833146-6-2

Second edition
First published in March 2013

Join the Readers List here and get your free Ebook:
https://cmuntjewerf.com

Other novels by Caroline Muntjewerf:

The Stories
Return To Les Jonquières
Of Dutch Descent

van Hollandse Afkomst (Dutch)
Avondstond (Dutch)

Holländische Wurzeln (German)

# Bel Amour

## ~1~

*T*o certain people, airports might hold a degree of excitement. Divides into the unknown, boundaries where just beyond adventure lies, but Kate is merely struck by their forlornness. Heathrow is no exception. Her eyes rest on a child who leans against a small suitcase. The little one seems to be alone. Shyly she catches Kate's smile who wonders where the child's parents might be.

A cleaner languidly turns over garbage bins. He doesn't empty them entirely, he wants to leave something for his next round. It's hard to find work nowadays.

'Darling, we're boarding.' Kate's partner nudges her with his elbow. She hates it when he does that. He jumps up and grabs her by the arm in an attempt to make her follow him.

'Why the rush?' she asks. 'There is still time, the plane won't leave without us.'

'You know I hate to be last,' he says.

There's reluctance in her demeanour when she stands up to wait in line with the rest of the first-class passengers who have the privilege of boarding before others.

Just as they walk through the gate, Kate turns her head. She sees a woman hurriedly approach the child and grab it by the hand. It's their turn now to board the plane.

'I still don't see why you want to buy in Tennessee,' he says. 'We have a great place here.'

'*You* have a great place here,' Kate says.

He draws her closer to him, not minding her long blonde hair. His grip pulls, and Kate feels a tweak at the back of her head.

'Yes, well. I assume it will be *ours* in the near future.

*Darling.*' Coming from his mouth, the endearing address has the uncanny ability to lose its meaning.

She releases from his grip when they enter the aircraft.

'I wish we had talked about this more carefully. I think it's totally unnecessary,' he says, and almost drops the bag, he is putting in the overhead bin, on his head.

'I told you, John, there was no need for you to come with me.'

'Darling. I couldn't let you travel all that way by yourself.'

Kate sighs and makes herself comfortable in her seat. She takes a file from her bag as she plans to catch up on arrears; the company she built with her brother Jacob takes up much of her time. They are now focusing on the American market.

'Can we have a drink, please?' John asks the flight attendant, who is welcoming the passengers.

'One moment, sir,' she replies.

He sits down in the seat next to Kate's and takes out his files and laptop. With a sigh, he decides to work on the laptop first.

'I don't understand this George Walker,' he says. 'What does he expect me to do with this rubbish?'

Kate makes a few annotations on her paper, then looks his way. 'You will like the property I've set my mind on in Tennessee,' she says.

'... Yes. Well. I suppose we could use it as a holiday hideaway.'

The flight attendant offers them a drink from the bar. Kate declines. John takes a scotch.

'Always the same,' he says. 'I'm always the one having to sort out the rubbish *they*'ve got themselves into.'

Kate rests her hand on his arm; she can't have him grumbling so early on in the journey. He closes the laptop and puts it away. 'Well, I suppose I can work on it while you're house hunting on the other side,' he says.

Kate continues thumbing through her folder, scrutinising specific passages, while the flight attendant takes the glass from John. Soon the security procedures are demonstrated as the aircraft backs away from the terminal.

'Have you switched off your mobile, John?'

He fumbles through his jacket and finds his phone in his pocket. He quickly checks a message before turning it off.

'Mother. Telling us to be aware,' he elaborates. She doesn't like America.'

Kate looks out the window and sees the plane manoeuvre on to the runway. The waiting time hasn't delayed them, and soon they're taking off. Kate watches the scenery slide underneath her and life down below diminishing until only fields outlined by green trees can be seen and minute houses where traffic snakes past. She looks beside her and sees John's eyelids fall. She then closes her folders to put them away and relaxes back in her seat.

Hours have elapsed when Kate opens her eyes and sees the city of Memphis coming into view. They're on final approach, and the touchdown is imminent. The aircraft slides onto the runway and the plane taxis towards the terminal building. Still somnolent, Kate tries to remember the last time she arrived here. It has been at least fifteen years since she set foot in the country she was born. Then, their grandparents accompanied her and her brother. Grandfather has since died, rather unexpectedly, no one had anticipated it. Strokes seem to come without warning. Grandmother appears to cope well with her son Henry living in the same manor.

Kate calmly shakes John. He had fallen fast asleep soon after a late breakfast was served.

'We're here, John.'

'What? Where?' He looks around in bewilderment.

'We have to get off the plane. We're here.'

'Where? ... And where's my hot towel?' he asks.

Kate gathers her belongings to disembark. John follows her example. 'We're flying First for Christ's sake. Not even a hot towel. How will I refresh myself?'

'We'll be at the hotel soon,' Kate says.

'Did you get one?' John wants to know.

Kate begins to walk to the exit door and exchanges the obligatory 'thank you, goodbye' with the flight attendants before going through the door and into the aisle. John follows close behind. 'I'm starving,' he says.

The wait at Customs is not long, and their passport check runs without difficulty. John doesn't waste time to get to the baggage claim where Kate takes a seat and watches him grab their suitcases off the baggage belt and swing them onto a trolley. He looks her way with an impatience that corresponds with his character and motions her to come.

When they walk through the doors leading outside, the warmer weather is instantly noticeable. Kate feels elated. She gazes up at the hard blue sky. The warmth of the sun strokes her face.

'Damn! It's hot here,' John blurts out.

'Cab?' a taxi driver asks and opens the door in front of Kate.

John leaves the trolley with the cases on the pavement and follows Kate into the taxi. The cabdriver lifts the luggage in the trunk and then sits behind the wheel.

'What hotel, ma'am?'

'The Madison. Downtown,' John replies. 'I shall have a shower as soon as we arrive, and then some food,' he informs Kate. 'I'm starving.'

'Of course,' Kate says.

'Where're y'all from?' the driver asks.

'UK,' John answers.

'What, sir?'

'UK. United Kingdom.'

'Aah.' The cabdriver appears to understand from where they originate. 'How d'ya like Memphis?'

'We don't know yet, we just arrived,' John says sharply and casts an exasperated look at the back of the driver's head.

'I'm sure we will like it very much,' Kate says.

'I'm sure y'all will. You've come the right time, y'know. Last week ...'

John looks out the car window uttering a wearisome sigh as the cabdriver tells them about all the events honouring Memphis' favourite son that have only just ended. Street banners still show signs of the week gone by when 'millions' of people flooded Memphis, as they do each year in August.

The cab comes to a halt in front of a corporate looking building. Before the cabdriver can open the door for her, Kate gets out of the car. A doorman swiftly helps to take the suitcases from the trunk and put them on a trolley.

'Be sure to visit Graceland now ya' hear,' the cabdriver says as he wipes the sweat off his forehead. Kate gives him a friendly nod.

'Let's get out of this heat,' John says and takes Kate

by her arm.

They enter the coldness of the air-conditioned hotel where muffled voices meet them in the busy lobby. John looks around and then steers Kate through to the reception desk where he registers and collects the keys, before shepherding Kate to the lifts.

On reaching their room, John throws off his clothes and enters the bathroom, while Kate tips the bellboy. She takes off her shoes and pulls up a chair to relax by the window overlooking part of the city and the Mississippi River. Despite her fatigue, a feeling of delight envelops her, delight encouraged by her return to where she hails from. Her blue eyes twinkle as she enjoys the view. It's just like she pictured the old town to be. The sun's rays frolic on the smooth surface of the dark water below, that's only rippled now and then by ships that slide across it. Distant traffic hurries over the bridge leading across this mighty river. From behind the large, double-glazed hotel room window, it radiates a peaceful panorama.

Kate turns her head when she hears a soft beep, coming from the pile of clothes that John left scattered half on the bed and on the floor. She ignores his mobile phone, casting her gaze towards a paddle steamer that has just made its way to the quayside.

'Are you ready?'

John's sudden voice takes Kate by surprise. She hadn't noticed the water flow stopping on the other side of the door.

'I'd like to freshen up first if you don't mind,' Kate says.

'Sure.' He rubs his damp fair hair, where Kate has recently detected the odd grey one. 'Won't be long myself.'

She takes a pair of jeans and a blouse from her

suitcase and lays them out on the bed before going into the bathroom. 'There should be a good restaurant not far from here,' she addresses John through the open bathroom door. 'Fine.' John tosses a few pieces of clothing from his suitcase until he decides on what to wear. He opts for his Lagerfeld trousers and Calvin Klein shirt.
'I think it's Greek,' Kate's voice sounds.
'What?'
'The restaurant.'
He looks at himself in the mirror. 'As long as they have food. I'm starving.'

'Darling, did I tell you, you look wonderful tonight?' John says as he looks from his plate over to Kate, who smiles at him, lifting her glass with white wine. 'Cheers.'
John does the same.
'To the house,' Kate says.
'What?'
'The house. You do remember why we came here, I hope.'
'Ah yes, the house.' He dabs some bread in the olive oil scattered around the salad leaves on his plate. 'Would you mind awfully, if I didn't come with you tomorrow to view it?' he says. 'You know how I feel about all this, and darling, to be honest, I'm not sure if it is ever going to materialise.' He looks at her. 'I hope you don't mind.'
'Of course not,' Kate says. 'But I do need to have a place to live when Jacob and I are expanding the business. You do understand?'
'Naturally. But you could get a nice, small apartment here in the city. The business will be here, not out there in the countryside.' He gives a cautionary nod.
'We'll see,' Kate says.
'Darling, I just don't want you to get your hopes up

and then be disappointed.'

Kate smiles at him. 'We'll see. Let's finish this lovely food.'

John shakes his head. 'Don't say I didn't tell you when things go amiss.'

On the eastern horizon, a pale pink sky tries to escape the dark blue sphere, which still carries some glittering sparks. A soft pink that the sun sends forth as she drifts to another part of the planet to announce a new day. The skies soon fade, paling to yellow until the sun bursts out in a brightness that blinds the eyes and warms the earth.

In her knee-length nightgown, Kate stands in front of the window, unaffected by jet lag. She slept well after the wine of last night had kicked in.

The peacefulness of morning is suddenly disrupted by the shrill sound of the ringing phone by the bed. John moans from under the cover, and sleepy-eyed he shows his face.

'What the ... '

Kate walks towards the bed and picks up the phone. 'It's for you,' she says softly and lays it down on the duvet. John sounds annoyed when his hand searches for the telephone. 'Don't these people know what time it is ... bugger.'

'Hello ... What? What message ... I never received ... Mother? Oh, my God ... Is she all right? I mean ... '

Kate now turns to face John, who sits up in the bed.

'I shall have to come back,' he says. 'Listen, I don't care, I shall have to. She's my mother. I will arrange for a flight today ... Yes, thank you for letting me know. Thanks, Ron.'

As he lets the phone slip from his hand, a worried look appears on John's face.

'I'll have to make arrangements,' he says as he glances up at Kate.

'What happened? How is your mother?' Kate wants to know.

'She had a fall when she was on that outing with the Ladies. They took her to the hospital.'

'Poor thing.'

'Yes. Poor thing. I keep warning her,' he says,' keep telling her she's getting too old for these outings. She never listens.' He throws the covers off and gets up. 'Will you come back with me?' he asks.

Kate shakes her head. 'No, you know I can't do that. I have things to arrange here.'

'I shall have to leave you on your own then,' he says with caution in his voice.

'I'll be fine.'

John starts looking through his bags to find the necessary documents.

'I'll order us some breakfast,' Kate says. 'I'm rather hungry now.'

'You ate like a horse yesterday. How can you be hungry?'

'It must be the air,' Kate replies casually, as she dials room service.

John shakes his head. 'I don't think I can eat right now.' He looks for his mobile and finds it in his jacket. 'There *was* a message,' he says. 'Last night. Have you not heard it bleep?'

'I didn't realise your mobile worked over here,' Kate says ignorantly. 'You said they have a different system here.'

'Of course it works. It works everywhere!'

Kate seems indifferent. She goes to the bathroom, where she runs the bath.

'Aren't you meeting the estate agent today?' John asks.

'Around lunchtime,' Kate replies, tying her long blonde hair in a knot. 'We'll go and see the property this afternoon. It's a shame you can't come.'

'That's totally out of the question now,' he says. 'I might be on a plane back to England this afternoon.'

Kate lowers her naked body into the refreshing water, as John walks into the bathroom and sits down on the edge of the tub.

'I don't like leaving you here by yourself,' he says.

Playfully Kate splashes a bit of water his way. 'I told you, I'll be fine. You seem to forget I lived here when I was young. This place is not strange to me.'

He leans over to kiss her. 'This is how I like you most. Sexy and wet.'

'Don't be so corny!' Kate responds.

There's a knock on their door.

'Oops, breakfast,' she says.

A gleaming blue Cadillac pulls up in front of the hotel. Kate remembers how she and Jacob used to watch cars like that drive by on the Interstate. They would make up stories about when they were grown up and had lots of money. Money that would buy them all the fancy things they wanted. A big house where they could live with their mum and daddy, who would then drive a fancy car too. But the bubble always burst as soon as they turned to walk up the dirt road, back to their trailer, wondering what they would have for supper. Bread and beans again?

This time it is for real. He might have aged some twenty years, but Kate recognises the man and waves at the former surveyor who will join her to view the property. He waves back from behind the wheel. By sheer coincidence, Kate had located this old friend of her father.

'Mr Jones,' Kate says through the open car window, '*so* lovely to see you.'

'Earl. Please,' he replies and opens the door for her. 'You look well, miss Jennings.'

'Kate. Please,' she insists and sits down next to him. 'You don't look too bad yourself, Earl.'

He smiles. 'Yeah, considering. My, I'm still in awe. When I heard it was you interested in the property. I still remember you and your brother, skinny little things, and look at you now.'

'It's good to be back,' she says with a cheerful glint in her eyes.

'I'm glad y'all have done so well over there in England. I tell ya, the folks around here have been worried about you and little Jacob after that tragic accident with your folks.'

'We were well looked after by our grandparents,' Kate says.

Earl drives alongside the river before following the route into the city to show Kate present-day Memphis. Kate sits back to enjoy the scenery, and she tries to remember her days growing up in this area as a child. Memories flash by, but much of it is blurred, like photographs that weren't focused correctly and are missing detail. She has never been back to the village after Daddy's funeral.

Her grandparents had insisted for their daughter to be laid to rest in England, where she belonged. She and Jacob went with them then. Daddy's family were too poor to look after them.

'Have you ever been back this way to see your folks over here?'

Earl's sudden voice startles Kate. 'Sorry?'

'Have you ever been back?'

'Uh, yes. We came with our grandparents about fifteen years ago.' She pauses a moment. 'Jacob and I were reluctant to go to the village … By the time we wanted to go, we had to fly back.'

'I can make a detour if you want,' Earl suggests.

Kate shakes her head. 'Better not. I'll be here a while yet.'

'It hasn't changed much,' Earl says. 'Still a backward town. Most young kids move on, nothing for them there.'

Kate recalls the years when she and her brother were growing up in England and learnt that their mother had received a good education and still she had decided to live in a town like Flat Junction, marrying a poor Tennessean. Something that had Kate puzzled, and to this day they're unaware of their parents' reasoning for remaining in the village after they were married. Summers were so hot you could see the earth crack in front of your feet. Winters were cold and wet. Her mum and daddy were always trying to keep the heater in the trailer from giving up, for they couldn't afford a new one. One day the heater broke, and Daddy had a hard time fixing it. Mum had wrapped her and Jacob in a blanket, snuggled close together, while they were trying to repair the heater.

Earl turns into a gravel road and drives on. Soon Kate sees the house nestled at the bottom of a knoll, surrounded by fields and trees. The house had always looked so distant, so far out of reach when she had looked at it from behind the windscreen in her daddy's beat-up pick-up truck.

'All this land belongs to the property,' Earl informs her. 'There's a swimming pool at the back.' He turns his head. 'But I suppose you'd prefer to swim in the creek,' he jokingly adds.

'It has a creek too?'

'Sure. All thrown in.'

They drive up to the front of the house where Kate notices an estate agent waiting by his car. Before they get out, Earl mentions that he has already had a good look around the property. 'It is certainly worth the asking price, but I would haggle. They have a bit of a hard time selling it,' he says in a soft voice.

They approach the estate agent, and Kate shakes the young man's hand before following him into the house. The homely feeling overwhelms her as soon as they enter.

She looks up in the spacious, bright hall, seeing the broad staircase run to the first floor.

'It looks like you're in awe, miss Jennings,' the estate agent says. 'Let me show you the rest of the house. It's an extraordinary property for that price.'

'I hear you have a hard time selling it,' Kate says. 'Why is that?'

The man shrugs his shoulders. 'Many people want it but can't actually afford it.'

Kate glances over to Earl.

'How long has it been on the market?' she asks.

'About ten, twelve years,' the man says. 'But, uh, we've rented it out most of the time. As you can see, no cobwebs,' he adds with a grin.

They walk onto the patio bordering the swimming pool. Kate admires the distant view.

'Isn't it spectacular?' the estate agent says. Kate turns to Earl. 'What is your judgement?'

'It needs some work here and there,' Earl replies.

Kate takes Earl by his arm to separate him from the estate agent. 'I didn't want to look too excited in front of *him*,' she says in a soft voice, 'but I want this place. As soon as we walked in the door, I felt I'd come home.'

Earl nods understandably.

'So, what's the real reason this property won't sell easily?'

'Hard to tell, he could be right. It might be above most people's budget. Did you know the Bakers that used to own this place?

'Vaguely. Their sons went to a different school from us.'

'Well, about a year after you and your brother had gone over to England, tragedy struck here too. It ripped the family apart, and Jon Baker was found dead one day. Shot himself.'

Kate looks shocked but is curious. 'What happened?'

'Same old story, the wife got estranged from him. It appeared that their happy family existence wasn't so happy after all. When he'd gone, Mrs Baker sold the property and moved back east with the boys. New owners claimed the house was haunted and eventually sold it, quite cheaply I must add, to the estate agency.' He nods in the direction of the man who is still waiting patiently.

Kate briefly considers. 'So, I could offer below the asking price?'

'You can try. Ghosts don't scare you?'

'Have you seen any around here?'

Earl smiles.

'Besides,' Kate adds, 'England is riddled with ghosts.'

Earl bursts out in a guttural laugh. 'I suppose it is,' he says guffawing.

Kate turns to the estate agent. 'I think we can do business,' she says.

A streak of sunlight streams brightly between buildings and onto the street. Kate shields her eyes as she exits the bank building, and is soon absorbed by late-afternoon shoppers and people on their way to after-work venues. She strolls along a pedestrian zone and sits down at an empty table of a street-side coffee shop.

'Soya cappuccino, please,' Kate tells the enquiring waitress.

Afternoons like these have a sense of pleasing friendliness, satisfied people in the streets, happy that another working day is over but equally pleased to go back the following day. Not everybody is pleased it emerges. A mother pulls an obstinate child by the hand, and when Kate wonders who cast the shadow over her table, she finds a woman in basic clothes asking her for money, her cupped hand close to her frayed dress. The woman can't be more than thirty-five. She might even be the same age as herself, but the worried expression on her face makes her look older. Seeing this woman in her simple dress generates recollections in Kate's mind about her own life when she was a child. Kate is tempted, but as she reaches for her handbag, the waitress anticipates her.

'Scat!' she says in a loud voice.

The woman disappears as fleetingly as she had appeared.

'I'm sorry 'bout that, ma'am,' the waitress says and puts the cappuccino on the table.

Kate gives her a friendly nod, but her eyes search for the destitute woman.

Quietly sipping her coffee Kate watches the area being draped in longer shadows as the sun slowly disappears behind inner-city buildings, leaving the square in a warm shade. She decides to walk back to the hotel and soak up the atmosphere of the city that is close to her memories.

Noisy cars rush from one traffic light to the next,

making way for pedestrians where obligated. Kate finds a way that leads her along the river, whereupon ships float past in the distance while the noise of the city is absorbed by the waters of the Mississippi. She soon reaches a path that leads her back to the hotel.

John opens the door to their room as soon as she puts the key in the lock.

'Kate. Darling.' He gives her a perfunctory kiss on the cheek. 'Where have you been all afternoon?'

'Hello John, and how was your day?'

'Darling, I'm glad you're back. I've had such a dreadful time. Can you imagine? I've been on the phone *all* afternoon, but you know those Americans, they speak in a most peculiar accent. You can't explain a thing to them. Only just now I managed to book us on a flight. Tonight.'

'Us, John?'

'I ... I couldn't reach you.'

'John, I have things to arrange here. I am *not* coming back with you.'

She takes off her shoes and walks into the bathroom.

'Kate, please, we can come back at a later date. I know how much you would like to buy a house here, but it's hardly a necessity.'

The shower starts running on the other side of the bathroom door.

'The flight's at midnight.'

Kate pops her head around the door. 'I'm sorry John. I told you before. I have things to organise here.'

'What things?'

He enters the bathroom. 'Kate?'

'I have to arrange for builders and painters to refurbish the house,' she replies through the sound of the streaming water.

'What?! What house?'

'Would you mind, John? I'm having a shower now.'

'You can't be serious,' John grumbles and sits down on the side of the tub. 'Kate, we do not *need* a house in this country.'

Kate reaches for her towel and wraps it around her. 'John, when are you going to realise that I am serious about this. You can live with me here and we can spend time in England,' she says while walking into the room.

John looks dismayed. 'You don't seriously think I could *live* here, do you? This is … America.'

Kate takes out a few comfortable pieces of clothing to wear. 'Have you heard any news about your mother?'

'… I suppose she's all right,' he mutters and comes in from the bathroom, hands bulging in his pockets, and surliness covering his face. 'They would have let me know otherwise.'

Kate brushes her long blonde hair and ties it at the back. 'Shall we go for dinner?' she asks.

'I'm not ready yet,' John complains. 'I have been busy arranging our flight.'

He walks towards her as he takes his hands from his pockets. With questioning eyes he puts his hands on her shoulders. 'Kate. Do you love me?'

His seriousness takes Kate by surprise. Never before have they spoken of love, whatever that means to John. 'John, don't be so childish. Just because I came here with a different purpose than you, doesn't mean I don't love you.'

She releases from his grip.

'All right,' he says. 'Will you see me off at the airport?'

Kate is halfway to the door. 'Are you coming for dinner?'

John looks down his plain white T-shirt. 'Don't you think I should change first?'

Kate's eyes glide over his attire. 'Nah, you're fine. This is America.'

Grey mist has wrapped Heathrow Airport in a muggy blanket as the plane bursts onto the runway. People who have come to see aircraft land and take off on this day, appear to be disappointed by the limited view. Whingeing children are begging for candy and crisps while their fathers try to capture some of the spectacle of aeroplanes that come roaring out of the clouds. In that respect, Jacob distinguishes himself from other onlookers, as he stands alone on the top floor of Heathrow's new terminal, hands loosely at his sides and receiving furtive glances from some women; their eyes are betraying a certain longing. Jacob watches the plane he has come to meet, land and taxi towards the terminal building. He then slides a hand through his dark, perfectly cut hair and disengages from the crowd before he makes his way downstairs, following the signs for the arrivals hall.

Time elapses before Jacob spots his portended brother-in-law emerging from the other travellers. He folds the newspaper he purchased under his arm, and walks to greet him.

'Hello, John. You had a good flight?'

'Ah, Jacob.' John's face briefly lights up before shadowing over again. 'Don't even ask. I'll never take a non-direct flight again … We need to talk, let's find a taxi.'

Jacob relieves John of one of his bags, and together they walk towards the exit doors. 'Kate sent me all the information about the house,' Jacob says. 'It looks fantastic.'

John doesn't listen to Jacob's expressions of approval. He covetously tries to elude other passengers who are engaging themselves to get transport to the city, and he attempts to overpower someone to get a taxi.

'Here's one free,' Jacob intervenes and motions the driver. John swings his bags on the back seat of the taxi and slides onto the seat alongside them. Jacob gets in next to the driver who speeds away from the terminal, only half-listening to Jacob's directions, indicating he is familiar with the route back to town.

'I think you will have to talk to Kate,' John begins when they are on their way, leaning his arm on a bag. 'It's preposterous. One day over there and she's bought a complete property. I don't think she knows what she's doing. Never mind her asking *me* for *my* opinion. Oh, no. I mean, I thought we were going to work on our future? Is not marriage part of that? How can our marriage work when she lives on the other side of the Atlantic?'

Jacob looks over his shoulder to catch a glimpse of John's face. 'I assume you will both live over there.'

'Damn, Jacob. You don't see me living in America, do you?' He casts an irritated glance out of the car window. Drizzle has started falling from the clouded skies. 'She didn't even see me off at the airport,' he grumbles.

'Well, it was rather late, John. Grant my sister her rest at least.' The taxi halts for another traffic light. 'I'm sure Kate knows what she's doing. I was sorry to hear about your mother, though. How is she?'

'I shall go the hospital tomorrow,' John replies, his face showing a recalcitrance not becoming his thirty-two years. He has his mind on a more pressing issue. 'Will you talk to Kate?' John asks.

'John, I'm not my sister's keeper. I can't tell her what to do with her private life.'

23

'I can't believe what I'm hearing!' John sounds indignant. 'Surely you should want what's best for your own sister?'

'Exactly, and if she is happy with the house she's bought, I'm happy for her.'

John had not anticipated Jacob taking such a neutral stand. Annoyed, he turns his head.

Rainwater currently streams along the car windows and splashes up from under the tyres. It doesn't seem to bother the driver who drives fast wherever it is allowed. The rush-hour congestion has a larger part in delaying the arrival at Jacob's office.

'Will you *talk* to Kate?' John demands before Jacob gets out.

'John. I don't think it's my place,' he replies and gets out of the taxi. Jacob casts a glance through the back window of the car, but John has turned his head away.

'Sir, where to next,' the driver asks John. 'Sir?'

'Victoria!' John snaps.

Jacob quickly rushes through the rain and opens the door to the building. His shirt has caught some precipitation, but he's not concerned, and he walks towards the lift. When Jacob reaches to press the button, the lift door opens and staff stream out, their working day at an end. Jacob gets in and soon reaches his floor.

'You're still here?' he remarks when he notices his secretary just getting ready to leave the office.

'Your grandmother rang, Jacob. Please phone her back as soon as you can find the time.'

'Thanks.'

'The rest I've put on your desk. I'll see you tomorrow.'

'Yes, thanks. Enjoy your evening.'

He moves towards the window and stands in front of

it, looking out at the Thames River below. Slowly but surely lights emerge from the clearing drizzle until a bright, late August evening appears along the Embankment and over the City of London. Not until then does he take his hands from his pockets and picks up the telephone.

Clad in jeans and gumboots and wearing a cream coloured jumper Kate enters the stables where she is met by the pleasantly warm smell of straw and horse manure. The stable boy is clearing out the stalls to make space for a few more animals.

'Hello Billy,' Kate greets him when she spots his black curly hair appear above one of the stall doors. His dark eyes briefly look at her. 'Morn' ma'am.'

Kate sees the horse's eager head looking her way over his stable door at the recognition of her voice, and happily throws his head back when Kate approaches. The Palomino has only been a resident here since last week, but he is quite at home. Kate reaches out and tickles him between his ears. 'You're ready for a ride, aren't you, Chief?' she says in a soft voice.

She slides her hand along the horse's neck before she throws the saddle on his back. The Palomino neighs briefly. She closes the straps and leads the horse from the stables to the field. Kate waves at one of the builders before she pulls herself up into the saddle and rides off. The rain of the past week has coloured the sloping fields around the house in fresh green. Yesterday the sun had seized the chance once more to spread warmth, and cheer the late-blooming flowers in the field.

On a straight stretch, Kate gives the horse free reins; she loves the feeling of being on the back of a horse that runs with such velocity. Free as the wind she lets herself fly across the fields, spreading her arms as Chief leads the way. He pushes up the knoll and continues the gallop, slowing down somewhat when the path slants downwards. Kate takes the reins with a satisfied feeling, and they come to a halt. She pets her horse's neck when her attention is drawn to something on the abandoned road below. The road is merely a track that separates her property from that of the neighbours. It's rather unusual for a pick-up truck to be parked on the track that is hardly used. A man emerges from behind the vehicle. Kate lets Chief slowly move a bit closer to the track and tread down the hill. She lifts herself in the saddle to be able to see better. The man is dressed like any old cowboy, wearing a chequered shirt with sleeves cut off and jeans.

'Oh my,' she whispers with sudden elation. 'Who might that damsel in distress be?'

She caught a glimpse of his face as his wavy long hair was blown aside by a breeze.

She can't help but feel amused when she sees him angrily hitting the side of his pick-up and kicking it. Kate leads Chief down towards the road and stops not far from the car.

'Can I help in any way?' she asks. Now that he is a mere few metres away from her, she guesses he must be in his early thirties. The man turns, and looks surprised. He glances beyond her, and in the distance as if searching for more signs of civilization.

'Excuse me,' Kate says, trying to catch his attention.

'Sorry, I just ... I never saw you come. Do you live around here?' His hurried glance meets her eyes, and for a few seconds, Kate is at a loss for words.

'... Uh ... Oh. Yes. Just, down there, on the other side of the hill.'

'You don't happen to have a cellphone on you, do

you? I never carry those things, but I think, now.' He makes a gesture towards the pick-up. 'I think it's given up on me.'

Kate regains her composure and shakes her head. 'No, I'm sorry.'

Disappointed, he looks down at his vehicle. 'You don't – '

'But you're welcome to come with me to the house and phone from there,' Kate interrupts him.

He looks around as if expecting more help to come galloping around the corner.

'It's no trouble at all,' Kate says.

'OK,' he agrees. 'I don't see how I can call for a tow truck otherwise.'

Kate dismounts. 'My name is Kate,' she says and holds out her hand.

'Much obliged,' he replies and shakes her hand. 'David.'

'Just follow me. David,' Kate smiles.

'Nice looking horse you got there,' he says.

'Chief. That's his name.'

David reaches out past her shoulder to stroke the horse on his neck; his arm briefly brushes Kate's hair.

'We can walk to my house, it's about half a mile as the crow flies,' Kate suggests. 'Or we can let Chief take us there.'

David shows a quick smile. 'All right.' He takes the reins from her and throws his leg over the back of the horse. Then he holds out his hand for Kate to take it and with his strength, he lifts her behind him in the saddle.

At a steady pace, the horse finds his way back to the house.

'You're not from around here, are you?' David observes over his shoulder.

'Sorry?' Kate says. She holds her arms loosely around his sides, his hair strokes her face.

'I mean, your accent, not from around here.'

'No. Well, I grew up in England, my brother and I. But I was born here.'

Her cheek brushes David's back when Chief slips into a small hole. In a reflex, she tightens her grip around his waist. David sends the horse back onto the path that leads over the hill where below, the house lies bathing in the morning sun.

'My,' David expresses when he sees Kate's home. 'Is that your house?' He stops for a moment.

'Yes,' is Kate's reply. She feels pleased that her new home impresses him.

David spurs the horse to move on. When they enter the yard, he leans slightly sideways to support Kate as she slides off the horse's back. They walk to the paddock where Kate relieves Chief of his saddle and bridle before closing the gate, and she thanks Billy who has come to take the gear from her.

'Nice hideaway you have here. If you don't mind me saying so.'

'Not at all,' Kate replies. 'Please, come in.'

She shows him into the kitchen where the intense smell of paint comes their way. The decorators are still busy painting the hall and the living area. 'I'm sorry about that smell,' Kate apologises. 'Would you care for something to drink?' she asks as she puts the telephone in front of him.

'No, thank you.'

Kate hands him an old telephone directory. 'It's no trouble,' she assures him.

'Thanks.' David quickly thumbs through the pages, then dials a number before he starts explaining his problem.

'Yeah,' he replies, 'it was just off Interstate … '

'Forty,' Kate subjoins.

'Forty, yes … follow this sign … ' David flicks his fingers.

'Bakersfield.'

'Bakersfield,' David repeats into the receiver.

The person on the other end of the line seems to think it rather amusing. 'Well, I thought it was a short cut,' David justifies himself, innocence spreading across his face. 'How was I to know?' he says and looks at Kate as he puts the phone down. Kate is entranced by his guileless charm.

'I think I should get back to the car and wait till they come,' David says, 'appreciate your hospitality,' he adds and makes to pass her.

'Are you sure I can't offer you a drink?' Kate asks again. 'I mean, they will take a while to get here.' She isn't tempted to let him go so readily. 'Make yourself at home.'

David looks doubtful. 'No, ma'am, I think I'd best go now. I mean, don't get me wrong. I appreciate your help an' everything … '

'Ma'am? What happened to *Kate*?' She goes to the fridge and takes out a soda. 'No one will *steal* your car in the meantime,' she says and hands him the drink.

David smiles at her and takes a swallow from the bottle. 'Is your husband still in England?'

'Sorry?'

'Oh, pardon me for askin'.'

'What makes you think there's a husband? Don't you trust a woman to be successful in her own right?'

'Oh no, ma'am … uh, Kate … It's just, well, pretty woman like you … don't expect a pretty woman like you to be single.' He takes another sip as he keeps his green eyes fixed on her face.

'Why thank you,' Kate says in her best southern accent. 'Are you? Married, I mean.'

David shakes his head. 'No ma'am ... Kate. Girlfriend, I'm seeing this girl.'

'Okay,' Kate is slow to express. 'Shall we? Start walking back to your pick-up?'

At a slow pace, Kate drives her rental car through rows of other cars, looking out for a free space in the dungeons of this immense multi-storey car park. She has driven around the city with the folder of potential business properties on the seat beside her. A few buildings she has looked at, seem appropriate to the new business venture Jacob and she have in mind. She manoeuvres her car between two oversized American car brands that make her own car look like a Mini squashed between two Mercedes. She exits the car park via the elevator that takes her to the ground floor, then crosses the street and enters the restaurant where she soon spots Earl at a table near the window.

'Hi, you look fine today,' Earl says with a smile.

'Thank you,' Kate replies and puts the folder down.

Earl motions a waiter who hands them a menu. 'No need for that,' Earl says. 'We'll both have a coffee and one of your American pies. If I remember correctly,' he adds, facing Kate.

Kate nods. 'That's fine.'

'What have we got here.' Earl reaches for the folder. 'I had a look at the copy you gave me yesterday. I think you can forget about the one in Lauderdale Street, not a good area for that type of restaurant.'

'I was quite interested in that building near Beale

Square,' Kate says. 'It looked good, with a lot of potentials.'

'Yeah … There was a fire there. That's one of the reasons why the former owner went out of business. Couldn't get it back on track after that. But it's a sturdy building, you can make a go of it.' Earl reaches for the sugar and milk after the waiter placed the coffee and pie in front of them.

'And the others?'

'Well, Elvis Presley Boulevard is a good area, so close to Graceland. All those tourists and Elvis-fans need to eat.' Earl strokes his corpulent belly.

Kate likes the idea of starting a takeaway restaurant near Graceland. 'You have a point,' she says. 'And in future, we could expand into the inner city.'

'Yep. Could work,' Earl admits. 'Don't forget, the tourists have set the pace in this town in the past. Once your business takes off, you can start another in the town centre.' He thumbs through the folder and takes out the photo that shows the property.

Kate peels another photo from under the potential business properties. 'I like this one too,' she says. 'It's off Jackson Avenue, near the centre.' Earl takes it from her and looks at it. 'I know this place, bit run down now. It doesn't look like this any more, I tell ya.'

'But we could have a look there?' Kate anticipates, wanting to explore more options.

'Sure, I'll come with you and have a good look at it,' Earl says, his eyes resting on Kate's pie. She takes a piece and then shoves the remainder towards Earl. 'So much for your dieting plans, Earl,' she says with a smile.

On the way home Kate finds herself resisting driving onward as she nears the turn-off for Flat Junction, but then indicates and directs the car off the Interstate and up the narrow country road. As she accelerates, she realises the road's surface has improved over the years. It is paved now. It does make the ride more comfortable than what she remembers from the past; bouncing up and down in the back of their daddy's pick-up. She notices an old farmhouse where her school friend used to live, it looks deserted, but it appears someone still lives there. There's a piece of clothing waving in the breeze on the line, and an ageing mule is standing by a fence, one hind-leg slightly lifted. The surroundings look barren. It seems the occupation of agriculture has been abandoned, with only grassy fields surrounding the humble houses that are scattering the area.

Kate slows down as she reaches the outskirts of the small town. A few new dwellings have appeared. Otherwise, the town shows no signs of a major expansion. Kate follows Main Street that still has the same abandoned feel to it with dust blowing up from its surface. She stops across from the small, wooden church and slowly gets out of the car. Mum and Daddy hadn't been frequent churchgoers, but Kate remembers the Sunday School classes she and Jacob were sent to in this small church. It looks like it could do with a fresh coat of paint, she observes as she opens the wooden gate to the graveyard. The sudden dry squeak of its hinges startles Kate. She hesitates but then, slowly, walks in the direction she can still remember. It was a confusing and sad time when she had walked through this gate last, years ago. Jacob held her by her hand, clutched it as if he was afraid to lose her, too. Daddy's family was here and an unknown elderly couple from a foreign land.

Kate stops when she sees the name on the gravestone. A very simple gravestone. It only shows Daddy's name and two numbers, the year he was born, and the year he passed on. Kate bites her lip, a silent tear appears and starts flowing down her cheek. She kneels to be nearer his grave. Only now it occurs to her that they left him behind, all those years ago. Deserted him. He should have been laid to rest with their mum. They loved each other so much. She slides her hand over the grave that is only a heaped layer of grass. Kate now notices the jar with fresh flowers at the foot of it. It pleases her that there is someone who remembers their daddy. She wipes her cheek dry and slowly stands up to walk back to the entrance gate.

She doesn't notice the woman in the cotton dress watching her. Kate makes her way into the street and strolls across to her car. Lost in thought, she gets in, starts the engine and turns the car around. For a brief second, her attention is drawn to the woman standing on the sidewalk by the fence that surrounds the churchyard. The woman looks at her, but Kate doesn't pay attention. She drives on and back to the main road.

Now that the builders and decorators have finished restoring the house, Kate looks it over with the foreman. She is content with the end result, but can't beat the feeling of forlornness.

'As you asked, we left the fireplace as it was,' she hears the foreman say. 'Just cleaned it up, it's safe to use.' Daddy *was* a skilled workman.

Kate looks at the fireplace and recalls the day she saw it when she was a child. The only time she was ever allowed inside the house. Mrs Baker was very pleased with her daddy's good work and showed her into this room. They didn't stay long, her daddy took her hand and soon they were on their way to their trailer.

'Well, ma'am. I'm off,' the foreman says. 'Good evening.'

'Yes. Thank you,' Kate replies absent-mindedly before he leaves her on her own. As the kitchen door closes, Kate looks up at the pastel-coloured walls and slides a hand across the mantelpiece. Suddenly there's a tingling in her hand. She quickly withdraws it and looks around quizzically. 'No ghosts, I hope,' she murmurs. She walks slowly through the spacious, empty living room. The tasteful pieces of furniture don't seem to fill the space much. She goes into the large hall and looks up before she puts her hand on the bannister and step by step walks up the broad half-circular staircase leading to the first floor. Her footsteps are absorbed and hushed by the lush carpet as she reaches the landing. Kate peeks into the bedrooms one by one. Six the house has, a few still need furniture. Kate stops in the middle of one of the bare bedrooms.

'Boo!' she exclaims. An echo is the only reply. She makes a little twirl but that too doesn't bring a smile to her face. With a sigh, she ambles back onto the landing. She hesitates and looks up the second staircase leading to the rooms in the roof. It used to be a large attic, but former occupants had renovated it into leisure rooms. Kate turns and makes her way down the broad staircase. The emptiness in her new house overwhelms her.

When the building was underway, she was unaware of its emptiness. Construction workers rushed in and out, and before the upstairs was finished, she'd slept in a hotel. This is the first time since she bought the house that she is totally alone here.

Maybe it had not been the right choice, buying such a large place. Maybe she had been too preoccupied with dreams from the past. Maybe John had been right when he said that with the business in the city, she did not need a big house in the country.

Kate strolls into the kitchen to make herself a drink. She lets her fingers slide lightly over the telephone; it's the middle of the night in London. She takes the remote control for the television and flicks it on. Her fingers play with the buttons of the telephone. Jacob won't mind her calling him at this hour and she dials the number.

A sleepy voice on the other end answers. A sleepy woman's voice.

'Oh, I'm *so* sorry,' Kate apologises.

'*What do you want,*' the voice asks.

'I'm so sorry. I must've dialled the wrong number.'

There's a fumbling noise at the other end.

'*Yes?*'

'Jacob?'

'*Yes. Kate? It's rather late here.*'

'I'm sorry, Jacob, I thought you wouldn't mind.'

'*It's all right, sis. Is everything OK?*'

'Yes. Fine. The house is finished.'

'*Good.*'

'You should come and see it.'

'*I will, soon.*'

' … I visited Daddy's grave today … I felt rather sad.'

' … *Kate, I will come when I have time. OK?*'

'Fine. I'm sorry for calling you so late. Give my love to John.'

She puts the telephone back on the charger and has another sip of her drink, then takes the bottle and slumps down on the couch.

The flickering television screen wakes Kate hours later. Somewhat bemused she slowly sits up in the otherwise dark room. Then she remembers. The house. With a sigh, she rises from the couch and switches on a light. She puts the cork on the bottle and places it back in the fridge. When she wants to turn the television off, she recognises a familiar face. She moves closer to have a good look at the man singing a song on her television screen. Her eyes light up. 'David,' she whispers. Without taking her gaze off the screen, she sits down again to watch the broadcast. 'My ... he sings,' she quietly utters. 'He's a singer.' Mesmerised, she watches him finish his song. *'Yes, folks, that was David Nelson,'* the announcer says. *'Creeping up the country charts. At fifteen this week but I foresee great things here.'*

With a peculiar feeling of satisfaction intertwined with inquisitiveness, Kate switches off the television. Delighted at what she has just experienced, she dilatorily makes her way up the stairs and into the master bedroom.

John and Jacob take their baggage from the overhead compartment and walk along the aisle towards the exit door to leave the aircraft. 'I hope Kate hasn't forgotten to meet us,' John says.

'She'll be here.'

'You said she might be busy. Signing contracts,' John says with caution. 'She could very well have forgotten. I shall not leave her on her own again. Now that mother is doing better.' He strides after Jacob, who has reached Customs.

At the baggage-claim, John soon has a trolley ready, but their cases take a while to come through.

'I can't wait to see the house,' Jacob says.

John still has his doubts, moaning as he loads their cases onto the trolley before they walk to the door that states 'Nothing to declare'.

Jacob is the first to spot Kate and greets her with a big, brotherly hug. John gives her a peck on the cheek.

'Kate. Darling.'

'So good to see you,' Kate says. 'I'm so happy! It was getting rather lonely without family around.'

'I told you,' John says. 'I told you, but you wanted to stay.'

'I had things to arrange, John,' Kate says matter-of-factly.

'Shall we?' Jacob proposes.

At the parking-lot, they load their baggage into the trunk. Kate takes the seat behind the wheel and puts the key in the ignition. Not for long, the car exits the busy car park at Memphis International Airport, and they proceed the journey to Kate's house.

Jacob sits silently in thought, taking in the surroundings and trying to recall familiarities of over twenty-three years ago. John has habitually taken a seat in the back. Despite having a drivers license, he does not ordinarily drive and takes chauffeured cars wherever he goes.

'Are there any new developments at home?' Kate asks.

'Mother is doing well,' John replies.

'Jacob?' Kate asks. 'I've had an unfamiliar lady on the phone twice already.' She turns her head for a brief moment. Jacob starts from his reminiscing and is brought back to reality. 'I suppose I can't make you believe she's a one-night-stand,' he says, grinning.

'No,' Kate declares.

'Her name is Maria. We met six weeks ago at a conference.'

Jacob hasn't been fortunate keeping women in his life after an engagement ended four years ago; she had found someone with even more money in the bank. Kate is pleased that her brother has someone in his life who has lasted longer than two weeks.

'There's the road to the village,' Kate suggests.

Jacob makes a subtle movement with his head. 'Not today, Kate.'

Jacob had witnessed the collision between the old pick-up and a truck on that horrible, fateful day. The truck had suddenly slid to the wrong side of the road and had hit the pick-up head-on. Mum and Daddy died instantly, while Jacob watched from the side of the road, to see them come home.

Kate turns the wheel and drives up the gravel road that leads to her house. Jacob remembers the scenery and the house where his father sometimes took him when he did odd jobs for Jon Baker. 'Even the sign is still there,' he says.

'That will be changed,' Kate says. 'I don't want to live in a place named Bakersfield. The Bakers have gone.'

'What will you do with so much land?' John asks. 'You weren't thinking of keeping cows, I hope.'

Kate stops the car in the front yard of the house. Jacob steps out of the car, his eyes fixed on the large house that arises in front of him. 'It's even bigger than I remember it to be,' he says. 'We could *all* live here.'

'I think that side room was added at a later date,' Kate explains. 'I turned it into an office.'

John takes his bag from the trunk and walks to the front door, Kate and Jacob in his wake, and allowing Kate to unlock the door for him to enter.

In the kitchen, Kate puts the kettle on and takes a tray of ready-made sandwiches from the fridge, as Jacob casts a glance into the large lounge room where the French doors divide the homely inside from the patio and the pool outside.

'I still have to let this sink in a bit,' he says, 'I could

hardly believe you actually succeeded in buying a property we only dreamt about having as children.'

Kate smiles. 'Well, we've done pretty well since. I'll show you around later.'

Jacob sits down at the table and watches his sister as she engages in preparing a late lunch, a mixed expression on his face.

'Jacob, we had to come back some day,' Kate says. 'You and I always knew we'd be back. We could have expanded the business anywhere, but we opted for this area.'

John interrupts their conversation by striding into the kitchen. 'I've put my suitcase in the master bedroom,' he says. 'I assume that's all right.'

'Sure, John.'

Jacob gives Kate a meaningful look.

'Tea anyone?' Kate asks.

The sun has barely shown her face when Kate and Jacob are strolling on the rolling scenery not far from the house. 'I think we might have to import from abroad if we are to get the right produce,' Kate says. 'I've looked into it and it seems a rather hard task to get the organic produce we need from the American states, let alone GMO-free.'

'If that's the case, let's just hope American bureaucracy won't make life too hard on us.'

'Yes,' Kate sighs. 'But, somehow, I'm sure we will succeed. I went to a Job Centre as well, specifying our policies and principles so now all we have to do is wait for applications to come in.'

When they stop on top of a rising field, Jacob lets his eyes glide over the scenery. He hasn't experienced the panorama from this angle. 'I'm sure, on a clear day you can see the village from here.'

'You can,' Kate says and points a finger in the direction. 'I go out riding whenever I have time and can see the village in the distance.'

Jacob puts his arm around his sister's shoulders. 'We did have happy times here, didn't we. Even though we were dead poor.'

A longing arises in Kate's eyes. 'Yeah, po' white trash,' she mentions with irony in her voice.

Jacob laughs. 'We probably still would be, if we had stayed.'

'Why didn't you bring your girlfriend?' Kate asks. 'For her to see the area too?'

'I'll take her next time. She's busy now. Besides, travelling with John is not something you'd want certain people to experience.'

Kate shows a feeble smile.

As the sun climbs higher in the sky, Kate and Jacob are moving further down the hill, back to the house. On entering, they find John in the kitchen trying to toast a piece of bread.

'Is the coffee ready, John?' Kate asks.

John looks at her, bemused. 'I was actually waiting for the maid to show up. I find myself struggling to even have a piece of toast! Where is the housekeeper? Or are they always late in this country?'

Kate starts preparing the coffee and puts more slices of bread in the toaster.

'Kate, don't tell me you haven't organised the staff yet!'

Jacob grabs the frying pan. 'How would you like your eggs, Kate?' he asks.

John drops his head. 'I knew we should've stayed in England!' he grumbles. 'At least there you can get decent staff. People who show up when they need to work!'

'John, are you implying that I'm too stupid to make my own breakfast,' Kate says.

' … Well, no. It's just. Well, there are certain things you shouldn't be doing … yourself. You're not a servant.'

Kate is not prepared to let John spoil their day and proceeds to pour them all a cup of coffee. 'Just right,' she tells Jacob who has finished with the eggs. 'Lovely.'

Jacob puts the eggs on a large plate while Kate feeds the toaster a few more slices of bread, and placing the browned slices on the breakfast table.

John sits down and takes a sip from his coffee. 'I would've preferred tea,' he sulks. 'I think I shall have to organise staff myself if we are to live in *this* house.'

'You're not very happy here, are you John,' Jacob says as he reaches for a piece of toast.

'I … well, I could be, I suppose,' John replies. 'It just takes time to get used to everything.'

'Try to enjoy yourself a bit more,' Jacob says. 'It ain't all that bad around here.'

John looks at him. 'Isn't,' he says. 'It *isn't* all that bad around here.'

'See? Now you admit it yourself,' Jacob wittily replies.

Kate suppresses a smile while quietly sipping her coffee.

Earl is just biting into his greasy burger when Kate and Jacob pull up. He quickly wipes his mouth with a paper napkin and walks towards the car as they get out.

'I can't wait to have you as my customer,' Kate says. She slaps his fat belly with the back of her hand. 'I bet this is craving for *decent* food.'

'Jacob!' Earl calls out. 'Good to see you.' He warmly shakes Jacob's hand. 'You're the spittin' image of your daddy.'

'You think so?'

'Yeah. Do you have a wife?'

'Excuse me?'

'Handsome cowboy like you,' Earl says. 'I'm sure you won't have a problem finding someone.'

Daddy once mentioned, Jacob recalls, how direct Earl could be.

'Shall we go in?' Kate suggests, but her face drops when she turns and sees the property she wanted to submit to closer inspection.

The former Seven-Eleven looks as if a local street gang has been occupying it for the past months. The broken windows are boarded-up, gravity is splashed all over the walls, rubble on the ground. Kate looks doubtful. Jacob is silent.

'Yes, Kate. I did mention it doesn't look like that photograph anymore,' Earl offers. 'It needs a lot of work. But the building is all right. It had a complete overhaul before the shop moved in here.'

'When was that?' Jacob asks.

'Three years – '

'It's not that, Jacob,' Kate says. 'I don't think this place is right.'

'Are you sure?' Earl asks.

Kate nods. 'And I'm sure that the shop owners had good reasons to discontinue their business here.' Kate gives the place one more look. 'I'm sorry to have dragged you out here, Earl.'

They walk back to their cars and get in. It's Earl leading the way as they drive to the southern part of the city. Jacob sits beside Kate, taking in the sights of the city they regularly visited as children when their parents went to the larger stores for cheap products. It was then that he and Kate were sometimes treated to new clothes and shoes, paid for with money from Daddy's overtime.

At a busy shopping area, Earl swings off. Kate follows as he manoeuvres through the rows of cars, and she parks her car beside his. Jacob notices the For Sale sign in front of an inviting looking structure amongst the shops and eateries. He looks at Kate, whose eyes glide around the area, and an approbatory expression appears on her face.

'Shall I call the estate agent?' Earl asks when he sees the satisfied look on Kate's face.

Kate turns to Jacob who nods. They walk towards the building to submit it to closer inspection, while Earl searches for the telephone number of the estate agent on his cellphone.

It doesn't require a long discussion to convince Kate that this building will do well to house their next restaurant, the first one in the United States.

'The Veg and the Vegan!' she says, gesturing with her arm to show her brother where the sign should be placed.

'Should we change the name for the American market?' Jacob proposes.

'No. Why?'

Jacob shrugs his shoulders. 'Maybe something more catchy?'

'No, if we want to continue the business as a chain,' Kate says, 'we'll just stick to the name we have. It works well in the UK.'

Earl puts his cellphone back in his breast pocket. 'She can be here in an hour,' he says. 'Shall we?' Earl points at a café. 'We can wait for her there.'

Jacob and Kate follow him when Kate notices a music shop. 'You go ahead, I'll be with you in a minute,' she tells them.

'Turn off here, Kate, please,' Jacob tells his sister on the way home.

Kate casts her brother a glance and then turns off into the road that leads to the village where they grew up. Jacob looks out the car window and sees scenery, he recalls from his childhood days, pass by. As they enter the small town he is surprised to recognise certain small shops.

'It's incredible how little has changed here. Let's park the car and walk the rest of the way,' Jacob suggests. Kate slows down and stops the car in Main Street that is bathed in bright afternoon sunlight. Jacob's hand searches for the door handle and he, too, steps out onto the sidewalk. Kate moves up beside him and together they stroll through the warm dusty street. The sun-bleached shops here could do with a fresh lick of paint, too. Kate sees that one of the shops sells fresh flowers. She reaches and takes two bunches from the bucket outside. While Jacob waits, Kate enters the small local equivalent of the News Agents so often seen in towns around England. A friendly old lady with pale blue, inquisitive eyes addresses her. 'Brought in fresh, honey. Nice bunch,' she says as she takes the money from Kate. 'Passing through, are you?'

Kate shakes her head but isn't inclined to tell her about her childhood days in this village. 'I've recently moved here,' Kate replies. The old lady casts a brief, studying look towards Kate before handing her the change. 'You moved here?' she asks.

'To the area, not here, not to the village,' Kate is quick to explain.

'Oh. Do you want those wrapped, honey?' the lady asks kindly. 'I've – '

'No, thank you. This is fine. Good day.' Kate has

spotted Jacob's glare through the shop window and quickly makes her way outside, feeling the shop owner's curious eyes nettling her back.

It's a short walk to the churchyard and, like Kate, Jacob doesn't need directions getting to the small church. He opens the wooden gate with its squeaking hinges, reaching for his sister's hand as he did all those years ago when they walked behind men carrying their daddy's casket to the burial place. Kate holds her brother's hand a bit tighter in hers when she feels his trembling. For Jacob, the walk to their father's gravesite is imprinted in his memory. Dirt scuffs beneath their feet while they follow the path. Kate wraps her hand around her brother's arm as they stop at the foot of the grave. Visions from years ago become vivid. That day when the wooden coffin was lowered into the muddy hole. Kate had watched it touch the puddle of water on the bottom and hadn't believed that the wooden casket contained her daddy. She could not understand why her daddy was put in a hole. Jacob hadn't spoken for days after the accident.

Presently he sighs, but cannot suppress a sob. He holds a hand in front of his eyes, trying to hide tears that have started to appear. ' … I'm sorry, Kate.'

'It's all right, Jacob. It's all right.' She squeezes his hand. 'I suppose, we never really said goodbye,' Kate tries to reason. 'We just left.'

Jacob sighs. 'Yes, that's it. We just left … Buried him and left.'

Kate bends to her knees, putting the flower bunches beside her, and starts breaking off the blooms from their stems. Then she spreads the flowers all over the grassy patch that contains their daddy's remains underneath. When the blanket of colour has covered their father's resting place Kate looks up at Jacob.

All of a sudden a breeze stirs and causes the flower petals to move.

Kate trembles.

'Come,' Jacob offers and reaches for his sister's hand to help her to her feet.

The following disturbance that can be heard behind them, sends a chill down Kate's spine. The slight dragging sound in the dust makes Jacob turn his head.

Behind them stands a woman in a plain cotton dress, observing them. Her chestnut, shoulder-length hair is pinned back behind her ears.

Jacob turns to face her. 'Yes?'

'Hello,' she says. She points at Kate. 'I've seen *you* here before.'

Kate has a vague recollection of a woman in a plain dress standing by the fence.

'I know you,' the woman says.

Jacob is distrustful. 'Uh, I don't think we know you.'

She points at Kate once more and then lets out a chuckle. 'You are Katy. And *you*,' pointing at Jacob, 'you are little Jacob.'

Kate and Jacob look at each other.

'Am I right?' the woman says.

'… Yes.'

'It's been a long, long time. I was only eighteen when it happened.' The woman holds out her hands. 'Emmy, I'm your daddy's youngest sister.'

Kate's mouth falls open. 'Auntie Emmy?'

'That's me.' The lady chuckles.

'You were our babysitter.' Jacob is just as astounded.

'I sure was,' Emmy says. 'You sweet kids you. Not a nasty streak in your bones. Here, let me give you a big hug. It's been way too long.' She grabs Jacob and Kate by their shoulders.

'Auntie Emmy,' Kate utters. 'How ... how long has it been?'

'Well, you can figure that out for yourselves. Your daddy's been gone now right on twenty-three years.'

'Yes,' Jacob says. 'That's right. Twenty-three years.'

'Last time I saw you, I waved goodbye when you left with your grand-folk, Jake senior's in-laws. Never heard from you again,' she says with regret in her voice. She dismisses the remark with a wave of her hand. 'Well what, you were just kids. But I still hold on to that one Christmas card you sent me!'

Kate gives her aunt another hug. 'Come, we must go somewhere, have a drink and talk,' she urges.

'Of course!' Aunt Emmy exclaims. 'I'm not letting you go so soon now! We'll go to my house.' She hooks her arms around Kate and Jacob and they move away from the grave and towards the gate.

'I've always kept my brother's, your daddy's, grave tidy,' she goes on. 'Mind you, I still think it wasn't right that they took your momma away. She should've been buried here, with her husband! They loved each other so ...' Aunt Emmy shakes her head.

'True,' Kate admits.

'They're together up there,' Jacob says, moving his head up towards the heavens.

'You got *that* right,' Aunt Emmy says.

The sound of the squeaking hinges accompanies them as they step out of the churchyard. 'It's not far,' Emmy explains. 'Then, nothing is in this town. Not much progress or expansion here, I tell ya.'

Not far from the churchyard, Kate and Jacob find themselves in a street just off the thoroughfare, and they reach Emmy's house that is nestled between other small dwellings.

'Is there an uncle as well?' It suddenly occurs to Kate that they could have a relative unbeknown to them.

Aunt Emmy makes a gesture with her hand. 'Oh yes, there was a husband all right. Gave me five kids too. Then he took off. Two of my kids now live in Memphis. One studies to be a lawyer,' she adds with a meaningful expression. 'One's in Nashville and the eldest moved up north.'

She opens the front door to her house and they enter directly into a plain but pleasant living-room. 'Please, make yourselves at home. I'll make us tea.'

A couch with a large colourful throw leans against the wall facing the entrance, the robust coffee table that stands before it doesn't match the rest of the furniture but Kate is certain that matching furniture is the last thing on Aunt Emmy's mind. She draws Jacob's attention to some family photos on the sideboard and points at one with five children. 'Those must be our cousins then,' she says to her brother.

'Sure are,' Emmy's voice sounds and she moves up behind them. 'These are the twins, they live in Memphis. My youngest is still at home. Should be back from school any moment. Please, sit.'

Kate moves away from the family photographs and sits down in one of the lazy chairs while Emmy takes cookies from a jar and puts them on a plate. 'Home-made,' she says. She notices Jacob looking at a picture of their daddy and mum. 'That's the only one I had.'

Jacob realises it might be the only one in existence for it's the same photograph that has been on display for years now at Grandmother's house.

Emmy pours the tea from her earthenware teapot and hands them both a cup. 'There's sugar and milk,' she invites before she sits down across from them. 'For a long time, I have wondered how you were, if we'd ever see each other again. And after all these years, I started hearing rumours … ' She slaps both her hands on her knees. 'And here you are, back home!'

'I'm … We're sorry, Aunt Emmy,' Kate says, 'but, as you said, we were just kids and our grandparents didn't really know. We lost the only address – '

'Never you mind. Important thing is that you're back and y'all look so well!' She shows them a broad smile. 'You have to tell me everything. Will you be staying long?' Aunt Emmy leans back into her chair.

'Uh … ' Jacob begins. 'Well, Kate will. She's bought a house here.'

'Here!'

'Across the Interstate. Do you remember the house where the Bakers used to live?'

'Well, I heard that property was sold and all this building going on. And now, Katy? It's your new home?'

Kate smiles. 'Yes. Do feel free to come by any time.'

'Such a big place … '

'Well, I don't intend to stay on my own all my life, Auntie Emmy.'

A door slams and the sound of an adolescent's voice rings out. 'Mom, I'm home!' Simultaneously footsteps stumble up the stairs.

'Hey, Danny!' Aunt Emmy yells. 'Get down here! We have guests!'

There is hesitation in the footsteps that have now reached the landing but then, gradually, they come down. A teenager shows his face in the doorway. His sleek hair could do with a cut; it's partly covering his face.

'Come in here,' his mother says. 'Come meet your cousins, they've come all the way from England.'

Shyly, Danny approaches the guests who look at him

with anticipation.

'Go on,' Emmy says. 'They're not from Mars.'

Danny shows a bashful smile.

'This is Kate and that's Jacob.'

Jacob stretches out his hand. 'How are you, Danny.'

The teenager nods. 'Fine, sir.' He goes over to Kate and clumsily shakes her hand too.

'It's their parents, in that picture,' his mother explains. Danny doesn't seem to be eagerly interested.

'I'm off now, Mom. Playing ball with Jimmy.'

'Don't be late for supper!' Emmy hollers after him. She turns her attention back to her guests. 'He's a fine kid.'


Darkness had fallen when Kate and Jacob left for home. From the moment Kate had turned the key in the ignition, their conversation had focused exclusively on their unexpected reunion. But now, as the beams of the headlights illuminate the gravel road, they notice the house is shrouded in darkness, save for the lit window in the master bedroom upstairs.

'Odd,' Kate says.

'Maybe John wants to save on electricity,' Jacob says as they get out of the car. Kate holds a home-made cake wrapped in cling-film that her aunt had pressed into her hands at the last moment.

As soon as they enter the hall, John's anxious voice calls out: 'Who's there!' Jacob detects a certain panic in his calling.

'It's only us,' Kate says. 'What are you doing upstairs?'

Quick footsteps come out of the master bedroom, followed by John's rushing down the stairs. 'Where have you two *been*?'

---

'And how was your day, John?' Kate asks, dryly.

'You never guess who we ran into today,' Jacob says.

'John? Is something the matter? You look a bit – '

'If I tell you, you won't believe me,' John interrupts.

'Don't be silly, John,' Kate says.

'See?'

'John, just tell us,' Jacob says.

John follows Kate into the kitchen. 'Kate, strange things are happening in this house ... I was sitting in the lounge room, and I must have dozed off. Someone tapped on my shoulder. That woke me up.'

'So?'

'There was no one there!'

'You probably *dreamt* it. Someone tapping you on the shoulder,' Jacob says.

'I knew you wouldn't believe me.'

Kate gazes at Jacob who shrugs his shoulders.

'Well,' Kate begins hesitantly. 'I suppose I should tell. There have been rumours going about ... Mind you, I haven't noticed a thing.'

'Rumours?' John demands. 'Kate!'

'One of the reasons why I could negotiate a lower price is because they say the house is haunted. It wouldn't sell.'

Jacob suppresses a smile. John looks astounded.

'A haunted house! With ghosts! Kate, have you gone totally mad!'

Kate shakes her head innocently.

'And you expect us to live here!'

'John, I don't see why you're making such a fuss over this,' Kate rebukes. 'Your mother's country house supposedly has a ghost. That never scared you off!'

'Well, that's different, it's an old house. Centuries old as a matter of fact,' he adds, not trying to conceal his conceitedness.

Jacob sees anger arising in his sister's face. 'Kate,' he says to calm her, but Kate runs outside and slams the door behind her.

Jacob turns to face John. 'I think that's enough already. Consideration has never been your forte, has it, John?' Jacob questions as he takes a drink from the fridge.

'I apologise,' John says. 'I shouldn't have said … it's just … ' He hangs his head before he walks out of the kitchen and up the stairs.

Five minutes later, he's back and finds Jacob in the kitchen, preparing to cook supper.

'Jacob? Can I … maybe, have a word?'
Jacob gestures for him to continue and at the same time gives him a cutting knife and some vegetables

' … I'm not really certain if I want to be here with Kate,' John says, inspecting the knife.

'You cut the vegetables with that,' Jacob instructs him as he slides pasta in the pan with boiling water.

John acts somewhat indecisive but puts a carrot down on the cutting board. 'I love her, but … I don't know. She does so many things on her own. Sometimes I don't know from one moment to the next what she's up to.'

'It's called *independence.*'

'I know that! But, we're in a relationship. I'm just not sure if I want a woman who's as independent as Kate is. Do you like your women to be independent?' John asks, struggling with the carrot.

Jacob shrugs his shoulders. 'I don't know. Depends, in what way. As long as you can keep up, I don't see any harm in a woman who likes her independence.'

John looks at him. 'Do you think that, that's it? Do you think … I should try harder to keep up with Kate?'

'Yes, if that's what you think is failing in your

relationship with my sister.'

John's face lights up. 'Thanks, Jacob!' he says. 'Yes, that's what I'll do. I shall try to keep up with Kate, show more interest in what she's doing.' He nods his head. 'But first ... How do you cut this blooming thing?'

'Here, let me. You wash the lettuce.'

'Right. No. First, I shall apologise to Kate.' John wants to walk outside.

'Oh, you won't find her there,' Jacob says. 'She's out riding. Wait until dinner.'

'Right,' John says. 'Riding? It's pitch dark out there!' He shakes his head, picks up the lettuce and lets water from the tab run over it, muttering: 'Independent, Kate is independent.'

Annoyed by John's thoughtless ways, Kate has taken Chief from the paddock. Does he ever think of her, about what she might feel? He can be such a snob! *'Centuries-old as a matter of fact,'* she mimics after him. *'Darling.* God, I *hate* that,' she murmurs.

The darkness is not the cause of her horse's edginess, rather Kate's annoyance. 'Sorry, Chief,' she says and pets him on his neck, calming him before she mounts. She is pleased the moon has appeared. It lights the field she aims to race across; it's the only way to let her anger subside. She gives the horse free reins, and he takes her where he wants to go. After a while, she finds that Chief has brought her to the top of the knoll. There where she can overlook the neighbours' property. The horse treads on along the rim. Kate glances down at the dirt road as it lies there in the greyness of the evening, lit up blueish by the moon's brightness. The track is empty as far as the darkness allows her to see. She pulls the reins and Chief stops, rather abruptly. Disenchanted, she lets her feet slide out of the stirrups, and she jumps down to the ground. Gently she pushes the horse aside and sits down in the damp grass. She rests her arms on her raised knees and allows thoughts to wander. Back to that day, not too long ago, when she encountered David on her land. She lets her eyes drift, searching. Searching, for beams of headlights from a pick-up truck but none can be seen. Kate lets out a sigh, then stands up.

'Chief, come. Let's go back.' She walks with the reins in her hand, taking the lead as they go back through the moonlit field. Once at the stables, Kate takes her time tending to Chief before reluctantly making her way to the kitchen door.

A pleasant smell of an Italian dinner enters her nostrils when she goes in. She looks at her brother, who is laying the kitchen table.

'Had an enjoyable ride?' he asks.

Kate nods. 'You've been busy. Smells good.'

'*I* made the salad,' John says as he enters the kitchen.

'Thank you, John,' Kate says.

Jacob glances at his sister.

'Kate, I have to apologise,' John says as he walks towards her and takes her hand. 'I'm sorry I was so … so. Well. You know what I mean.' He gives her a peck on the cheek.

'Shall we eat?' Kate suggests. She looks for her bag and digs up the CD that she has bought that afternoon and puts it in the CD-player.

'A touch of local culture,' she says as she presses the start button on the player. After the intro, David's strong, rich voice wafts into the kitchen. Jacob nods approvingly. 'Nice,' he says.

'An upcoming country star, apparently,' Kate replies, rolling the spaghetti around her fork.

'A far cry from what we're used to,' John says. 'But I suppose that's all Americans can come up with.'

Jacob shoots him a look.

'I'm sorry,' John says, 'but it's just *not* to my taste.'

'Well, John, have you ever thought about that it *might* be to someone else's taste?' Kate says.

'Kate, you never listen to this kind of music. You're too well-educated for this.'

Jacob taps his knife on his plate. 'We're having dinner now, John. Please?'

'I apologise,' John says, lifts his glass and takes a sip of the wine. Fortunately, it meets with his approval.

At Jacob's direction, John now helps clear the dishes and puts them in the dishwasher, while Kate walks unsteadily into the living room. She slumps down in a chair and closes her eyes.

'Are you all right, Kate?' Jacob asks. 'I'm just making coffee.'

Some incoherent mumbling sounds emerge from the chair where Kate is sitting.

'I think we should take her upstairs,' John says. 'She shouldn't have been drinking so much wine. Silly girl, she knows she can't hold it.'

Jacob walks into the lounge and shakes Kate's shoulder. 'Sis, shall we take you upstairs?'

Kate makes an indistinct gesture with her arm.

'Better leave her,' Jacob says and goes to the kitchen to get the coffee.

John pulls Kate by her arm. 'Kate, we are going to take you upstairs,' he persists.

' … Leave me! Don't … *touch* me,' Kate utters and slams her hand in the air.

Jacob puts the tray down and pushes John aside. He

addresses his sister in a soft voice. 'Katy, come, let me take you upstairs.'

Kate smiles up at him. 'Katy,' she slurs, 'nobody … calls me Katy … anymore.'

Jacob puts her arm around his neck and pulls her out of the chair to then help her up the stairs.

'Jac … Jacob,' Kate whispers in his ear as she stumbles alongside him. 'Can't you … ss .. send him away.'

'Send who away?'

' … *Him* …' Kate sounds annoyed. 'I don't … *want* him … here.'

'Kate, if you mean John. You will have to take care of that yourself … ' Kate slumps to the left, and Jacob pulls her upright. 'When you've sobered up.'

Holding his sister tightly, they enter the master bedroom. Jacob lowers Kate down on the bed, takes off her shoes and leaves her to sleep.

John has already poured himself a cup, even though it is coffee. 'Rather uncivilised, isn't it?' he says. 'She should take care not to drink so much. It doesn't suit her.'

Jacob pours out a cup of coffee as well and adds sugar. 'I think it's all been a bit much. Coming back here. The house. The memories of the past.'

He sits down on the couch. 'If you are really serious about my sister, John, I think it's time to show her a bit more consideration.'

'What are you talking about?' John says defensively. 'I told you this evening, I hardly know what she's doing most of the time. She shuts me out!'

'Try, John. Do you ever talk?'

John looks at him. 'Of course,' he says, sulkily. 'I tell her … a lot.'

Jacob sips his coffee. 'Try harder,' he says while he

plays with the remote control of the CD-player. Soon Kate's latest addition sounds from the speakers once more.

John raises his brows and lets out a sigh. 'How hard can a man try?'

It's late in the evening when John slips into his pyjamas and slides under the covers beside Kate. He lies on his back, his arms outstretched under his head, and looks over to Kate, who is fast asleep, still wearing her blouse and slacks. Then he silently gets up, takes his pyjamas off and slides under the covers again. Quietly he moves closer to Kate, and cautiously starts undoing the buttons of her blouse. He gently pushes the blouse aside and starts playing with Kate's lace-bra. He looks at her face as he lets his fingers slide down her tummy towards her slacks and undoes the zip. There is a soft moan, and Kate rolls onto her side, her hand falls to her stomach. John touches Kate's face with his lips and softly whispers her name. There's no reaction. Carefully he wriggles his fingers under the front-closing hook of her bra and opens it. He slides his fingers around her breasts and he kisses her nipples. Her soft moaning makes John look up at her face. 'Kate,' he whispers. He kisses her again, this time on her lips. 'Kate. Oh, Kate,' he satisfyingly groans, but Kate's eyes remain closed and she turns over. John sees his chance and slides her arm out of the blouse and bra-strap. From behind he starts caressing her breasts and kissing her neck. Kate moves her head as if to chase off an annoying fly.

'Kate,' John sighs. His lips reach for her mouth.
'Nng.'
' It's me Kate. John. Are you awake?'
'What do you want?' Kate mutters; the slur is gone.
His hand moves down to her panties and between her

legs.

'John, what are you doing?'

' … Well, I thought, you might want to.'

She rolls onto her back and glances down her half-naked body on the bed. 'How … How did I get here?' she asks, bemused.

'Jacob took you up. You had a bit too much to drink at dinner.'

' … I doubt that my brother would leave me half-naked on the bed. John? Are you taking advantage of me?'

'Of course not! I just thought. Well. We haven't done it for a while, and I wanted to please you.'

'Please me?!' Kate collapses her head back in the pillow.

'Alright then,' she says. 'Please me.'

'What? Do you mean …?'

She bends over and takes her slacks and panties off, flinging the items halfway the bedroom and lies down again.

' … Are you sure?' John wants to know. 'I mean … '

'Well, get on with it! Please me!'

'Alright then,' he says.

He bends towards her and kisses her lips. Kate finds it hard to kiss him back. Slowly, John moves his lips down her chin and towards her breasts, his hand caressing her hips and thighs. He slides on top of her when he's ready. She can hardly enjoy it with the habitual moaning and groaning creature irritatingly destroying the moment. Soon Kate feels him inside of her. Fortunately, it doesn't take him long.

John lets out a gasp of breath as he rolls over to the side. 'How was that then?' he asks with a satisfied grin on his face. 'Darling.'

Kate rolls over and turns her back. Should she tell

him to leave the money on the bedside table when he goes out?

Kate's bare feet touch the cold patio paving the following morning. She wears an oversized T-shirt and jogging pants, her head feels numb, her hair is in tangles. It's close to noon. She can hardly remember the last time she overdid it on the drinking. It must have been in college, a binge-drinking evening. Then the reasons had been merely for kicks. She had vomited the contents of her stomach all over the marble hall floor.

She squints against the sun's glare in the hard blue sky. The cold breeze doesn't bother her. She goes back inside and makes her way to the kitchen, where she pours a large glass of orange juice. Looking out the window, she notices her car missing from the yard. Jacob probably took it. John wouldn't dream of driving on the 'wrong' side of the road.

For a moment she feels relief when at the end of the hall a door slams, but her alleviation evaporates when she realises, it is John coming out of her office.

'Kate. Darling. Good morning,' he says. 'Or should I say, good afternoon?' he adds with a grin. 'I hope you don't mind, but I have checked some agencies on the Internet, to find housekeeping staff in the area. I've wri – '

'Are you all packed, John?' Kate interrupts him.

It takes John by surprise. 'Packed? What do you mean?'

She looks at him and hopes he won't make a fuss. 'John, I don't really care if you're staying in a hotel tonight or are flying back to London. I just don't want you around me.'

'But … Kate,' he says, a feeble smile on his face, 'you can't be serious. You're not serious. I mean, after last night.'

'What about last night, John?'

'Well, you and I. You know.'

'No, John, I don't know. And I don't feel the slightest inclination to recall.'

She walks outside and sits down on one of the patio chairs, not in the mood for his boyish overindulgence.

'Kate!' He follows her behind. 'Kate, if there's *anything*, anything at all that I've done wrong. Just tell me. I do apologise.'

Kate glances up at him. 'John, I do not want you around me now. Go upstairs, pack your bags. Will you call for your taxi or shall I?'

John gives her a piercing look. 'Will you then please explain *why* you want me to go? I think I *am* entitled to an explanation. I mean, I know I'm not a Casanova but, we've had some good times. You have to admit. And it was you who was drunk last night. I can't help it if you didn't enjoy us ma – '

'John! Have you *ever* thought about why you want to be with me? Have you *ever* given a thought about what I mean to you?'

'But Kate, I love you!'

'Do you?'

'Of *course* I do!'

'Then maybe it is time for you to distance yourself from me for the time being. For now, I need space. I need to be on my own for a while. Don't blame yourself. You can't help the way you are.' She has a pleading look in her eyes.

John shrugs his shoulders. 'Well, if that's how you feel. Well then. I'd better … pack … my bags.'

John puts his suitcase down on the gravel when the

taxi pulls up. He dithers when Kate appears in the
doorway. She looks pretty in the dress she's now wearing,
her hair tied at the back with a ribbon. The cab driver gets
out and puts the case in the trunk. John glances at Kate as
he reaches for the car door, then sits down in the back
seat.

'Are you sure about this?' Jacob's quiet voice sounds
as he emerges behind Kate. Kate nods.

The tyres crunch on the gravel when the cab turns
and drives towards the main road. Kate slowly raises a
hand to wave goodbye. John doesn't notice.

She sighs. 'Yes, quite sure.'

They watch the taxi gradually picking up speed and
turn onto the Interstate.

'I'm sure he'll find a woman who suits his … ways
beautifully,' Kate says.

Jacob rests a hand on her shoulder. 'What about you?
What will you do now?'

Kate raises her eyebrows. 'Fancy a country show this
weekend?'

2

*T*he atmosphere at the venue is one of feverish activity.
Different women at different stages in their lives wear
smiles of nervous yearning on their faces. After the gates
open, the rush towards the stalls in the concert hall is
hectic, and fans try their best to be the first to purchase
items and collectables donned with images of their
favourite singer. Currently, the foyer and corridors are
teeming with fans. A situation that motivates Jacob to lead
his sister away from the crowds, and towards the
auditorium. Kate can't suppress a nervous smile when she
and Jacob enter the enormous hall to look for their seat
numbers as stated on their entrance tickets. 'Beats Royal
Albert Hall,' she says in a loud voice to overpower the
noises of anxious activity all around them. Jacob is more
reserved: 'I wouldn't go that far, Kate,' and takes his sister
by her elbow. 'This row,' he notices. They slide along the
seats and soon sit down.

'Good view of the stage,' Jacob observes.

'Yes,' Kate replies with a happy and satisfied
expression on her face. Jacob looks at his sister. He hasn't
seen her so excited since their grandparents had taken
them to see the last Wham! concert, but that was at a stage
in their lives when one could expect such indulgence. 'I
hope you're able to control yourself once it starts.'

Kate nudges him with her elbow. 'Of course,' she
replies coyly.

Jacob glides his gaze along the rows that are now
swiftly filling up with audience members, all decked out
in their favourite 'colours' and carrying banners with
singers' names unknown to him.

'If it were England playing, I'd understand,' he states.

The audience bursts out in incoherent screams when a man appears on the stage. Kate rubs her thighs in anticipation. 'Is he the opening act?' Jacob remarks.

Kate gives him a scrutinising look.

'Sorry,' Jacob says.

'There'll be some good singers on, you know,' Kate says. 'They might not be Andrea Bocelli or Sarah Brightman, but that's because they sing a different genre.'

Jacob nods empathetically.

The announcer on the stage clarifies that apart from the main act 'special surprises have been thrown in'. The crowds go wild, it appears that *that* is what they've come to see. Jacob bends over to Kate. 'Have you come to see a *special surprise*, too?'

'I can tell you're really starting to enjoy this,' Kate answers back.

Jacob stands up. 'I'll get us some drinks,' he says, 'before the real action starts.'

Kate looks up at him as he meanders his way through the throngs of people, but almost instantly her attention is drawn to a calling out of the name *David*.

Her eyes search the stage, but all that appears is a group of people that in her memory is stored as *hillbillies*. They burst out in whining song accompanied by steel guitars and fiddle. Kate feels undeniable embarrassment while the crowd bursts out in cheers and screams. She melts back in her seat and tries to enjoy that what is, after all, part of the cultural tradition she grew up in. She looks about her at people with smiles of excitement on their faces, and wonders why on earth someone could get excited over this repetitive rambling supported by such simple musical arrangements. Maybe John was right when he said she was too well-educated for this. All things considered, what person in his right mind would call a violin a fiddle? Or was this perception too snobbish?

'Oh, please God, save me from becoming a snob,' she whispers softly to herself. Maybe she has merely outgrown all this and has been fortunate enough to gain more knowledge than the average person here. She has seen more landmark theatres on the inside and has been to more beautiful, mainly classical, concerts in her lifetime than these people perhaps only dream about; given, one would have an affinity with classical music.

To her relief, the hillbillies have soon exhausted their oeuvre, but what appears on the stage next can hardly be called a significant improvement. It makes her wonder what the general conception of 'special surprise' presently is in her old home country. While the people around her join in for more audience participation, Kate starts to move about in her seat; those drinks do take long. For a moment she wished she had joined Jacob getting them. Composedly, she sits through this act as well when all of a sudden Jacob's hand is in front of her face offering her a paper cup with non-alcoholic beer. 'Sorry, they don't pour the other. Did I miss something?'

Kate shakes her head. 'Thanks,' she says and holds up the drink in a toasting gesture.

When the last act leaves the stage, the crowds express a more hushed mood, but ready for the next irruption with the appearance of the following artist. As the lights dim, there's an excited murmur going through the auditorium. A voice sounds from the loudspeakers, announcing the singer Kate has been anxious to see. She shoots up in her seat, but she has to stand up to see the stage because people in front of her block her view with their banners. Jacob looks up and about him when he finds himself surrounded by bodies. He soon follows Kate's example and stands up, too.

'This is like bloody Last Night of the Proms!' he yells in his sister's ear.

'I knew you would like it!' Kate calls out.

The band starts off the first tones of David Nelson's latest hit single when the man himself leisurely walks onto the stage, his guitar is hanging loosely from his shoulder. He waves at the crowds and takes his place in front of the microphone. Then he starts singing. Much to Kate's delight, the audience deservedly lets him, so she is indeed able to hear his appealing voice. With a smile on her face, she gazes captivated at the man on the stage. His wavy hair is tied at the back and he wears a cowboy hat. The shirt with the cut sleeves has made way for a light-blue jeans shirt with a design typical for singers of this genre. The sleeves he has rolled up to his elbows. Jacob looks around the room and at his sister, behaving in a way that's not her usual. Excitedly, she claps her hands after each song, scarcely able to keep the floor under her feet and hardly noticing what's happening around her.

'I *really* had no idea country music could turn you on like this,' Jacob manages to say in between two songs. Kate gives him an enigmatic look.

'Have you … met, before?' He makes an indistinct gesture with his hand. 'I mean, the CD and … '

'I found him on my land,' Kate says in a loud voice.

Jacob looks at her. 'Yes, of course.'

The man on stage introduces his last song of the evening, dedicating it to the wonderful crowd: 'You make a man feel at home.'

When the final notes fade, the audience irrupts in applause not heard so loud earlier on in the show. The cheering completely deafens David Nelson's 'Thank you very much'. He gives the audience a final wave and is gone.

Kate sits down and slides her hands across her face, then looks at Jacob. 'Wasn't he great!'

Jacob nods, 'I must say, he can sing,' he replies but his worried eyes rest on his sister. 'Are you all right?'

Kate lets out a sigh while people all around them find their way to the exits. Her face is brimming with happiness as she glances up at Jacob. 'Couldn't be better,' she says. Jacob notices the dreamy look in her eyes. 'Shall we go?' he suggests.

When the crowds have dispersed a little, Kate follows her brother to the nearest exit.

'Souvenir?' Jacob points at the groups of people seizing last-minute memorabilia from the stalls. Kate smiles. 'No, thanks. I hope you enjoyed the evening.'

'It was good fun,' he says as they try to find their way through the throngs of people. 'I haven't had so much fun since, well, since the last Last Night of the Proms.'

'You can't compare, Jacob.' She pulls his sleeve. 'Let's go this way.'

Kate shepherds them to an exit that won't lead them to the usual main exit doors.

'Kate … '

'Come on.' She opens the door, and they see a passage that leads away from the main stage. Kate pulls her reluctant brother by his arm, and with quick steps, she leads the way. Jacob's voice sounds subdued as he hurries after his sister. 'Kate, I don't think we're supposed to be here.'

They're almost at the end of the long passage when behind them they hear the sound of a door opening. Kate and Jacob turn around and see a man step into the corridor. There's a subtle sign of incredulity in his face and he gives them a scrutinizing look. 'Lost your way?' his deep voice booms towards them.

Jacob notices the security badge glistening on the man's broad chest.

'We're terribly sorry,' he says and takes Kate's arm to lead her back the way they came. 'Wrong door.'

The man keeps his eyes fixed on the two, his fists resting on the spare *tyre* around his waist.

'Terribly sorry,' Jacob apologises once more and makes to lead Kate away from the imposing security guard when another male voice sounds, asking what the commotion is about.

'All under control, sir. The way's clear,' the security guard's voice resonates, looking at Jacob with a penetrating glare, while the latter tries to remove his sister from this situation, but she pulls her arm away from him. The man who has just stepped through the doorway gives Kate a quick smile. He tips his cowboy hat. 'Ma'am. Kate.'

Jacob gives his sister another look.

Kate moves closer to David and holds out her hand.

'So glad we meet again,' she says.

'It's all right,' David tells the security guard as he shakes Kate's hand. 'We're old friends.'

Kate notices the twinkle in his eyes.

'We *so* enjoyed your show,' Kate utters. 'Me and my brother, Jacob.'

'Very good,' Jacob says convincingly when he too shakes the singer's hand.

'My pleasure.'

Jacob takes Kate's elbow to escort her to the correct exit door. 'I think we should go now,' he whispers in her ear.

'Won't you join me and my band?' David asks. 'We're done for tonight.'

Jacob shakes his head. Kate nods hers in anticipation.

'Kate, I don't think this is appropriate,' Jacob says in a hushed voice.

Kate shoots her brother a look, but before she can say something, David has taken her by her arm and leads her away, a bit further down the passage.

'Brothers,' he sympathises. 'Look, I hope you don't think I'm bold or anything but I would like to see you again.'

He moves his hand to his chest pocket and takes out a small card. 'We're almost at the end of a promotional tour, after that I'll have time. Call me. Please?' The beckoning raising of his eyebrows makes Kate's heart melt but she quickly regains herself. 'What about your girlfriend? I don't want you to think – '

'There was a girlfriend, nothing special. Hanger-on, more than anything.'

For a brief moment they stand, as David's green eyes meet Kate's shiny blue ones.

'Dinner okay with you?' Kate then suggests as she removes the business card from David's fingers.

David shows her a broad smile. 'You tell me where 'n when and I'll be there.'

He tips his hat. 'Ma'am.'

'Please. Kate,' she urges facetiously.

Before he turns to walk back to the dressing room he takes off his hat and gives her a warm kiss on her lips.

Jacob looks around, through the windscreen of the rental car, as he approaches the building where he currently has an office rented. He notices ample parking spaces by the side of the futuristic-looking building. It was opened only last year. After he has parked the car under one of the young trees, that nevertheless cast enough shade, he strides across and enters the building through the glass doors where he makes his way to the Reception of the cool, almost cold, interior. A coldness that isn't only caused by the air conditioning. His office in London is quite modern but it still has contained its warm atmosphere owing to the centuries-old structure. Supposedly, one cannot expect that of a new building. He tells the receptionist his name.

'Fourth floor, sir. Number 19.'

Jacob gives her a friendly nod and walks to one of the many elevators that conveniently keep clients from having to walk up the broad staircases in this glass, inner part of the building.

Not before long, he enters the office that, until now, he has only observed via the Internet. Hardly has he made himself at home in these unfamiliar surroundings, when there's a knock on the open door.

Jacob looks up at the young woman who is standing in his doorway. 'Yes?'

'Sorry, sir?' She looks at him expectantly. 'I'm here for the interview?'

Jacob checks his watch.

'I might be a bit early, sir?'

'No, no. Sit down, please.' He points at a chair in front of his desk.

She straightens her skirt and slides onto the chair. With a smile, she shoves the envelope she was holding towards Jacob. 'My reference, sir? And my CV?'

Jacob looks at the young woman and wonders if he has to sit through these antics all morning. He rests his hand on the envelope.

'Your name please?' he asks.

'Oh, I'm sorry, sir,' she smiles shyly. 'Earlene, sir,' and stretches out her hand. 'Earlene Parker.'

Jacob shakes her hand. 'Have you done this often?'
She looks at him as taken by surprise. 'What sir?'
'Going for job interviews.'
The girl's face drops. 'I'm sorry, sir. I ... I just want
to make a good impression.' She tries to resume her
former cheerfulness. 'You see, sir. So far I have only
worked for my uncle, sir. Never had to go for ... job
interviews.'

Jacob opens the envelope to inspect the information it
contains. Without looking up he asks her why she left her
uncle's employ, noticing the two sheets of paper barely
have any information on them. His eyes catch the heading
on the reference 'Parker Meats'.

'Were you sent here by the Job Centre?' Jacob wants
to know.

'Yes, sir?'

Jacob looks at her. 'So, you are familiar with our
policies and principles.'

The girl nods with a smile on her face. 'In my uncle's
business, I only worked in the office, sir.'

'Do you know what vegetarianism entails?'

'Sir?'

Jacob lets out a sigh. 'Do you know anything about
vegetarianism?'

'I know that vegetarians don't eat meat, sir. I have
been trying to become vegetarian myself, sir. Don't like
them killing all these cute little critters, then, after all,
we're all *God*'s creatures, ain't we, sir? But at my uncle's
it hasn't been easy at all, sir, all these people there, always
eating that meat. *After* they killed all these cute little
critters. God's creatures, sir! I'm telling you. It hurt my
heart, sir!'

Jacob tries to keep a straight face.

'Sir? So, then the Job Centre told me about your

business and I thought,' and she points a finger at Jacob, 'I'd be a lot better working for y'all. Sir.'

Jacob slowly runs a finger across his eyebrow, then hands her a sheet of paper.

'Would you, please? Just fill out your details. There's a small table in the hall.'

'Oh, thank you, sir.' Gratefully, the young woman makes her way there when the phone on Jacob's desk rings.

'Yes, thank you. Send them up, please.'

Not long after a young man takes the seat in front of his desk. Despite his young age, he has desirable qualities to work in a vegetarian business, having gathered experience in restaurants in London and Berlin, and holding certificates from the Vegetarian College in Manchester. It doesn't take Jacob long to decide who will be one of the cooks at the restaurant to be opened here in Memphis. He ticks off Matthew Yardley's name on his list before the next applicant enters.

Four hours have passed and Jacob has slowly started to pace up and down his office, thumbing through the forms that all the applicants were asked to fill out. He feels satisfied and occasionally smiles when certain applications remind him of certain applicants. There have been quite a few, sent by the Job Centre, but not all would be suitable or needed. The right qualifications don't always ensure a motivated employee. The woman who came in with only a reference that stated her excellent cleaning abilities might stand a better chance than the man with years of experience working in an office cafeteria. He takes another glance.

'Earlene Bongi Mkeba Parker,' he mumbles. '*My momma thought it was a good idea to remember our*

*African ancestors that way, sir.'* Jacob chuckles, takes the pile of applications and puts them in his briefcase before closing the door of his office.

On entering the parking lot he realises he has misjudged the rotation of the sun. His car is now in full glare. Warmth envelops him when he opens the doors but the cool autumn breeze soon makes the interior of the car more comfortable. He remembers to switch on his mobile phone that he'd switched off before the interviews. It bleeps straight away and Jacob notices a message from Kate. It takes him a few seconds to read it before he starts the car. He pushes down the accelerator, drives off the parking lot, and onto the road heading downtown. Honking horns startle him, and he realises just in time he was about to ghost drive. He quickly throws his wheel around and squeezes into one of the lanes on the right side, accompanied by more honking. 'Bloody Americans,' he mutters under his breath.

Jacob has never been a keen driver and it has taken him some time to get used to driving on the right-hand side of the road. He glances beside him to see a boy pulling faces at him from the back seat of a car. The mother behind the wheel pays no attention. She is too busy steering with one hand and chattering in the cellphone she holds against her ear, with the other. Jacob is glad when he finally reaches the inner city where it doesn't take him long to find the large parking garage, following the instructions Kate gave him. After a long search, he finally turns into a free space in the multi-layered car-*storage*.

'Waste of time,' he tells himself. He is always so much better off taking taxis that drop you where you need to be. He grabs the briefcase and locks up before he finds his way out of the maze, taking in a deep breath as he enters the street. His eyes search for the coffee shop Kate mentioned in her text message.

'Oh, excuse me,' he stops a passer-by. 'Café Paris?'

The man nods his head in the right direction. 'Cross. Through that narrow street. It's right behind there.'

Jacob thanks the man and soon finds the establishment.

'What took you so long?' Kate greets him. After the aggravation getting here, he wasn't waiting for his sister's vexing questions. 'Sorry, can't get used to the traffic here.' Jacob motions the waitress and orders a cold beer.

'It's actually better than driving around London.'

'I never drive around London. I *am* driven.'

Kate looks at her brother, then focuses on his briefcase. 'Any luck this morning?'

Jacob takes out the applications and hands them to her. Kate reaches into her bag to give him her findings.

'I talked to the architects,' she says before starting to read through the applications. Jacob opens Kate's folder and instantly shows an approving nod.

'I like this,' he says, eyeing at one of the drawings Kate gave him. 'This arching front looks nicely … organic.' He lets his finger slide over the drawing before looking at the rest of them.

Kate half listens as she works her way through the forms, noticing that some Job Centres would send any unemployed individual for a job interview. She sorts the applications into a 'yes' and 'no' pile. Jacob leans back when the waitress puts the drink in front of him. 'Are you having lunch here?' he asks his sister.

Kate ignores the question. 'Who's this, Charlene Presley? Any relation?' Kate queries.

'Cousin, she claimed. A hundred times removed, more like.'

'Clearly hasn't benefited from the estate. Look at her address and she's only worked in a launderette.'

Jacob takes a gulp of his beer. 'I've marked the ones I think we can train, and there are a few we could put to work straight away. Now, what about lunch. Here? Or would you rather go home.'

'There's also the matter of stock,' Kate mentions as they are pulling onto the Interstate to drive back to the house. 'Getting the right GMO-free supplies in.'

With Jacob driving, Kate has her hands free to select some music for the way home. A moment later David Nelson's voice is sounding through the speakers.

Jacob glances sideways. 'You're quite taken by this chap, aren't you?'

Kate merely looks at her brother.

'You weren't thinking of starting something with this guy, were you? I mean, John wasn't the right one for you, really. But, a country singer?'

'As I mentioned,' Kate chooses to disregard her brother's attempts to start that conversation, 'I've looked into GMO-free suppliers in this country and will contact them.'

Jacob shakes his head at his sister's denial and steers the car, that he imperceptibly started pushing above the speed limit, along the road. Kate lays her hand on his arm to make him slow down. 'Careful, Jacob.'

The trees by the side of the road are getting ready for their winter slumber. Leaves have begun to fall and blow against the windscreen.

'If it makes you feel better, I'll invite David for dinner one evening,' Kate says.

'In that case, I might ask Maria to come over,' he says. 'She's just finished her talks on nutrition.'

Kate's fingers tap along with one of the upbeat songs on David's CD and she gazes through the car window. The scenery around the area where they were born, pleases her senses.

'If we can't get the right supplies in this country, with all the bureaucracy,' Jacob mentions, 'I'll fly back to London and call a meeting. See what we can accomplish elsewhere.'

Kate agrees. 'We can look at all the options over lunch.'

As the CD is sounding one of its last songs, Jacob turns into the driveway to the house.

Nashville's skyline appears into Kate's view and soon she reaches the city boundaries. Finding the venue is not a hard task with the announcer on her car radio bellowing out this night's main event and giving directions. Shortly, she nears the concert hall and finds a space to park her car. With her backstage pass, she has no problem being admitted into the hall and is led to the dressing rooms by one of David's personal assistants.

'Kate, you made it!' is David's reaction when he lays eyes on her.

'Of course.'

David pulls her towards him. 'I'll show you around. We'll be rehearsing soon, you can watch.' Before Kate can answer he kisses her. 'OK?'

Kate nods. 'That's why I've come, to see you, and listen. I *really* like your CD,' she adds with a smile.

'I don't want to sound cocky, but you're not the only one,' David assures her. He opens a small fridge. 'Drink?'

'Sure. Do you have anything soft?'

David hands her a mineral water. 'Let's go, I'll show you the building.' Kate allows herself to be led by David as they walk through the large concert hall. Sound engineers and technicians are busy preparing the venue for tonight's show. David leads Kate to the centre of the stage. 'Here's where it all happens!' he informs her gladly.

Kate observes the seating in the auditorium. They resemble seats in a football stadium. She recalls the time her uncle took her onto the stage of the Royal Albert Hall before he was to conduct the Royal Philharmonic. That looked so much more imposing.

Kate stands in front of the microphone. 'So this is your spot?' she asks.

'Yep.'

When David's band members assemble on the stage, David takes Kate's hand and leads her to the front row. 'You just sit right there and relax. Enjoy the show,' he tells her with a wink, to then join his band on stage. After tuning their instruments the musicians start playing. No matter her upbringing -John couldn't resist pointing out to her- Kate finds herself starting to love an entirely different genre of music than what she is used to when listening to this country band. The pleasure is enhanced when David starts singing. It might be just a rehearsal but Kate thoroughly enjoys this private show, even without the nervous anxiety of an audience intensifying the atmosphere. Familiar songs waft towards her, and she applauds each one. Halfway through the rehearsal, Kate senses someone moving into the seat beside hers. She looks and sees a chubby man sitting next to her. Without acknowledging her he, too, watches the rehearsal. When the last song has sounded he offers Kate a fleshy hand.

'Fred,' he says.

'Hello,' Kate replies shaking the hand; it feels clammy.

'David's friend?' Fred asks without facing her.

Kate looks at him. 'Yes, I'm a friend of David.'

He turns to face her. 'Pleasure,' he then says. 'Not from around here, are you?'

'London,' Kate replies.

'That's England, right?'

'Yes.'

'Great soccer players come from there.'

'I'm not very familiar with football,' Kate says, her eyes drifting to the man she has come to see and who now walks towards the edge of the stage.

'I see you've met my manager,' David says. 'Ready to go?'

The endomorphic man lifts himself from the seat. 'David, a word,' he demands.

David jumps down to follow Fred away from the stage. 'Excuse us,' he addresses Kate over his shoulder.

From a distance Kate observes the manager making constrained hand movements and looking at David as if he were addressing a ten-year-old.

She confronts David when he returns to her side. 'What was that about?' she wonders. David takes her by the arm. 'Nothing. Manager talk. Let's go somewhere, have something to eat before the show.'

Prior to leaving the auditorium, Kate looks over her shoulder to see Fred watching them.

David shows her through the passages and corridors of the large concert hall until daylight reveals the parking lot. They walk to a dark green four-wheel-drive.

'I see you got rid of the pick-up,' Kate says.

'It's just on loan. Can't really show my face in this town with my old run-down pick-up, can I?' He opens the door for Kate to get in.

'Where do you live, anyway?' Kate asks as they drive off. Before he can merge with the traffic Kate notices a few young women pointing at them and they start waving their hands excitedly.

'It's him! It's him!' Kate hears through the open car window. 'David!' the women cry out. One of them is nervously aiming her cellphone at the four-wheel-drive to take a photo. 'David! This way!'

Kate swiftly turns her head in the opposite direction.

'Fans,' David explains. He waves at them and at the same time sees a space that allows him to drive away.

'Let's get out of here,' he says and soon they're in the fast lane. 'Jackson.'

'What?' Kate says.

'Jackson, where I live.'

'Oh.' Somewhere halfway between her house and Nashville, Kate realises.

'Have you been making music long?' she asks him.

'For years, but it took a while to get noticed.'

'Well, I'm glad *I* noticed you,' Kate assures him. David briefly faces her, and a quick smile plays around his lips before he returns his focus on the road. Shortly after, he turns off and parks the car in an area with a few shops and takeaway burger places.

'What can I get you?' he offers.

Kate looks at him. 'I'm fine, thank you.'

'You sure?'

Kate nods. 'What if I take *you* to a nice restaurant, after your show,' she suggests.

David shakes his head adamantly. 'No, no.'

Kate doesn't understand. 'Why not?'

'Kate, let's make one thing clear. When I invite a woman to dinner, *I* pay for that dinner.'

'Fine. I take you, you pay.' Kate smiles at him.

'Is that how it works in your country?' David is not persuaded. 'If you don't mind I'll get myself something to eat now. I still got to work tonight.'

Kate watches him as he gets out and walks towards the nearest burger joint. Although the man intrigues her she's beginning to think she's being too precipitate, too eager. Maybe she shouldn't have gone this far, but it was *he* who phoned *her*, asked her if she wanted to join him at his last concert of the tour.

She browses through the CD collection that she has spotted under the dashboard and finds one that doesn't contain David Nelson songs.

'Elvis! Great choice,' David says when he's back with his pre-dinner snack. 'Wanna go over there?' He nods towards a bench.

'OK,' Kate replies and gets out of the car.

'Leave the door open so we can hear the music.'

Accompanied by 'Suspicious Minds' Kate follows David and sits down next to him on a bench that's partly wrapped in the shade of a nearby tree. David puts the container beside him on the bench to then take an eager bite from what he has just purchased. 'You sure you don't want anything?' he asks between two bites.

'No, thank you. I'd like to keep my appetite for later.'

'All right,' David says.

As he indulges in his food Kate recalls the strange situation between him and his manager. David doesn't strike her as a person who would allow others to intimidate him. He has given her the impression of being someone with a healthy dose of self-confidence and despite his strong, trained, body he emanates kindness and a charm that those around him, and not in the least his fans, must perceive as compelling. Still, as she sits here with David, who hasn't taken long to eat his burger, his attitude appears to conflict with her initial feelings about him. 'Does going on stage and sing in front of all those people never make you nervous?' Kate asks.

David wipes his mouth and looks at her. 'Yeah, it does.' He stuffs the paper napkin in the used container. 'But the feeling you get, the energy coming from the audience,' his eyes glisten, 'there's nothing that equals that.'

He gets up and throws his garbage in the trash-can. 'Shall we?' It sounds more like a demand than a request. Kate stands up and follows him to the four-wheel-drive.

After David and his band had disappeared from the stage, the final applause from the audience has sounded, and the cheerful screams have faded, Kate gets up to find her way to his dressing room. Security guards in the passage behind the auditorium push a few female fans back to the exit doors. Kate, wearing her pass, has no problem getting through. As one of the guards moves aside for only a few seconds to allow Kate to walk on, one young woman seizes her chance and squeezes past Kate. She makes a run for it towards the dressing rooms with the security guards yelling after her to stop as they cannot leave their station. Kate finds the situation rather amusing and follows the fan who soon makes it to David's dressing room. One of David's band members is just opening the door, and with a bemused look on his face watches the young woman fly past him and burst into the room. When Kate arrives at the door, she witnesses the fan holding her arms tightly around David's neck. Members of his band rush towards him and free David from the entanglement. They have a good laugh about the situation. As Kate looks on, David starts an amicable conversation with the woman and he hands her a signed photograph. Before she's led outside by one of the guards, David thanks her and kisses her on the lips. The scene disconcerts Kate, and she suddenly realises that this is not what she anticipated her relationship with David to be. She feels she's not wanted here and tries to make a quiet escape.

'Kate!'

Kate hastily walks into the passage but David is right behind her and grabs her arm. She gives him an apathetic look. 'I enjoyed your show tremendously but I have to get back now,' she says.

'Kate, what's going on?'

'David, I think we shouldn't become too friendly,' she says collectedly, removing David's hand from her arm.

'You're not offended by that fan, are you? For heaven's sake, Kate, that doesn't mean anything. All in a day's work.'

Kate gives him a cool glance before she turns and begins to walk to the exit doors, but David grabs her arm once more and leads her away from the dressing rooms. 'Don't behave like a darn highfalutin English snob,' he says under his breath.

Kate rips her arm free. '*Don't* call me a snob! Who's lapping up women here?'

David gives her a harsh look. 'I really thought you had more class, Kate, but I suppose I was mistaken. It's all a facade isn't it?'

'And your behaviour? All a facade too?'

David shakes his head as he looks at her. 'No. What you see is what you get.'

'So, you mean that this,' she gestures with her hand, 'situation, with your female fans, is normal?'

'Yeah. And now that you bring it up, male fans can get really excited too. Only they don't get so physical,' he whispers close to her ear.

Kate distances herself from David.

'Now don't tell me that over there in England people

don't get excited at pop concerts.'

'Of course they do,' Kate affirms. 'But – '

'But what? Not in your circles?' he deduces with irony in his voice.

'There you go again,' Kate says. 'There's nothing wrong with my circles. I wouldn't be where I am today if it hadn't been for *my circles*.'

'I'm sorry,' David says and holds out his hand. Kate hesitates but then puts her hand in his.

'So where's this highfalutin restaurant you were going to take me to,' he says as he folds an arm around Kate's waist. Kate nudges him in his side. David twitches.

'I should have told you,' Kate says. 'I'm a vegetarian. I never eat stuff from those places we went to this afternoon.'

A fresh drizzle softly descends from the darkness above Nashville. The tiny drops give the road a gleaming appearance that's made more colourful by streaks from the neon lights. Most restaurants have closed and Kate and David find their way between others who have made a night of it. David holds Kate firmly close to him.

They hadn't foreseen the rain, tucked away all evening in a superb vegetarian restaurant David had never known about and they only happened upon this evening.

'I could've sworn I had the best steak,' David says close to Kate's face. 'They could've fooled me.' His breath still carries the smell of the French wine. Kate snuggles up closer to David. 'I should've brought a jacket.'

'Never mind, darling, I'll keep you warm … What's wrong?'

Kate has frozen in David's arms. She stops and looks up at him.

'Please, David, promise me one thing. Don't *ever* call me *darling*.'

'Sure. If that's what you want. Honeybun.'

'Unpleasant connotation,' Kate explains.

He pulls her close once more. 'We'd better go where it's warm,' he says softly.

When they've gone up the few steps of the hotel where David is staying, a doorman welcomes them and holds the door for them to go through.

'Do you want to go straight up or have a drink at the bar?' David questions.

'Up, please.'

David takes his key and then Kate's hand. He gives her a quick kiss as they go into the conveniently empty elevator. As soon as the doors have closed Kate slides her arms around David's neck and starts kissing him. David moves his hand along Kate's neck as he returns her caresses. They are abruptly disturbed when on the first floor the door opens, and a nanny with a sleeping baby in her arms enters. She smiles at the couple, then has a closer look at David.

'Ain't you … ?'

'No,' David is quick to say.

'I can swear you're – '

'I always get that,' David says. 'It's my brother.'

'You're kidding me!' the girl exclaims. The baby moves in her arms. 'Oh, I *so* wish I had a pen so I could get the autograph of Billy Ray Cyrus' *brother*!'

The doors of the elevator open and David and Kate make a swift exit. 'Good night,' David wishes the girl.

Kate bursts out laughing. 'Oh my, picture me on a night out with … mmmpff.' David puts his hand over her mouth. 'Ssshh, hush, don't let the whole hotel know.'

He moves closer and lowers his hand to kiss her, then

softly moves his lips down to her neck, pulling her jumper aside to reach her shoulder.

'David … David, there's close circuit television here,' she says in a breathy voice.

'Darn.' He looks around. 'Are we on the right floor?' and checks the numbers on the doors.

'Here,' Kate says, taking the key from him and opening his room door. Barely inside and Kate kicks off her shoes and takes off her jumper and bra.

'Wait!' David says. '*Not* so fast.'

Kate glances at him, bemused, grabs her jumper and holds it prudishly in front of her naked breasts. David looks at her and very slowly starts undoing his belt and one by one undoes the buttons on his shirt. Roguishly, he slides the item off his shoulders and lets it swirl to the floor exposing his muscular chest. Kate can't suppress her sniggering. The extreme slow unzipping of his fly evokes a nervous giggle from Kate as David's behaviour titillates her feelings. He slips off his jeans. Kate drops her jumper and unzips her slacks. As the clothing falls to the floor, she moves close to David to feel his strong body touching her soft skin. Gently he caresses her lips with his, slowly moving down to her neck, sliding his hands along her back, Kate touches his gently with her fingertips, his long hair caressing the back of her hand leaves her tingling, the smell of his skin excites her. David moves closer to the bed and tenderly lowers Kate down. His kissing her skin kindles her emotions, he strokes her breasts and slowly moves on top of her. Kate slides her leg around his as David starts making slow thrusting moves. She feels the warmth of their bodies and gasps for breath as David arouses her. She wants to kiss him, but it's the electrifying tingling all over her body that connects her to this man.

Kate's head rests near David's shoulder as she watches the morning sun gradually light the room; sunlight accompanied by muffled traffic noises. She wonders how she could have ever lasted so long with John. She can't think of anything else than that they're both from the same circles. She has to smile at the thought and looks at David as he lies there, breathing steadily. *They* both come from the same background, in a way. But does it matter? What she feels for David she has never felt for John, or anyone else. John just appeared in her life when his mother thought it was time for him to be married. The man lying next to her is a different matter. She rolls over and slides her arm across his chest, still half asleep he lets his hand rest on her arm. Kate feels she never wants to let him go when a knock on the door interrupts their togetherness. David slowly opens his eyes, then closes them again. The knocking sounds harsher the second time.

'What the hell … ' David mumbles.

'Shall I get it?' Kate offers.

David slides out of the bed. 'If it's Fred, he's knocked his last.'

'Fred? What would *he* want?'

David grabs his dressing robe from the bathroom and walks to the door. Still tying the robe around him, he opens the door.

'Ready, my boy?' Fred barks and walks into the room.

'Fred … '

'Don't tell me you forgot your interview at WMRB at seven-thirty,' and, noticing Kate in the bed, 'morning ma'am.'

'What's the time?' David's inquiring voice sounds annoyed.

'Almost seven.'

'Fred, go downstairs,' David says pushing his manager towards the door, 'get yourself some breakfast and let me get ready.'

Fred looks at him and casts a glance at Kate who has pulled the sheet up to her chin. 'Ten minutes,' he says and walks out.

David shakes his head, goes to the small fridge, takes out a bottle and gulps some water down.

'Pity,' Kate says. 'I was looking forward to a nice long breakfast with you.'

'Sorry, Kate.' He walks into the bathroom and the shower starts running.

Kate slips out of the bed and walks into the bathroom, too. She opens the steamed-up shower door and moves in front of David. 'Let me at least wash your back,' she says and slides her arms around him. David gives her a contented look. 'He only came to check up on me,' he says. 'That radio station is just around the corner. Enough time.'

He kisses her as her hands massage his back with the foam, but the harsh streaming water brings him back to reality. It not only washes away the remnants of soap but also their time together. David turns off the shower and reaches for the towels. He wraps Kate in one and the other he ties around his waist. Water drips from his wet hair to the floor.

'I'm sorry, Kate, but I don't think it's a good idea to come with me. There'll be photographers.' He grabs his boots off the floor and rummages through his wardrobe, seizing a pair of jeans and a western shirt.

'I understand,' Kate says. She struggles to suppress her disappointment. 'I need to get back anyway.'

David hesitates at the sight of the Stetson but leaves

it. He kisses her and then walks to the door. 'I will call you,' he says. 'Get room service to send you up some breakfast. Eat something before you drive back.'

The door slams and Kate, wrapped in the towel, her wet hair encircling her face, is left in the deserted hotel room.

While the pebbles in the driveway crunch underneath the tyres, Kate switches off her car radio. She has listened to David being interviewed, an interview interspersed with his music. David in his world and she, Kate, just a businesswoman listening to a broadcast on her car radio while driving home. How serious is he about her? When they're together, she seems to be his whole world, but he switches back to his so easily when he needs to comply with his work. But she can't ignore last night, she would give a tremendous amount just to have him by her side this very minute.

She steps out of the car as her stable boy Billy comes out of the house. He walks across to the fields where Kate notices Chief and her latest purchase by the fence.

She enters the house by the kitchen door. 'Kate?' Jacob's voice sounds.

'Morning, Jacob.'

He comes in from the lounge room. 'Where were you? I'd hoped you'd be home when I brought Maria.'

In his wake a pretty, slender young woman enters the kitchen, her Asian visage hemmed in by bobbed black hair.

'My sister, Kate. Kate, Maria.'

Kate feels the smoothness of the subtle handshake. 'Welcome,' Kate says. 'Pleased to meet you.'

Maria's perfect teeth show a white smile. 'Likewise, likewise.'

'Will you please, excuse me,' Kate says, 'I'd like to freshen up.' Before the others have a chance to say another word, Kate is gone.

Upstairs in her bedroom, Kate drops down on the bed and closes her eyes.

Then remembers her phone and reaches for her handbag. There is one message, from Jacob, none from David. She sits on the side of her bed before rising to look for a comfortable outfit to wear, hoping her brother hasn't planned anything that involves the business. The last thing she feels inclined to do is work. Maybe she should call David now, he might be wondering if she has made it home all right. Or would he? Wouldn't he have called her already if he was truly worried about her? She throws a jumper over her head, straightens it, and walks onto the landing.

Reaching the bottom steps and entering the kitchen, Kate finds her brother in harmonious cooperation with his girlfriend while they are organising lunch. She takes a cup from the tray and pours some freshly brewed coffee in it. Maria is industriously preparing a rice dish at the stove while Jacob slides cut vegetables to the dish, much to Maria's approval who gives him brief instructions. Without a doubt, her knowledge of nutrition should create a very nourishing meal.

Out of a desire to make herself useful, Kate starts laying the table and sits down to finish her coffee.

Maria gives her a friendly smile when she puts the dish on the table.

'I hope you like it,' she says, 'it's made with tofu.'

'It smells great,' Kate replies.

Jacob starts filling up their plates while Maria pours Jasmine tea in cups Kate hasn't seen in her household before. She observes the two who are busying themselves in compatible collaboration. They'd make a great team, Kate contemplates.

Jacob holds up his cup. 'Cheers,' he says and the other two follow suit.

It dawns on Kate that Jacob has spoken little since she arrived home. Is he too absorbed in his recent relationship?

'So when did you arrive?' Kate asks Maria.

'Last night.'

'I don't like to mingle in your affairs, Kate, but you had me worried,' Jacob interferes. 'You could at least have left a message.'

'I'm sorry. I was in Nashville to see David's show.'

Jacob doesn't know whether to be surprised or circumspect; he gives her a searching look.

'It became a bit late so I stayed over.'

'You should have let me know,' Jacob merely says.

Kate looks at her brother with moderate guilt in her eyes. 'I am sorry,' she says. He is right, she hadn't thought, too preoccupied with the possibilities of a new relationship. She knows how worried Jacob gets when she's out on the road.

'I have builders starting the renovations tomorrow,' Jacob says. 'I hope they can finish the job in the coming month.'

Kate is only half listening. Did she hear her mobile ring? She'd put it down in the lounge room.

'Kate,' Jacob's voice sounds. 'I thought you were going to look into the colour scheme.'

'What? What colour scheme?'

Jacob looks at her. 'For the restaurant.'

'I thought we were going to pursue the same scheme as in the UK? Brand recognition.'

'Oh,' Jacob says, 'we've agreed on that now?'

Kate glances at him and nods. 'I think it's a good idea.' She faces Maria. 'Very tasty dish, Maria. Thank you.'

David feels content about the interview he has just given until he notices his manager when he steps out of the studio. 'Satisfied?' David pounces upon him.

Fred's eyes turn icy cold. 'Don't you talk to me like that, boy. You'd never have made it this far if it weren't for me.'

David returns the look. 'You wouldn't have earned a penny if it weren't for me.' He pokes a finger at Fred. 'And don't ever call me *boy*.'

Fred's face loses its cold glare as the muscles relax. 'Alright, but I – '

'And don't *ever* burst into my hotel room again like you did this morning,' David warns and turns to leave.

Fred grabs him by his arm. 'Yes, I think we should have a word about that.'

'About what?'

'About your getting too close to certain … creatures from the opposite sex.'

David's eyes turn to anger.

'I'm telling you,' Fred goes on, 'at this stage in your career, your up and coming career,' he says, pointing a warning finger, 'I don't think it's a good idea. You've got a lot of female fans that are bloody head over heels over you. *They* buy your albums. *They* come to see your shows. If they find out – '

David whacks Fred's pointing finger aside. 'They come to see the shows because they love the music,' David says with restrained anger in his voice. 'They buy the CD's because they love the music. Don't act like a godforsaken pervert, Fred. You just can't take it that I'm getting the best end of the deal.'

Fred's face freezes. 'I'm telling you for the last time, don't pursue anything serious with anyone from the opposite sex, or you can kiss your career goodbye.'

David moves close to Fred's face. 'You know what I think, Freddy boy, that you're jealous, that I *can* have a love life and that you, with your pathetically hiding your sexual preference, cannot.'

David casts one more look at Fred's face, then turns and walks to the exit doors. Hearing Fred's busy footsteps following his stride, David makes for the reception to go outside, but before he can reach the revolving doors Fred has caught up with him.

'What were you implying just now,' Fred demands in a low voice.

'You know very well what I'm talking about, Fred, and I'm warning you for the last time. Keep away from my private life.'

'I was hired to see to it that your career was led along the right channels,' Fred says sharply, 'to see to it you'd get the best deals.' He bangs his fist against the wall. 'Damn it! I'm one of the best in the business. I'll be damned if I let you ruin that.'

'Then do what you have to do. But stay away from my private affairs.' He gives Fred one last hard look and then walks out of the building.

David steers the four-wheel-drive to the left, exits the Interstate, and drives onto a road that will take him to the south side of Jackson where he turns off into one of the suburbs. At a steady pace, he passes neighbourhoods and sees the local Mall. He flicks on his indicator to make for its parking lot but when he sees a huge poster displaying his face in a record shop window, he drives on.

On the corner of a side street, he notices a small flower shop. He pulls up in front of it and jumps out, leaving the car door open. He opts for a bunch of colourful flowers, pays the shopkeeper, jumps back into his vehicle and speeds off.

He drives through a leafy area that has pleasant-looking houses with neat gardens on both sides of the street. The driveways of the quatre-acre properties lead to garages that are attached to the houses. David turns into one of the driveways and stops behind the dark red Chevrolet that is parked in front of the garage. On the top floor of the house, a face is visible in one of the windows. David grabs the bunch of flowers from the seat and quickly walks up the few steps to the back door.

'Ma?' he hollers when he doesn't find his mother in the kitchen.

Footsteps sound from the hall. 'David? Son, I thought you were on this tour thing.'

His mother is dressed in a pair of white pants and a colourful blouse in shades of blue when she enters the kitchen, her dyed hair in a neat do around her head.

'Good to have you home,' she says and embraces him.

He holds up the flowers. 'Tour's finished,' he replies.

'Thank you, son,' his mother says and smells the flowers. 'Did you get a new car?' she continues as she peeks in the cupboard under the sink and takes out a vase.

'No. It's on loan.'

She fills up the vase with water and puts the flowers in it. 'Can I get you anything? Coffee?' She gives the arrangement a brief tidy and then places the vase on the kitchen table before she switches on the water kettle.

'Fine,' David replies.

'So, what did you do on this tour? I hear your record

on the radio all the time,' she adds with pride.

'Ma, you should've come. I told you, I could've had someone collect you when we did Nashville.'

'I don't need collecting. I can drive myself, but I had to work, you know I had to work. I can't just stay away from the hospital.' She pours the boiling water over the freeze-dried coffee in the mugs and places one in front of him.

'Next time,' she promises. 'I'll make sure to be there next time.'

'It went really well,' David says, 'sometimes too well. Sometimes I think things go too fast. Just last year we were doing bars and clubs and now it's stadiums.'

His mother rests her hand on his arm. 'Be glad, thank the good Lord. You've waited long enough for this to happen.' She stirs some sweetener through her coffee. 'How long are you home for?'

'We have a few TV appearances coming up, few interviews, maybe another show and then we'll be in the studio, rest of the year, working on the next CD … In Nashville,' he adds.

'You will barely see little Sam,' his mother cautions him.

'I'll go over on the way to my place.'

His mother looks at him. 'You should go more often. The boy's only three, he won't remember you when you're always gone.'

'He will – '

'You know Melanie's gotten married, do you? Sammy will think her new husband is his dad.'

Dejected, David looks at his mother.

'I'm just saying, son. You'll have to bear these things in mind.'

'Do you see him?'

'Thank God I do. Melanie calls me when she needs a sitter. Rest of the time she probably puts him in day-care. Don't know about *his* parents, I think they live in Florida.'

David takes a final swallow from his coffee. 'I'd better go.'

'Your plant died on me but I got you a new one,' his mother says. She rummages in a large bag she has by the pantry. 'Here, give Sammy this from me. He asked for one,' and hands him a colourful teddy-bear.

'Don't they come in brown anymore?' David wonders.

'He wanted this one,' his mother replies. She holds his face in her hands and kisses him on both cheeks. 'Please, come by any time while you're here,' she says. 'Don't forget your momma. With Pete all the way in Hawaii, soon I won't have any of my sons here.'

'Ma, you know we come by as often as we can,' David says. He hugs his mother and then walks out the door. 'I'll be seeing you.'

He looks at the teddy-bear before he puts it next to him on the front seat of the four-wheel-drive. He sees his mother waving at him from behind the kitchen window and with a brief honk from the horn he backs out of the drive.

On the other side of town, David parks his car in front of an apartment building. He looks up towards the third floor at one of the flats before he gets out and locks the vehicle.

Even though this is a thoroughfare, children play in the street of these unsafe surroundings. When a basketball rolls his way, David kicks it back to the boys playing on the sidewalk. He notices an alleyway with a small courtyard where a basket is attached to a wall. David crosses the street and rings the bell for the third floor flat. He announces himself when he hears a noise through the intercom. A male voice sounds: 'Mel's not here.'

'I come to see Sammy,' David says. For a few moments, there is no response. David rings the bell again. When a buzzer sounds, he pushes the door and enters the building. The hall looks clean but remnants of gravity are still visible through the thin layer of paint on the walls. David presses the button for the elevator, the doors open and he gets in.

When the doors open on the third floor he sees his little boy waiting for him in the hall. 'Daddy!' he cries. David lifts Sammy off the floor and into his arms. 'Sammy, my boy.'

David looks about him but sees all the doors around the hall closed. 'Where's Mummy gone?' he asks Sammy.

'To the stow,' the little boy replies.

'Why are you here by yourself in the hall?'

'Stuwat said, Stuwat said, wait.'

As he gives Sammy the present from his grandma, David walks to the flat and rings the bell. After a moment, the door opens, and a bald man with a well-trimmed goatee opens the door. Above his right ear, its rim pierced with studs and rings, a tattoo is visible.

'Well, if it ain't our famous singer!' he exclaims.

David looks at him. 'Why do you leave a three-year-old alone in the hall?'

Stuart's piercing brown eyes lose their former glee. 'Well, it was Sam you came to see, not me.'

David gives him another look. 'I want to take Sammy out for a bit. I hope his mother won't mind.'

'Well, uh, David. We had plans and Mel can be back any moment. I don't think now is a good time.'

'I go with you, Daddy,' Sammy says and puts his

arms a little tighter around his father's neck.

'Know what,' David says, 'Sammy can stay with me tonight, then you two can have all the time to yourselves. I'll have him back tomorrow first thing,' and he wants to go back into the elevator but Stuart pulls him by his sleeve. 'Like I said, now is not a good time. Mel won't like it.'

'Look, I hardly get to see my boy. I think now is an excellent time.' David steps into the lift holding Sammy close to him.

'Mel will be mad!' Stuart yells as the door closes.

'Let's get some food and then we go over to my house,' David says as he straps Sammy into the seatbelt of the car seat. Out of sheer excitement, the boy dangles his legs and claps his little hands. 'Daddy's house, Daddy's house!' David smiles and walks around to the driver's seat with a happy demeanour now that he has his son with him. He starts the engine and accelerates.

He is about to turn the corner, when David notices his former girlfriend driving up from the opposite direction. She is not aware of the two, and David drives on without allowing himself to be recognised. 'You haven't told me if you like Grandma's present,' David says. 'Shall we take it back to the store?'

'No!' Sammy cries. He grabs the teddy-bear and hugs it. 'I like it!' he laughs.

'Do you like living with Mummy and Stuart?'

The boy's attitude changes and he wriggles his small shoulders. '*You* have to live with us,' he says.

'Sam, I can't live with you. Mummy is married to Stuart, not to me.'

'Stuwat is stupid,' Sammy says.

David briefly glances sideways. 'Who taught you that

word?'

Not far from his house, David drives the four-wheel-drive onto the parking lot by a Health Food store. Sammy wriggles impatiently in his seatbelt. 'Daddy. Daddy.' David unclasps the belt and lifts his son from the child seat. Sammy holds his new bear by a paw as his father gives him a ride on his shoulders to walk across to the shop.

'Do you know what you want to eat?' David wants to know.

'Nice things.'

'OK, we'll get some nice things.'

He lifts Sammy back to the ground. 'Now, let's see.' David grabs a shopping trolley and instead of Sammy, the teddy-bear gets to sit in the child's seat. Sammy walks next to his father and helps him wherever he can, carrying vegetables and fruits, yoghurt and cheese, bread and butter. Sammy carries some things he has found on the shelves, too.

'Are you going to eat that?' David asks.

'Yes.'

David has a closer look at the jars of peanut butter and jam. 'OK. Let's pay.'

'Let's pay,' Sammy happily repeats after his father and puts his jars in front of the check-out girl who smiles at the boy.

David pays as Sammy helpfully puts groceries in a bag. Father and son leave the store and walk back to the four-wheel-drive. 'Now we go home,' Sammy says.

'Yes, now we go home,' David concurs and lifts his son onto the front seat.

Only a lamp sheds light into the room as David sits on the couch, his feet relaxing on a small stool in front of him. Sammy's head rests on his lap and David gently strokes his fine, blond hair. Soon after supper, the boy had dozed off. Currently he lies sleeping, his grandma's latest gift under his arm, totally at peace. David wonders if his three-year-old was so tired because of so many unfamiliar situations happening around him lately, that he only feels at ease with his real dad, or whether it's just what three-year-olds do, fall asleep straight after supper. He should put the little one to bed but for now, he just wants to enjoy the moment. He reaches for a folder that contains song material for his next CD and starts reading through the lyrics, occasionally humming the music. Mostly country-rock songs he notices, and a few fine ballads, too. Love songs, with happy endings. In his own life, he has not been handling things in a discerning way. After he broke up with Melanie he jumped on a roller-coaster of relationships, sometimes with more than one woman at the same time. No woman stands for that. Kate for sure would have sent him packing had he not handled the situation the way he had done. 'Kate, Kate,' he mumbles, 'poor little rich girl.' He leans his head back, realising he has to polish his attitude if he wants to hold on to her for here is one with a real head on her shoulders. He takes one of the sheets and reads:

*You know you love me, I can't express how much I love you*
*But you must know I do*
*When we met I knew, the room lit up because of you*
*I want you near me always, let nothing come between us*
*For I love you and you must know I do*

Chorus: *Linda, Linda marry me...*

David reaches for a pen and crosses out the girls' name, replacing it with 'Kate'. In a soft voice he continues:

*Kate, Kate, marry me. We won't ever be apart, I know*
*We are meant to be together, let go of that other guy*
*and come with me*
*We are meant to be together, you must know so let go, let*
*go*
*We belong together so come and stay by my side ...*
*forever*

Sammy's head moves, but he remains sleeping. David puts the music sheets aside and gently lifts his son off the couch. He slowly walks up the stairs, and in the bedroom, he puts the boy on his bed. Half woken, Sammy reaches for his father's hand. 'Read stowy,' he utters, 'stowy.'

'Sure, son, a story,' David replies in a soft voice. 'Now, where'd we put that book.'

He takes their latest read off the shelf and sits down on the bed next to the pillow. 'Here we are, the doggies were just out to rescue the little boy, so he could come home to his daddy ... '

Sammy's eyelids have fallen again and, holding his father's arm, he is fast asleep in seconds.

With a jump on his father's bed, Sammy wakes him the following morning. 'Daddy, it's time.'

David turns his sleepy head. 'No, no ... too early,' he mumbles.

'Not eawwy, it's light.'

David grabs the boy and pulls him near. 'You know what that means, don't you?'

'What.'

'I have to take you back to your momma.'

'No, I stay with you,' Sammy says.

David pushes himself up and he glances at the clock by the bed. 'Hand me that phone there, Sam,' David says with a sleepy voice.

Sammy's little hands take the phone from the charger and he gives it to his dad. David pushes a few buttons and soon Melanie's voice sounds loud and clear through the receiver. 'Good morning to you too, Mel,' is David's reply. 'Li ... Listen ... Yeah, but you weren't there.'

While David tries to have a conversation with Melanie, Sammy makes attempts to take the telephone from him as soon as he learns who is on the other end of the line.

'Well, I thought, there's no harm in Sammy staying with me for a few days ... '

David moves the receiver away from his ear as Melanie's voice becomes a pitch too high.

'So, you agr ... ' David attempts. 'You agree ... '

Sammy takes his dad's hand again to try and get the phone from him.

'Sam ... ' David soothes. 'OK, I'll have ... I'll have him back before you're off to Florida ... Yes, promise.'

He holds the receiver to Sammy's ear. 'Mummy wants to have a word.'

Sammy puts his hands around the receiver. 'Hullo Mummy. I'm with Daddy now ... yes ... good boy ... Love you, Mummy ... bye.'

David takes the phone from him and puts it down before he gives Sammy a good cuddle. 'It's just you and me, Sam. Your mom says you can stay for a whole week! But then you have to go with her on holiday.'

'What's holiday?'

'That's when you go to a place where you can see

nice things and relax.'

'You come too.'

David looks at Sammy with a disappointed face. 'No, Sam, you're going with Mummy and Stuart. They won't want me there.'

He gets up off the bed and takes Sammy on his arm. 'Well. We'd better make the most of it. First, breakfast.'

'Bweakfus,' Sammy repeats after him.

'That's right, bweakfus, then shower ...'

'Showah.'

'Then ... We'll think of that later.'

'Latow.'

The rolling scenery around Kate's house has not been entirely freed from its nightly darkness when Kate's bare feet find the way to her office. Her dressing gown hangs loosely around her shoulders, revealing her knee-length nightgown underneath. She sits down at her desk and switches the computer on. She is soon absorbed by different websites that inform her about GMO-free goods and which companies supply those. As she's focused on the screen the printer produces the hard copy. She sends a few replies to earlier emails, then reaches for the pile of paper generated by the printer. Leaving her office, she flicks through the pages while walking towards the kitchen. In the hall, she glances in the mirror at her tired face and dark-rimmed eyes. Thoughts of David have robbed her of sleep. Conflicting thoughts, a yearning to want him near and at the same time, doubt. Her feelings for him couldn't possibly be so misleading. How did he feel about her? Or is he with someone else now, telling *her*: She was just a hanger-on? He still hasn't phoned. What has he done after his interview? Drive home to Jackson? Or was his time commanded by other commitments?

She takes some juice from the fridge and goes into the lounge room. Should she call him? Her heart tells her she should, her mind tells her it's a bad idea. Things were so much easier with John. He was always there, even though it was a relationship out of convenience more than anything. Not for long, her fatigue prevails over her thoughts, and with her head resting back in the cushions she dozes off.

'I see you've been busy,' Jacob says, not aware Kate is sleeping. He's holding the sheets of paper Kate had left on the kitchen counter. Kate blinks her eyes and turns her head. 'Oh, morning Jacob.' With a sigh, she straightens her back.

'When *did* you work on this?' Jacob asks as he observes his sister's face.

'Just now,' Kate yawns. 'Couldn't sleep so, thought I'd make myself useful.'

'Sis, why don't you have a shower and a good breakfast. Then we go out and show Maria around Memphis. Drop by at the building site.'

Kate nods. Distraction is what she needs now more than anything.

Enjoying the surroundings en route to Jacob's office is not what keeps Kate's mind occupied as she drives through Memphis. Four days have passed since she joined David in Nashville. Since then, it is as if he disappeared from the planet. Not even a text message has he sent her. The one she sent him yesterday is still left on hold. She remembers he hardly carries a mobile and his landline number was not on the business card he had given her, only his management's, where she has tried to reach him but she soon realised that they weren't going to inform her of David's whereabouts. What for heaven's sake did she mean to him? She hasn't had a proper night's sleep since that day – The harsh sound of the warning system in her car stirs her back to reality; she catches herself going 40 in a 30-mile zone, and she quickly applies the brakes. If something awful has happened to David, she is sure she would have heard about it through the media. Why has he not phoned her? She cannot believe she doesn't mean a thing to him. And where is that damn office? *Second road off Jefferson Avenue*, she reads on the post-it stuck on the dashboard, *keep going 'til you're halfway, large industrial area, you can't miss it. Jacob.* Keep going? Keep going for how long? And why does she have to be there anyway? Jacob is very capable on his own at arranging the contracts with the newly appointed employees.

An untraditional looking building arises before her eyes. That must be it, the only structure around the area that can't be missed, unless you walk around with your eyes in your pocket. She parks her car and paces towards the glass doors of the building. The lady at reception turns her head in Kate's direction who walks straight towards the elevators. On the fourth floor, Kate leaves the elevator and makes her way to Jacob's office. A few of the people who have applied for jobs are there with him.

'Ah, Kate,' Jacob welcomes her. 'May I introduce my sister? Kate Jennings. She'll be your boss on this side of the Atlantic,' he says, addressing the small group.

As they begin to introduce themselves, Kate starts shaking hands.

'Matthew, ma'am.'

'Do you have a last name?'

'Yardley.'

'Earlene Parker, ma'am.' Earlene in fact courtesies. Kate tries to keep a straight face and gives Jacob a brief questioning look. A robust-looking man is next and introduces himself as Nicholas Poulos.

'He'll be the chef,' Jacob clarifies, 'he has years of experience in vegetarian nutrition. Matthew will be his right hand.'

'Raj Lakshmani.'

'Pleased to meet you.'

'Marianna Schröder.'

'I hope you'll agree, Kate, she'll be mostly working with you,' Jacob says.

The young woman gives Kate a quick smile as she shakes Kate's hand.

'And this is,' Jacob checks his list, 'Alejandra Ramirez, she'll be working in the kitchen as well as at the counter ... We have a few more kitchen and counter helps, I'll see them this afternoon.'

'Excellent,' Kate says. 'Very pleased to meet you all and I hope we'll form a great team so we can establish a great business.'

'I'll be in touch with you all in the next few days,' Jacob then says. 'Thank you for coming in this morning.'

After more handshakes have been exchanged the group withdraws from the office, leaving Kate and Jacob to discuss the latest developments.

With a cheerful face, Jacob grabs his sister's shoulders. 'It looks like things are falling into place.'

Kate can't bring herself to share his enthusiasm. 'Jacob, I hope you won't mind but I'd rather not wait around for the next employees. I can meet them at a later date.'

Jacob agrees. 'I think that's not a bad idea, Kate. To get your act together, I mean. Take some time off.'

'Jacob, please ... It's just these ... these emotions of the last few days – '

'Weeks,' Jacob corrects her.

'… I'm sorry, Jacob. Matters of the heart … just don't mix with business,' Kate sighs.

'OK, sis, better sort yourself out first then. We do have a business to run. I don't need to remind you of that.'

Jacob places a hand on Kate's shoulder. 'Take a few days off. You have my permission.'

'I'm sorry Jacob but, I never expected this to happen.'

Jacob leads Kate to the door. 'Who does? Until it hits a person in the face.' He strokes her hair and opens the door. 'Go home, take Chief for a ride, whatever.'

'Can I expect you home for dinner?' Kate asks.

'No, I'm meeting Maria later on, in town. We'll have dinner there.'

Kate's face betrays regret when the elevator door opens.

'Sorry,' he says as she steps into the elevator. While the door closes, Jacob sees Kate briefly wave a hand from her waist, perhaps a gesture for him not to feel guilty.

A cold breeze catches Kate's hair as she gets out of the car and walks to the kitchen door. Clouds have gathered above the landscape and cooled the atmosphere. Once inside, she drops her bag and laptop on the couch and goes upstairs to change. The house feels desolate with no one else there. She puts on a pair of jeans and a warm jumper before wriggling her feet into her riding boots.

When she walks out through the kitchen door, she feels a few raindrops touch her cheeks, something she chooses to ignore. In the stables, Kate collects Chief's gear and proceeds to walk towards the field. Chief has heard her come home and now waits by the fence. His companion grazes at a distance.

'Hello, you old faithful,' Kate says, and pets his neck before putting the bridle on him. After she has strapped the saddle on his back she pulls herself up and slips her feet into the stirrups. At a steady pace, they ride onward over the knoll and further along a path that the horses have trodden over the weeks. The surroundings darken, and Kate glances up to see the rain clouds threateningly near, but she won't permit that to make her feel perturbed. She spurs her horse on to move faster. Hooves clatter on the hard soil and pieces of mud fly up. There's a sudden shot of lightning ahead and Chief jumps aside nervously. Kate pulls the reins to stop him, and the horse lets out a loud neigh.

'OK. It's okay,' Kate says, calming the horse. 'All right, Chief.' She strokes him on his neck, 'we'd better turn back,' but as she pulls the rein her eyes catch movement in a distance. Dark clouds above give away sufficient daylight for her to be able to distinguish the path down below. She lifts herself in the saddle in an attempt to be able to see that, that is the divide between her property and the neighbours'.

She sees an old pick-up truck. Beside it, a figure with long hair, tied in a ponytail.

Kate keeps her horse steady and despite the chilling breeze, warmth flows through her, triggered by an incident not long ago. She stands breathless. 'David?' she utters.

For a moment, she doesn't know whether to race towards the lone figure or turn and go back to the house. She lets Chief slowly tread along the rim of the knoll until she is closer to the dirt road below. When the figure turns, looks up and waves at her, she trembles but rides down the slope at the same time.

She looks at David as she moves closer to the pick-up, a barely visible smile plays around his mouth.

'How'd you – '

'Rough guess,' David interrupts.

He holds out his hand to help her down from her horse. There is no other way but to practically jump into his arms. The warmth of his body feels good, and she allows herself to be held for a moment. Then, she pushes him off.

'Kate, I'm very sorry. I plead guilty. I should've called you but …' He sighs. 'I had a family matter to attend to.'

Kate discerns the seriousness in his eyes as he looks at her.

'I want you to know, you've been on my mind constantly,' he continues. 'It drives me crazy.' He moves closer and makes to circle his arm around her waist but Kate takes a step back.

'Alright. I understand if you don't want to see me again … But, it won't change the way I feel about you.' He doesn't make any attempts to get back into his pick-up. Instead, his eyes look into hers.

His attitude is confusing. Kate wants to slap him after what she'd been through because of him, but that feeling momentarily evaporates now that he is standing there in front of her, confessing how much he has missed her. Or has he?

'I think we need to talk,' David says.

'David … ' Kate begins. Again he gives her that look. 'David … I'm not the kind of woman who shares her man with other women.'

She lets out a relieved sigh.

He looks at her with some disbelief. 'You don't really think – '

'David, I don't know what to think anymore!' Kate retorts angrily. 'For days I've been worrying, thinking.

Wondering! In the meantime not a word from you! I tried to reach you, called your office. Nothing! And why do you carry a bloody mobile if you never switch it on!' She pushes him against his shoulder. 'What do you want me to think!'

'Kate, I'm sorry. I … As I said, family matter.'

'That's no excuse not to call!'

He averts his eyes and digs the heel of his boot into the soil, then, he looks up. 'I'm here now. I drove here to see you, *talk* to you. Face to face.'

Kate looks at him with angry eyes and clenches her hands to fists, but his sincerity makes her anger melt away. She can't help but move towards him and put her arms around his neck. His arms embrace her. 'I have missed you,' David softly says. 'You have to believe that.'

Kate's eyes have filled with tears. She rubs her face against his shoulder not to let him notice.

'I wasn't sure if you felt the same about me,' David's soft voice sounds close to her ear. 'It took me a while to gather the nerve to come up here and tell you. Tell you that I love you.'

He takes her face in his hands and Kate lets him kiss her.

'I hope that feeling is mutual,' David asks of her.

Kate looks at him and kisses him back. 'Of course, silly,' she whispers. 'Will you stay for a bit?'

David's apprehension makes Kate feel uncertain. 'I'm sure there are things for us to discuss,' she says.

'Kate, I need to get back. I just drove up 'cause I had to be sure, I had to know.'

'Okay … Now you know,' she reacts in her business-like manner. 'Where do we go from here?'

David looks at her with questioning eyes.

'I mean, mostly you'll be in another town. I have my

business to run here. When will we have time to be together? Will you come home here or are you going to your own house?'

David holds up his hand to put a brake on Kate's verbal waterfall. 'Kate, please, can we just take it easy for a while? For Christ's sake, don't start solving problems that haven't even arisen yet.'

He takes her hand. 'We'll work things out.'

'Work things – ' David pulls her towards him, presses his lips to hers and kisses her passionately.

Kate needs to catch her breath when they are done kissing.

'I really need to get back now,' David says and opens the door of his pick-up.

'Wait!' Kate says. '*Not* so fast.'

David looks at her as Kate holds out her hand. 'Your phone number. And make it one where you can be reached?'

David smiles, searches for a pen under the dashboard and pulls one out. He takes her arm and writes his private numbers on it, in full.

'What about an address?'

David complies. 'But call first, I'm not there a lot.'

'What about your mobile? Will you change your attitude towards that ingenious piece of technology?'

'I promise.'

Kate grabs him by his collar and kisses him before he steps into the pick-up.

'I call you as soon as I'm home,' he says and closes the car door. He smiles at her through the open window.

She watches as he drives off down the darkening road. Drops of rain splash in front of her feet as David's pick-up slowly moves out of sight. A feeling of emptiness overcomes her, but the increasing raindrops drive her to find her horse, and she spots Chief not far from her. He has wandered off into the field. Kate gives a brief whistle and starts strolling back along the track. Soon Chief is following her faithfully. Despite the threatening clouds, she wants to take her time to move away from the spot where only a moment ago, David met her. She pulls her sleeve and reads what he has written on her arm. His mum's phone number too, that's useful. Mums always know where their brood hang out. Apparently.

When she walks down the hill towards the front yard, she sees an unfamiliar car drive up on the gravel road towards the house. She can't recall anyone she knows driving a Plymouth. She's halfway down the sloping field when the car stops and someone gets out. A person Kate now recognises as her aunt Emmy. She quickens her pace. 'Auntie Emmy!' she says in a raised voice.

Emmy turns and waves. 'Hello there!' she hollers and starts walking towards the fence.

'How are ya?' Emmy greets her. 'Thought I'd take you up on that offer to drop by anytime.' She hugs Kate and kisses her on the cheek.

'Good to see you, Aunt Emmy.'

Kate calls the brown mare and takes both horses from the field.

'Here, let me,' Emmy offers as she takes the mare's lead. She follows Kate to the stables where the latter relieves Chief of his bridle and saddle before leaving the horses into their warm, dry stalls.

'Beautiful place, this,' Emmy says as they rush through the rain to the house. 'Pfui! They hadn't foretold this rain!'

Kate opens the door and they quickly make their way inside.

'Who'd have thought, one day this would be in the

family,' Emmy finds. 'Jake once told me, he'd give the world to be able to live in a place like this. Give his family a proper roof over their head.'

'Ironic isn't it,' Kate says. 'What can I get you? Tea? Coffee?'

When there's no answer Kate looks behind her to see Emmy with open mouth gazing around the spacious hall and the sweeping staircase.

'Hoowee! Look at that! This is like that house in … what's it called, this movie? Gone with the wind.'

'I'm glad you like it,' Kate smiles.

'Like it?! I think that's understated. Jake would have been proud.'

It had never occurred to Kate before, that for Aunt Emmy witnessing this house in all its glory must not only awake memories of her brother, but also bring home to her the Spartan background they hail from.

'Coffee, if it's no bother,' Emmy says, and follows Kate into the kitchen. Kate prepares the coffee machine and as they wait for the coffee to percolate she shows Emmy the fireplace in the lounge room. 'I didn't want to change a thing about it,' Kate says. 'I still remember the day Daddy finished it. Mrs Baker allowed me into the house to show me what a good job Daddy had done. She was very pleased with it.'

'Jake made this,' Emmy slowly utters and slides her hand along the mantelpiece. The sensation that she touches something, the hands of her brother so skilfully put together before he was killed, evokes a brief moment of sadness in her eyes.

'I think the coffee is ready,' Kate says and proceeds to the kitchen.

'Jacob gone back to England?' Emmy asks.

'No, he's still in town. Business. And his girlfriend

came over.'

Emmy removes a tin from her bag. 'Here, brought you some home-made cookies.'

'Thank you, that's very kind, Aunt Emmy.'

'Please, let's drop the formalities. We're only … what? Twelve years apart? Emmy will do.' She pours a drop of milk in her cup and stirs it through her coffee. 'Your dad was a proud man. I want you to know that. Hated it, that he couldn't provide for his family the way he wanted.' She shrugs her shoulders. 'But what can you do? I'm glad my kids have better chances.'

'Au … Emmy, have you ever known that my mother had a university degree?'

Emmy shakes her head. 'No. Though, I'd heard them talk once, that your momma was thinking of taking on a teaching job, but … This was right before the accident.'

Kate lets out a sigh. 'Isn't it bizarre how perverted fate can be. She might've just waited for us to grow up a little before she took on a job as well. Knowing things would come right in the end.'

Emmy agrees. 'She was a sweet thing, your momma. At first, we were quite in awe of her. Her accent, you know. So … dignified. But she adjusted so well, in no time she was as one of us. Taught me a thing or two about English, I tell ya. Passed that with flying colours because of her.'

Emmy empties her cup with one last swallow. 'Well, I'd best be off. Danny will be home soon, better get him some food ready. Those kids, always hungry.'

She wants to put the newspaper she carried, in her bag but decides against it. 'I've finished with it. If you want to have a flick through? Else you can always use it for kindling.' She points a finger at Kate. 'Be sure to invite me when the days get cold and you're lighting

Jake's fireplace.'

'Of course, Emmy,' Kate says and walks her aunt to the door. She kisses her on the cheek. 'Thanks for dropping by.'

Emmy looks up to the sky while she walks towards her car. 'Storm's blown over,' she determines.

Outside, Emmy's car can be heard turning and then drive off as Kate sluggishly moves away from the door and resumes her seat at the table in the kitchen that only a moment ago was bubbling with Emmy's animated company. Some people can fill the biggest houses with their presence, and her aunt is one of them. She reaches for the paper Emmy left, a local daily, Kate notices. With one hand turning the page and the other holding her cup she reads a few headlines that don't particularly feed her appetite for knowledge. The last sips of her coffee taste bitter and she pulls a face. As she puts the paper aside her eyes catch a name, David Nelson.

'*David Nelson taking time out with his son*', the headline reads, with it a photograph of a father helping his small son on a ride at a playground.

'What?' Kate utters. '*After his successful tour, country singer David Nelson is spending quality time with his three-year-old son ... Here he can be seen ...*' Kate reads. 'What! And he never bothered to tell me?!'

Kate jumps up. Agitated, she starts looking for the phone. His *son*? What else does he keep hidden from her? The mother of the boy? She remembers what David wrote on her arm less than two hours ago and pulls up her sleeve. She seizes the phone from the charger and is halfway through dialling the number when she casts it aside. She has another look at the photograph in the paper and then grabs her handbag, locks the door behind her, rushes to her car and jumps in. Despite the moistness that has nestled between the pebbles in the front yard, dust and dirt spit up from under her tyres as she speeds off. At the end of the gravel road, she turns right onto the Interstate in the direction of Jackson. A soft drizzle begins to fall and fogs up her windscreen.

He can be so bloody secretive. Why hadn't he just told her? She switches on her windscreen wipers. Perhaps there was a simple explanation as to why he hadn't ... but perhaps he didn't want her to know. No, that doesn't make sense. A man in his position can't keep situations like that hidden from a wider public. Was she becoming too possessive? He wanted to take things easy. Easy with whom? She slows the car down. No, she has to see him now, clear the issue. Does he live with the boy's mother? Does he just come to *her* when he fancies? No, she won't believe he'd be like that. He wouldn't use her.

Or would he?

Just off the road, Kate spots a restaurant and she drives the car onto its parking lot. When she has come to a halt, she leans her forehead against the wheel. Wasn't she exaggerating the whole situation? This erratic behaviour was not at all her usual manner. She takes the crumpled paper lying on the seat next to her and looks again at the benign picture. David seems so at ease, a good father to his son. A sweet little boy. She takes her phone from her bag and soon has David's number on the display. He kept his word, it's ringing. Then it goes to voicemail. Kate rolls up her sleeve and tries the land-line number he wrote down there. That too rings on the other end of the line, but that is all the response she gets. She tosses her mobile aside, starts the car and drives back onto the Interstate.

David looks most surprised when he finds the woman he said goodbye to only a few hours before, standing in front of his door.

'Hello, David.'

'Kate … Come in.' He lets her lead as they walk into the hall. 'What brings you here so soon? I mean … '

Kate turns to face him. 'I was just wondering *when* you were going to tell me about your son.'

'Uh, well. Now is as good as any. Come in, he's just watching his favourite kids show.'

Kate holds him by his arm. 'That's not what I mean. Why didn't you tell me?'

'Kate,' David appeases the issue, 'would it have mattered?'

'It would've been nice to know you have a child,' Kate rebukes. 'And what about his mother?'

'We split up before she even realized she was pregnant,' David calmly says, 'if that is what you're worried about.'

Reservedly Kate turns and proceeds down the hallway.

'He lives with his mother,' David clarifies, 'I only have him with me for the week.'

Through the open-plan kitchen, Kate notices the boy lying on his belly in front of the TV screen. He seems too preoccupied to even notice his father has a guest.

'Sammy,' David introduces his son, who remains focused on the screen. 'Can I get you anything?'

'Cup of tea, if it's no trouble,' Kate replies.

'I don't get to see my boy a lot, so, I hope you understand I'd rather spend time with him now.'

'David, you could have just told me. What did you expect me to think when I heard it 'through the grapevine', shall we say?'

David looks at her. 'I'm sorry if it has upset you.' He flings a teabag in a mug and pours boiling water over it before he places it in front of Kate who gets a distinct feeling that coming between David and his son is not a good idea. She wonders if she has done the right thing by coming here.

'Look, I tried to call you on your phones,' she says, 'but it seems you have some kind of allergy towards these things.'

'Allergy?'

'I tried to call you but you don't pick up your phone.'

'We were out, just got back in fact before you knocked on the door.'

'And your mobile?'

'Forgot to take it.'

The credits have started rolling across the TV screen but Sammy doesn't make any attempts to remove himself from his spot.

'Sammy,' David says, 'finished. Come say hello to Kate.'

'Not finished,' Sammy says without looking up.

'Turn it off, Sam. That's for big kids.'

Sammy jumps up and presses the on/off button on the set, and then comes over to the kitchen. 'Can I have a dwink?'

'He has a problem with the r,' David explains. 'Sam, this is Kate. Daddy's friend.'

Sammy looks at her with a certain curiosity in his blue eyes. 'Hello, Daddy's fwiend.'

'Smart ass, here have your juice.'

Sammy holds out his little hands to take the glass of juice from his dad.

'Sit down first, Sam. No drinking and walking at the same time.'

The boy slides onto the bench at the corner table as David places the juice in front of him.

'Thank you,' Sammy says.

'You're welcome.'

Kate's face softens when she watches David attending to his son and witnesses yet another side of the man she is in love with.

'Is that a problem with children his age?' Kate asks, not very familiar with the mannerisms of young children. 'I mean, the r-thing.'

David takes another stool and sits down next to her, his back leaning against the counter. 'I don't really know. Sometimes I think it's his way of saying that he doesn't agree with his situation.'

Kate looks surprised.

'He's a clever kid,' David says.

'Yes,' Kate agrees, 'but maybe he needs a speech therapist?'

'He'll grow out of it.' David turns her way. 'Look, Sam has to go with his mother next week, to Florida. Why don't you come over for a few days?' He brushes a lock of her hair away from her face. 'Spend some time together.'

Kate's eyes shine and amenably she rests her hand on his arm.

3

$A$ stark blue sky bathes Nashville's airport in bright
daylight. From behind one of the large windows in the
airport lounge Kate, resting her head on David's shoulder,
watches planes take off and land. They have taken a few
seats in a quiet area, away from whining kids and
screaming mothers, and where businessmen can plug in
and do arrears of office work on their laptops. In the past
week, Kate has divided her time between Memphis, her
house and David's, and now they find themselves on the
brink of another parting. The pain of David's
commitments taking him to another state while hers
remain in Tennessee. David slides his arm around her
shoulder. 'I need to go, hon',' he whispers close to her ear.
With dread, Kate lifts her head as David stands up and
takes her hand.

With arms wrapped around each other, they walk
towards one of the gates for domestic flights. They spot
David's band members in the line ahead. One of the
wives, heavily pregnant, watches her husband leaving
with a solemn expression on her face.

A final kiss, an embrace and Kate, too, looks on as
David walks through to Customs to go onward to the
plane that will take him to New York this afternoon. She
sees him join the rest of the band as they disappear among
other passengers.

Kate strolls back to the spot where a moment ago she
sat with David and gazes out the window.

After a while, she sees his plane backing away from
the terminal and roll towards the runway. She watches as
the roaring engines push the plane onward and then lift it

off the tarmac. Soon it has diminished to a gliding bird, shining silvery in the sun. She gazes until only a sparkle is visible and then turns to go down to the exit doors.

Once in the parking lot, she tries to recall where David parked the old pick-up. She had scarcely paid attention when they arrived earlier but then spots the vehicle, gets in and follows the directions back to the road where, after a while, she pushes up the Interstate. The long monotonous ride on the highway gives Kate ample time to keep her brains otherwise occupied. She hardly takes in the journey back to her house. Her mind is on the one she said goodbye to a little over thirty minutes ago, and the feeling of ambivalence has resurfaced. For most of the week, she has had him to herself, but what would keep her love engaged when she was not around him? 'All in a day's work' he has once said, but that was before they became intimately involved. He would not be disloyal to her now. Not now, she was sure of it. Marriage. Not the subject they have spoken about but would not that be preferred? Then, it wouldn't change a thing about the way they both lead their lives. Their independent lives.

A few miles before the city of Memphis, she turns off to her property and drives up the gravel road to the house. Jacob must be home, she determines, when she sees a rental car by the stables.

Kate walks towards the house and catches sight of two figures in jumpers walking along the green slope in the distance. She enters via the kitchen door, deposits David's car keys in the tray on the counter and puts the kettle on. At least she won't be alone tonight with family around. She throws off her coat and takes a mug from the tray.

The boiling water sizzles over the tea-bag and Kate carries her cup to the lounge room, looks for the remote control and switches the CD player on. Relaxing back into the cushions of the couch she listens to David's latest hit, wondering if this is how her relationship with him will be. A few days together and then he is off again? While she might even be as far away as England? How will it ever work? But she loves him, and he loves her. He should have landed by now. She has hardly ascertained that fact when she hears a soft sound from her mobile.

'*miss you, hon,*' she reads, '*wish I had you with me. Flight on time, now on way to tv studio.*' Kate smiles, he's finally getting the knack of the art of text messaging. She replies by sending him a picture message of a flying heart and a line of x's.

Stumbling feet in the kitchen announce Jacob and Maria, who are back from their walk.

'Hiya,' Maria's voice sounds. 'Did you have a good time in Nashville?' she asks, untying the shawl she wears around her neck.

'Great, thanks,' Kate replies.

'Hi, sis.'

'Hi, Jacob.'

Jacob takes off his jumper and throws it onto a chair. In passing Kate, he strokes her hair briefly before he goes into the kitchen to help prepare dinner. Quiet tête-à-tête emerges from there and soon after, subdued sounds of clanking pans being placed on the stove. Kate checks the time on her mobile. She wasn't aware of how late it has become, not feeling any need to fill her stomach by eating.

Jacob walks into the lounge room and hands her a folder. 'I thought you might want to catch up on proceedings,' he says before returning to the kitchen.

Kate places the material on her lap and starts reading what her brother has accomplished during the days she occupied herself in other ways. A print of a computerised animation of the inside and outer front of how the restaurant will look like, snapshots of the renovation progress, the list of employees with calculated wages, bills and estimates of the whole operation, lists of suppliers ... She sighs, Jacob has been busy. Her eyes glide over the sheets of paper, as she makes an effort to focus on the business side of her life, but her mind keeps drifting. What if she'll be spending more time at David's and Jacob is in London? She has been thinking of asking Emmy to look after her house, keep it clean, for she isn't satisfied with the cleaner she has hired. What if they decide to have a child? She surprises herself with that thought. It's something she has never consciously considered before, but since she has been with David, feelings have emerged she has never been aware of earlier.

Never had she considered children when she was with John, not because she wasn't ready, rather she never saw John as a father figure who, after all, hadn't really outgrown his teen years.

Kate's eyes stare at the pages but her mind doesn't register what she is reading. She puts her work aside, rises from the couch, and walks out of the room. She looks for her jacket on the stand in the hall. It seems more coats pile up here every day, all two sizes smaller than hers. How many warm pieces of clothing does a person need anyhow?

'I'm going for a bit of fresh air,' she lets Jacob and Maria know before stepping outside.

Even though Jacob and Maria prepared a very appetising dinner, Kate has eaten little of it.

'Love-bug got you, Kate?' Jacob inquires as he gently pushes his sister towards the lounge room where they will have an after-dinner drink. 'Can I be your best man?'

'I don't recall mentioning a wedding,' Kate says stoically and sits down in a spacious lazy chair.

'I've contacted a few journalists to cover the opening – '

'What opening?' Kate asks petulantly.

'The Veg and the Vegan, Kate. Or have you forgotten all about that,' Jacob states.

'Am I missing something here? For what date have you planned the opening?'

'Not exactly certain yet, Kate. I just wanted to see if you still cared.'

Kate grabs a cushion and hurls it towards Jacob who can barely avoid it. Maria lets out a shrill sound, busily she starts salvaging the glasses with wine from the side table.

'No need to worry, Jacob,' Kate says, 'business as usual as far as I'm concerned.' She reaches for the last glass before Maria makes off with that too.

'You never guess who called me today,' Jacob says.

Apart from business associates, Kate can't think of anybody. Grandmother maybe?

'John. He sends his love.'

Kate looks at her brother with certain indifference while Maria determines the coast clear from flying objects, and sits down on the couch next to Jacob who puts his arm around her shoulder.

'I'm not kidding,' he says. 'He gave me the impression that he still likes you a lot, kept asking after you.'

'Honestly Jacob, you don't see me going back to him, do you?'

Jacob shakes his head. 'No. And I'd prefer the country singer for my brother-in-law any time.'

'Are you getting married?' Maria is happily surprised.

'Please, Maria, we haven't even *thought* about that,' Kate says.

Maria's face shows a touch of naivety and embarrassment at the same time. A quick smile slides across her face.

'Well, in that case, we have all the time to plan for the opening,' Jacob says.

The facade of the first The Veg and The Vegan restaurant in America is decorated in green and yellow balloons. Jacob finds himself surrounded by curious people while being interviewed by a few journalists from local newspapers. Some photographers are taking photos of the building and Kate talks to the staff who are also attending the opening of the restaurant that will be their future workplace. To celebrate the opening, Jacob and Kate are allowing the public to sample the food for free these few hours, to familiarise them with their vegetarian produce.

Inside, an ambience of peacefulness prevails owing to the placid atmosphere that has been created here. The staff is busy serving people and telling them about the food that is on offer. Kate oversees the room with a studying yet cheerful look on her face. Their cousins Daisy-Lou, Anna-May and Danny have come with Aunt Emmy and are presently walking alongside the buffet with inquisitive eyes, pointing at dishes and putting food on their plates. Emmy, who is standing next to Kate, is nibbling on a burger. 'Very tasty,' she munches with a mouth full, 'never knew it would be so good.'

'I'm glad,' Kate replies. 'Tell all your friends.'

Emmy nods. 'Sure will.'

They are joined by Jacob who has invited the journalists in and offered them drinks.

'Things look promising,' he determines with a satisfied smile.

'It won't be long before the whole of Memphis is eating here. Mind my words,' Emmy says, wiping her mouth. 'This is very good stuff.'

'We'll take your word for it,' Kate says. Her eyes have wandered and her gaze rests on a woman in a plain cotton dress, covered with a coarsely knitted cardigan. She stands in between other people, but at the same time, she seems to be trying to hide her presence. She looks around skittishly as she eats the hamburger she is holding, with quick bites. When she has finished, Kate notices her putting more food in a ragged cotton bag that she is carrying, all the time agitatedly keeping an eye on those around her as if afraid of being caught in a criminal act. Kate feels an urge to reassure her and moves towards the woman who begged her for money weeks before, but with her bag now filled with food, it is as if the woman is wafted out of the restaurant by a breeze. Not looking up she leaves with swift movements. Her curiosity now ignited, Kate makes her excuses and follows the woman into the street. She has to walk fast in her high heels to keep up with the woman who moves quickly, clutching the cotton bag in arms that also tightly hold the cardigan around her body. Kate shivers for the chilled breeze. She only wears her pale mauve two-piece lined with white lace, wishing she had grabbed her coat before so impulsively following the woman out of the restaurant, eager to know where she would take her free shopping. Kate sees the woman slip into an alley and when she reaches it she notices it's a through-fare. Kate steals into the alleyway, keeping eyes out for events unawares. At the far end lies another street, a back street and she notices the woman to her right still moving along with quick steps.

She crosses the street and disappears into another alley. Kate sends a studying glance into the street and sees a few run-down shops where some children in shabby clothes hang around. She is glad to leave the street and goes into the narrow alley as well. It must be some twelve meters long and to Kate's relief, she meets the other end unscathed. Some bushes that no one ever bothered to cut back block her passage. Kate's hair is caught in a branch and it releases a lock of her hair from the so accurately tied plaited bun. While trying to push the strand of hair back, Kate sees the woman walking onto an untidy green where a small, dilapidated trailer stands underneath an old leafless tree. At least she has a roof over her head, Kate establishes. She hesitates, wondering if she should go to the woman. Here she stands fiddling with a lock of her well-attended hair, wearing clothes that cost more than two months' rent for that awful looking trailer, while others … The sudden sound of an angry barking dog startles Kate. The animal's invisible presence on the other side of the shrubbery makes her gasp for breath. In a reflex, she puts a hand to her chest, then quickly takes to her heels and walks back through the alleyway. She has almost reached the light at the end of it when a shadow is cast her way. A roughly clad, grubby looking old man blocks her passage to the street. He stinks of stale liquor.

'Excuse me,' Kate says, 'could I pass, please?'

The man shows a line of rotten teeth when he tries to smile. His clothes resemble rags that never see a washing machine. Carefully, Kate attempts to slide past him.

'Sorry.'

A gurgling sound emerges from the man's throat. Kate is quick to leave him behind and steps onto the street. With a relieved sigh she continues, throwing an investigative gaze along the road, then crosses it and walks through the alley that takes her back to the shopping area.

Soon she enters the restaurant where, by now, more people have gathered to try the food that is on offer.

'Where did you go ... Went for a roll in the hay?' Jacob asks her as he removes a dead leaf from her hair.

'Don't ask,' Kate replies, 'but I hope our alarm system works well. Excuse me.' She walks in the direction of the restrooms followed by Jacob's inquisitive gaze.

A hectic atmosphere surrounds David as he strolls from the set to the cafeteria in the TV-studio after yet another interview. There was a phone-in during the broadcast with a few fans making inquiries about his professional *and* private life. The latter had brought thoughts of Kate to his mind but he had kept tight-lipped about his relationship with her.

In the busy cafeteria, he takes a soda from the icebox, then makes his way to the entrance to go back to his hotel.

'David!' someone yells out. David turns to see a man approach and he shakes his proffered hand. 'Hi,' David says. 'Great interview, David,' the man says. 'Good luck with your CD.'

Before David can answer the man has gone. It is strange how everybody seems to want to be acquainted with him nowadays. Complete strangers who want to be part of his success and want to be seen with him. Sometimes it makes him want to hide. All *he* aspires to do is make good music and bring some pleasure to people's lives through his music.

David flags down a cab and gets in when one stops in front of him. He tells the driver the name of the hotel he is staying at, and off they speed. Among the sound of honking car horns, they merge into a sea of yellow and metallic. 'Yeah, yeah, arsehole, a bit more consideration would be nice!' the driver cusses.

The busy traffic that David sees pass by through the car window doesn't entice him; he's just not a big city person. He allows his thoughts to wander and a blonde-haired lady he left behind in Memphis enters his mind. Her pretty face with those shiny blue eyes looking at him, her laugh. That immaculate porcelain complexion she must have inherited from her English mother. In thought, David brushes his hand along her long blonde hair.

'Holiday Inn!' the driver reminds him and the car stops in front of the hotel. David checks the meter and hands over a ten-dollar bill, as the driver spots his next customer. 'Keep the change,' David says.

With a swift movement, the driver pockets the money. 'I'm sure I've seen you somewhere,' he says. 'Do you live near Queens?'

'No, sir,' David replies half smiling, 'I'm not from these parts.' The driver casts him another look. 'All right, have a nice day.' The cab driver stops a few meters away and lets the next passenger get in as David walks up the steps and into the hotel. He goes to the reception desk to collect his key and is about to make his way to the elevators when Gene, one of his band members, approaches.

'Dave! How'd it go?' Gene says. Without waiting for an answer he suggests a drink in the bar. 'Fred mucked up our schedule, he booked us an extra gig tonight,' Gene informs him.

'But, we're doing that TV show tonight.'

'Yes, and after, we're rushed off to Washington for a live show – '

'Washington!? What time are we due there?'

'Midnight.'

'Chrissakes,' is David's reaction. He had hoped to be flying back to Memphis early the following morning. Gene orders them both a beer. 'I'm not happy about it either,' he says, 'with my wife about to give birth.'

'Right. When's she due?'

'Yesterday. I was just thinking this mornin', it's as if the little guy is waiting for me to get home before he pops into this world.'

David sips his beer. ' ... Gene, don't you think everything's going ... too fast? I mean, as I was telling my mother, just last year we were doing bars and clubs, now we're doing stadiums. And our lives seem to belong to someone else.'

Gene looks at his watch and plays with his cellphone, expecting it to ring any moment. 'Well, we have now what we've worked for all these years.'

'My mom's words exactly.' David takes another gulp from his beer before he informs Gene: 'I want to get married.'

Gene looks at David to establish whether he's mocking him, but the earnestness in David's face tells him otherwise.

'I'm serious, Gene. I love this woman. I want to marry her.'

'Does she know? That she's getting married, I mean.'

'I want to ask her tomorrow.' He unbuttons his shirt pocket and takes out a small box. 'Just hope that nothing else intervenes.'

'You really have made up your mind over this, have you? But, I mean, getting married? Now? On top of all our new responsibilities?'

David briefly opens the small container, looks at the ring and then puts it back in his shirt pocket.

'I suppose old Freddie's made all the arrangements,

got us a hotel in the other place.'

Gene empties his glass. 'Yeah, I suppose that's all been arranged.' He motions the bartender to fill them up again.

'I thought we were free of commitments the next four weeks,' David says. 'Supposed to stay put and rehearse for our next CD.'

'I wouldn't want it any other way, Dave,' Gene says. 'Then at least I'd be near my wife and kid.'

David looks into his half-empty glass. 'And I'd be near Kate.'

At the back of the restaurant, Kate is seated in her small office, focusing on her computer screen when Marianna enters.

'Miss Jennings, I'm sorry, but Earlene hasn't shown up this morning. Shall I call Alejandra, ask her to come in?'

Kate stares at her screen and makes a few mouse-clicks before she looks up at Marianna.

'Earlene?'

'Yes, she hasn't come in. Hasn't called either.'

'I hope she's all right,' Kate says. 'Earlene is never late. She's always early.'

'Do you want me to give her a call?' Marianna asks.

'Marianna, we didn't hire you to have others make the decisions for you,' Kate states. 'Do what you feel is best in this situation.'

Marianna looks at Kate as if desiring more encouragement but then walks away from the office towards a phone on the counter, leaving Kate to resume her administrative tasks. The latter sighs, as if she hasn't enough on her mind. David hasn't called, even though he should have finished his commitments in New York by now. She left a message on his mobile phone to which he has not responded. Kate lets out another indecisive sigh, looks at her organised desk to then switch the computer off. She gets up and grabs her long, warm coat. She is in need of fresh air.

As she walks out the door of the restaurant, it is Earlene who bumps into her.

'Oh, ma'am! I am *so* sorry!' Earlene exclaims. 'So sorry, I ... '

'Earlene, you were supposed to have started an hour ago.'

'I am so sorry, ma'am. So sorry. My momma is ill, and – '

'Alright, alright. Just don't let it happen again,' Kate warns, and she walks into the street. A taxi is honking beside her. Kate hesitates and then gets in. She doesn't feel like having to worry about traffic herself. She requests of the driver to take her downtown where she asks him to stop somewhere in the city centre. Kate continues on foot, keeping her hands warm in her pockets as the wind blows cold gusts through the streets. Now and then, she stops to admire shop windows that are decorated for the Christmas season. Time has flown by since she came back to Memphis. Christmas is already around the corner. Kate stops in front of a jeweller where her eyes fall on the wedding-ring section. She stares at the golden bands and sighs. Who was she kidding? But, perhaps she should get grandmother a nice necklace, she is sure she will be in England spending Christmas with the family. Family. They were reunited with their family here, too. She doesn't really know what she should buy David, he seems pleased with anything. Kate looks at a few more items in the window and then wanders across the street, following the sidewalk that eventually leads to a path along the mighty Mississippi River. She remembers, it was here where she walked months ago. Then, dreading to go back to her hotel, knowing who was waiting for her there. Now, she misses someone she wants with her. Kate gazes across the water that looks muddy and black, reflecting the dark clouds overhead. She resumes following the path when, quite unexpectedly, not far from her she sees a woman sitting on a bench. The woman in a plain cotton dress, her coarse knitted cardigan wrapped around her. Kate moves closer and now notices an old suitcase by the woman's feet. Her skinny pale calves are bare. She only wears a pair of well-worn brown shoes. Kate shudders at the sight.

'Hello,' Kate says. It is now that she also notices a child huddled against the woman. It makes Kate feel horrified. 'Hello,' she utters again.

The woman looks up. 'We were here first,' she says with a tired voice. 'Go find yourself another place to sit.'

'Oh, I'm sorry, I'm not chasing you off. I … I – '

'Leave us alone,' the woman says, looking at Kate with steel grey eyes that appear as cold as the wind itself.

Kate is slightly taken aback by the woman's reaction. 'Look, I'd better explain,' she then says, 'I know where you live, and, it reminded me – '

'We don't live anywhere, lady, so stop troubling us.'

'Oh, but I'm sure I saw you. You live in that old trailer – '

'We don't live in any trailer. Anymore,' the woman softly adds.

Kate looks at the child, she can't be more than four years old, her dark hair encircling a pale complexion as she wipes her runny nose with the sleeve of her jacket that's not exactly a good fit. At least she wears slacks and isn't going barelegged, Kate determines.

'Excuse me,' Kate says and slides onto a corner of the

bench. 'Let's go somewhere where it's warm, and then we'll talk.'

'Talk? Talk about what, the weather?' Kate hears the sarcasm in the woman's voice.

'When was it you last ate?' Kate continues. 'I could buy you lunch.'

'We don't take hand-outs,' the woman says.

'I'm not offering any,' Kate replies. 'Please, at least do it for the child. It seems to me she could do with a good meal.'

The child's eyes light up. 'Please, Mummy,' she whispers barely audible. 'Maybe it's warm there, too.'

The woman looks at her child. 'Okay,' she agrees.

She slowly gets up from the bench, stiff from the surrounding cold, and grabs her suitcase.

'Come with me,' Kate says. 'I know just the place.' She tries to take the child's hand but the latter quickly withdraws and walks to the other side of her mother. Kate then takes the suitcase from the woman for her to have one hand free to hold her cardigan closed.

'I'm Kate. What may I call you?'

There is hesitation in the woman's demeanour but she then relates to Kate her name is Lynn. 'And my daughter's Ashley.'

'That's a pretty name,' Kate tells the girl. 'Come, we need to take a taxi. It's too far to walk.'

When they approach the restaurant Lynn realises where Kate is taking them. She slows her pace and pulls her daughter near. 'I … I don't think it's fittin' for us – '

'Oh, but it's fine,' Kate interrupts. 'Come, don't worry.' Decidedly, Kate takes the woman's arm and opens the door of the restaurant before she changes her mind.

Lynn looks around in the same skittish way Kate saw

her do when she was filling her bag at the opening.

'Come, let's sit over there.' Kate shows them to a table at the back and asks Earlene to prepare two plates for Ashley and her mother Lynn. Kate goes behind the counter and pours a few mugs full with hot tea. 'Please,' she motions. 'Sit down, it's nice and warm in this corner.'

In a shy way, Ashley slides onto a chair next to her mother, her pale face briefly lit up by a subtle cute smile. She holds the mug with hot tea and warms her small hands with it. Lynn looks at Kate with a worn gaze in her eyes where Kate spots uncertainty.

'I can't pay you now,' Lynn says. 'But I'll pay you back … We're honest folk.'

'I don't doubt that,' Kate says. 'You only came in here when the food was free.'

Kate detects Lynn's fright. 'But, good for you!' Kate is quick to add. 'I was a bit cheeky too, then. I followed you. That's how I discovered where you lived, or rather, *how* you lived.'

Lynn's reaction is one of embarrassment. The lines in her worn face don't diminish when Earlene puts a large plate with delicious warm food in front of them. The little girl starts eating the veggie-burger with such eagerness that it has Kate wondering if they have had breakfast at all that morning.

'We had to move out of that trailer,' Lynn softly says. 'The man sold it, and we were put out on the street … We sleep in a shelter now.'

Kate motions Lynn to eat her food before it gets cold.

'Look,' Kate says, 'you can pay me back. How about, if I offered you a job?'

Lynn looks up from her plate. 'A job? Lady, I've been in so many different jobs, low-paid, mind. If I *was* hired, they shortly after kicked me out. Lack of schooling, they

keep telling me. Who needs schooling for washing dishes?
Who needs schooling for working in a laundrette? I ask
you, lady.'

The woman surprises Kate, elaborating about her
life's situation in that way. The food and warmth must do
her good.

'Lynn, I own this restaurant, we *train* people. If you
want you can have a job here, so you can provide for
yourself and your daughter.'

The revelation elicits some astonishment, and Lynn
looks curiously at the environment around her. The
restaurant with its pleasant atmosphere seems to remind
her of something that once was familiar to her.

'Well? Look, Lynn. I grew up in a trailer, I know
what it's like to be poor. I just want to give you a chance.'
Kate looks at Ashley, who has but one thing in mind and
that is not to leave a crumb on her plate. The little girl
behaves as if she is afraid that this will be their last proper
meal for a few days.

'Lady … '

'Please, call me Kate.'

'… Kate. I appreciate what you try to do, but … Well,
I'd better tell you. We don't have anything. The clothes we
have are the clothes we wear. I only just applied for a new
benefit, but don't know if we'll be getting anything, you
understand? I've only got a few household things in that
suitcase that I rescued before … Well, what I'm trying to
say is that, we don't have money to buy clothes and I
don't think you would want to train a person wearing
rags.'

Lynn takes another bite with an attempt as if to make
it clear that *that*'s her final word, despite her dismal
situation, but the argument does not convince Kate.
Wearing rags should not be a hindrance for not desiring to

improve one's situation. Was it Lynn's pride maybe? Or is it insecurity that dissuades her from accepting this opportunity.

'If that's your reason for not accepting my offer, then, we will have to do something about that, won't we?'

Lynn finishes her tea and looks at Kate who has turned her attention to Ashley.

'Would you like some more tea, sweetheart, or maybe dessert?'

The girl nods shyly. 'Go to Earlene,' Kate says, 'ask nicely and she'll give you something. OK?'

Kate turns to Lynn with expectation. Lynn's former worried expression has softened. 'That's settled then!' Kate says.

The city is submerged by darkness when Kate puts the key in the ignition and starts her car. It is close to ten, she has had more admin to take care of, and the new development, hiring Lynn, has been on her mind. She will have to take Lynn shopping for clothes. The poor woman hasn't a thing. Kate wonders how she got herself into this situation. She is certain that there must be facilities for women who are left with a small child, other than wandering the streets and sleep in a homeless shelter. They stayed at the restaurant almost until closing, escaping the cold conditions outside. Before they left, Lynn had promised to meet Kate the following morning.

Kate turns into another street and drives towards the Interstate. With eyes focused on the road, she switches the car radio on, hoping to hear David's hit record. She hasn't heard from him, and she feels slightly annoyed that he hasn't contacted her upon his arrival. What sounds from her radio speakers is the news-at-ten intro. Not what she wanted to hear and she only half listens to the announcements. '... *flight to Memphis from New York's JFK ... engine trouble was the probable cause of the crash ...* '

It takes Kate a few seconds to realise what the news bulletin is about but then her attention is drawn to the announcement and she turns the sound up. ' ... *So, that was the flight from New York that was due to arrive in Memphis at twelve noon today ... It's not yet known how many casualties ...* '

Kate starts to feel tense. A plane crash! *Casualties*, it races through her mind. She speeds up along Winchester and follows the road to Memphis International Airport. Not David! It can't be his flight. '*Emergency numbers were released for relatives ...*' There must be more than one flight from New York coming in daily. Kate quickly calculates, David was to leave New York at around 10 am. How long would the flight have lasted? Three hours? And then there's the hour time difference. No, not David's flight. Not her David. Nervously she merges into the fast lane, barely able to keep to the speed limit even there. 'Oh, step on it,' she mutters under her breath. Other drivers seem to move at a snail's pace. She quickly glances at other cars as she leaves the ones behind that drive alongside her. A tail light comes alarmingly closer and Kate jumps on the brakes. She utters a relieved sigh. She almost hit the driver in front of her. 'Oh, hurry up.' She notices the turn off to the airport and races towards it, heading another driver off. She hears the screeching tyres and the annoyed honking, and somewhere from the side, lights blink. 'Sorry,' Kate mumbles and she follows the sign that states *Arrivals*. In such a rush to find out what happened to the flight David was on, she does not allow herself time to think the worst. There must be survivors! And he's a celebrity, she was sure they would have mentioned his name if he's among the casualties. She reaches for her bag under the seat and puts it on her lap. With one hand on the wheel, she rummages in her bag with the other and takes out her mobile. A quick glance establishes there still is no message from David. Kate turns onto the parking lot and finds a space to park. She closes the door and rushes towards the exit and on to the Arrivals Hall. She doesn't even remember which airline he was flying.

The information desk can hardly be seen due to the many people around it. She walks towards the monitors to see if there are any messages posted on there. She finds the arrival time of flights from New York, but they are for flights that recently came in. Kate looks about her and it is now that she notices that perhaps she should not be here at all. She doesn't see any people in despair. What if relatives and friends were brought elsewhere? Not to distress other passengers? The only people there, are busying themselves to meet their flights or are going outside to flag down transport to the city. Kate walks towards one of the airline desks and asks the attendant if anything is known about the flight that has met with misfortune this afternoon. The lady looks at her with questioning eyes.

'Oh ma'am,' she then says, 'wasn't that just awful. I'm so sorry, ma'am. Was a relation of yours on that flight?'

All of a sudden Kate feels weak, her legs tremble. 'I uh ... Well, a very good friend, madam,' Kate says. Her eyes become moist. 'I just heard about ... Is anything known?'

The woman behind the desk gives Kate a compassionate look. 'I'm sorry, ma'am, I can't tell you much.' She shoves a form in Kate's direction. 'Here are the emergency numbers to call. It happened over Virginia, not here.'

Kate wipes a tear from her cheek. 'Thank you,' she says, and then slowly moves away from the desk. She sits down on a seat in the arrivals hall and gazes at the sheet of paper with the phone numbers. There is nothing she can do. She doesn't want to call any of those numbers and then be told … the name on a list. The numbers become hazy as tears fill her eyes. She takes a tissue from her bag and wipes her face. With a miserable feeling, she sighs and slowly stands up when a TV-screen at the far end of the waiting area draws her attention. CNN shows the latest re-run of the happening that afternoon. On the large screen a plane is lying in a field, broken in two, with its wings cracked like rotted branches beside the cabin, but otherwise intact. The commentator mentions nine casualties of the 98 people that were on board the plane. Nine. Kate casts another glance at the sheet of paper the lady has given her. Should she make the call?

'Kate! Darling!'

Kate turns her head to look beside her when she hears the familiar voice.

'Kate! And I was just on my way to surprise you! Darling, how did you know I would be arriving?'

Kate wishes she would dissolve into the carpet of the arrivals hall. She inattentively turns her head away from him when he tries to kiss her.

'Hello John,' she says by force of habit.

'I bet it's fate,' John states.

Kate regains herself. 'What brings you to Memphis, John? And I certainly am not here to meet you.'

'Well, let's just put it down to coincidence then,' John says, spreading his mouth into a broad grin.

His hair is a bit longer, Kate notices, but he still wears

his ill-matching outfits.

'I missed you, and I just wanted to see how you were,' John says. 'I do worry about you, you know.'

'That's sweet of you, John, but I manage just fine without you.'

He shows her a meaningless smile. 'Well. Would you mind having me around for a few uh … days? Maybe we could try and – '

'John, I really have no idea why you came here. I showed you the door, remember? I didn't want to see you anymore.'

'Oh Kate, that's months ago! We could start over and try our best to make it work.'

Kate feels her heart ache when she thinks of the reason why she came to the airport. David. She has no idea. He cannot be among those nine, he *has* to be one of the survivors. She pushes John off. 'I can't talk to you now,' she says. 'I need to … '

She rushes towards the exit doors. 'Better check yourself into a hotel!'

'Kate! Kate!' John takes his bag and hurries after her. Kate has reached the doors and quickly walks to the parking lot, hurrying past rows of cars until she spots her car. It is now that she looks behind her and witnesses John getting into a taxi. Thank God he's not following her. She does not want to deal with him now. What on earth is he thinking? Nervously she fumbles at the lock of her car door. She does not want him back. She never loved him. Kate feels tears well to her eyes when she thinks of the one she does love.

When she sits behind the wheel she takes a deep breath and focuses, before backing out. She wipes some tears from her cheeks with one hand as she pulls her car out of the parking lot, continues to the Interstate, and accelerates to drive home.

Home, where no one waits for her.

Jacob has gone back to London with Maria. She would be all alone in the big house again. 'The big house', yes, it does feel like a prison when she is there, all alone, imprisoned by loneliness. Maybe she should have let John stay. But, that doesn't feel right, having him in her house. She wonders if John has spoken to Jacob, who would certainly have told John about his sister's new love. Then, perhaps not. Her brother doesn't tend to be a blabbermouth. She is still shaken by John's sudden appearance. He was the last person she needed to run into, always so self-centred and he has not changed one bit. *'Darling, how did you know I would be arriving?'* For Christ's sake, what was he thinking? That the whole world still revolves around him?

Kate follows the red tail lights of the car in front, her car radio quietly sounding in the background but no song of David is played.

Her stomach feels as if some invisible hand has it tight in its grip. Anxiousness and uncertainty numb her and she has to take great effort to try to keep her head clear. Fortunately, the traffic is not too heavy. Her headlights catch the sign for the turn-off to Flat Junction. It makes her briefly turn her head in that direction but all she sees is pitch darkness beyond the headlights of the oncoming cars, their beams blinding her when there is a slight curve in the road. Shortly, she sees the first signs of her house halfway the fields. The night lights come on as soon as darkness falls. She hopes Billy has put the horses in their stables. He comes by a few times a week. When he's not looking after her horses, he is working at the training stables of a rich horse owner just south of Memphis.

As soon as she is inside, she will try and contact David. The thought alone makes her shiver. It's fright, she is afraid of what she might discover. The gravel starts crackling under her tyres. Should she have the drive to her house paved? It's not such a bad sound, the crackling underneath one's tyres. She stops her car in front of the garage door. She hardly ever puts it inside and she does not feel like parking it inside tonight. Before she takes the key out of the ignition, the clock on the dashboard tells her it is almost midnight. The cold wind shrouds her when she walks to the kitchen door. She locks it behind her as soon as she is inside. She switches a few lights on and, in passing, takes a bottle of wine from the pantry. After she has kicked off her shoes and thrown her coat over a chair, she walks to the lounge with a glass in one hand and the bottle in the other.

Holding the telephone, she takes a deep breath and then dials David's home number. It rings but no one answers. Kate tries his mobile number. It feels like the blood is draining from her face when she hears the message: *This number cannot be reached at the moment.* OK. OK, that can happen, that mobile numbers cannot be reached, Kate convinces herself. His mother, she hasn't tried his mother yet. Nervously, she reaches for the little notebook on the side table. 'David's mother,' she mumbles. 'Here it is.' She dials the number. After she has let it ring for some time, it is clear that no one will answer that phone either, but Kate is sure there must be an explanation for that, too. His mother works in a hospital. She will have the night shift. That's it. Irregular hours. The thought, though, does not ease her mind. With uncertainty still plaguing her, she takes the bottle and pours herself a full glass. Her free hand reaches for the remote control and she switches on the television. On CNN the information about the plane crash doesn't give her any more news than that what she already knows. Those reporters can't tell anybody anything than that what they know themselves and if there are no new developments they just keep repeating what they have already reported on. A local channel shows distraught people anxiously waiting for news, some are crying, others have worried looks on their faces. Kate switches the TV off and takes another swallow from her drink. Perhaps she should eat something. No, she can't eat now. She lets her head fall back into the cushion and closes her eyes. If only she had an answer. It doesn't make sense, nothing makes sense any more. Why was John there all of a sudden? When the only one on her mind was David? Was he injured or ... among those nine? No. She does not want to think the worst.

She opens her eyes and looks around the dimly lit room. Sluggishly, she gets up and reaches for the switch on the lamp that stands beside the couch and extinguishes the light.

As she slowly walks towards the stairs that will lead her upstairs, a strange feeling overcomes her. A feeling that there is something else in the room. *Someone* else. Kate stops where she stands. She is lit by the hall light but behind her in the dark lounge room, there is something. Someone. The thought makes Kate's skin crawl. Was somebody hiding? All that time she had been sitting there? Someone in her house? She stands as if frozen, but then she forces herself to turn around and check the lounge she left in obscurity behind her. Her eyes are wide open. Every muscle in her body is tense as she is standing there. Looking into the darkness, peering around of the room.

Then, suddenly, a shimmering light emerges beside the fireplace. She is gripped by fear. Her eyes shoot around the darkness as she tries to determine where it came from. It is as if fog descends. An oval-shaped cloud, settles next to the fireplace. The foggy cloud intensifies, developing into a brilliant bright light. A blinding light. Kate shrinks back when a man appears in the cloud. She stumbles against a chair. Then, her feet gain ground when she recognises the image that has appeared. The man, she has known so well as a child, looks at her. 'Daddy?' she whispers in disbelief. She feels as if she is instantly wrapped in a comforting blanket. Kate cannot take her eyes off the image that is so clear now, as he is standing there, lined by a thin white light. She reaches out with her hand, wanting to touch her father. He is smiling at her and keeps smiling as he slowly disappears and dissolves into nothingness. Only a dark space remains.

Kate keeps her eyes fixed on the spot next to the fireplace, and a sense of reassurance envelops her. Her eyes search the room, search for another sign of her daddy who died all those years ago. She feels surrounded by great comfort. He knew. He knew of her distress. It seems a long while before she finally draws away from the spot. Slowly, she walks up the stairs. Her came daddy to comfort her. The anguish that had so forcefully taken hold of her earlier, has now evaporated. In a haze, she prepares to go to bed.

She has heard stories like that, about dead relatives visiting. She never paid much attention. Always thought it must be people not able to let go, who might have *dreams* about their deceased family members. But now, her own experience was too vivid to ignore. Kate crawls under the duvet and rests her head on her pillow. 'Goodnight, Daddy,' she softly says before she closes her eyes.

*Jon Baker was murdered.*

Kate shoots up in bed with her eyes wide open. 'What? Who just said that!' She surprises herself as she, still half asleep, looks around the room. Jon Baker was murdered. What is that all about?

Daylight spreads through her room; she never closed the curtains, she now realises. She must have dreamt it. With a sigh she lets herself fall back into the pillow. Her mind is muddled and numb, and she tries to recall her experiences of the evening previous. It appears so unrealistic. There was a plane crash. Was David hurt? She was at the airport when all of a sudden John was there. Then, her daddy … Kate jumps out of bed and rushes downstairs. The chill in the house makes her shiver. She enters the lounge room. There, there is where he stood. She sees the bottle of wine and the half-empty glass on the occasional table. She walks towards the couch and sits down, there where she sat last night. She now remembers it all. David's plane *was* in a crash. John *was* at the airport. And then, the apparition of her daddy who had come to comfort her.

Kate shivers and doesn't understand why it so cold in her house. She gets up and checks the thermostat that is fixed to the wall just before entering the kitchen. She adjusts the switch and then makes to go back upstairs when the shrill, sudden sound of her telephone ringing on the kitchen counter makes her jump with fright. She turns and tries to keep her hand from shaking when she reaches for the telephone. She lifts it off the charger but is slow to answer it.

'*Kate?*' The familiar voice on the other end of the line makes Kate tremble. She wants to answer but the words are caught in her throat. Her trembling hands clutch the phone. The same phone he used when they first met. She holds it tightly. '*Kate? Are you there?*'

'D … David?'

'*Kate, are you all right? You sound –* '

'Yes! Yes, I'm fine! David! A … are you all right?'

'*Kate, I know it's early, sorry if I woke ya. Listen, I didn't want to disturb you last night. We only got back from Washington early this morning, Fred had mucked us about and –* '

'Washington? I … I thought you were in New York?!'

'*No, hon', we had a few extra gigs in Washington. Listen, how about you drive my old pick-up to my house and I meet you there. OK? I'm driving home from Nashville, hitching a ride with the guys.*'

'Nashville. I thought … '

'*Yeah, sorry hon'. Never got to Memphis. What do you say?*'

'Of course! Of course I'll meet you at your house!'

The reality is sinking in. He never flew from New York! The morbid haze she was surrounded by all these hours has dissolved.

'David!' she yells into the phone. 'David, I love you! I will always love *you*!'

'*Kate, I love you too. Now get your pretty little ass over to my house. OK?*'

'I'll be with you as fast as an arrow from a … oh, what was it again.'

She hears him chuckle. '*Breakfast at my place, Kate. Love you hon'.*'

Kate stands by the kitchen counter in her nightshirt, her bare feet on the chilly floor, but she feels warm all over. She slowly puts the phone back on the charger as she realises: He never flew to Memphis!

Did he say she had a 'pretty little ass'? Isn't that a bit … ? Oh, what the heck. David was all right, he was fine! That's all that mattered. She has to get ready and drive to

Jackson. That is all she needs to do now. Everything is going to be all right.

As Kate rushes upstairs she pulls her nighty over her head, throws it on her bed when entering her room and jumps into the shower. With the freshness of the water that runs down her body, the last remnants of her unsettling thoughts wash from her mind and flow down the drain.

Before the clock strikes 8.30, Kate is standing dressed in the kitchen. She puts on the coat that is still draped over the chair where she threw it the night before, grabs her bag and David's car keys and rushes outside.

She turns her head when she hears a car approach. It's Emmy coming to tidy up the house.

'Morning, Em!' Kate calls out to her.

'Hellooo! You're up early! Business?'

Emmy has reached Kate and hugs her.

'I'm meeting David for breakfast.'

'Ahh, David. Well, enjoy yourselves!' Emmy walks towards the kitchen door. She turns and watches as Kate opens the door of the old pick-up and sits behind the wheel, wearing an outfit that doesn't really match her surroundings. Rich girl, but not afraid to be seen in an old run-down pick-up truck. She still remembers her roots. Emmy waves as Kate accelerates and drives away.

On the way to Jackson Kate feels as if she is driving on soft clouds instead of the hard asphalt that passes underneath the wheels of the pick-up. She can't recall ever having felt happier and she catches herself making plans for a future with David. They will find a way to work around their different schedules.

She has almost reached Jackson when she remembers Lynn. Drat! Completely forgot about her. She was to take her and Ashley shopping. As soon as she has reached the city's boundaries, Kate pulls up and searches for her mobile in her bag. She calls the restaurant and hears Marianna's voice who answers the phone. Kate explains the situation and tells her that she has been held up. 'So, when they come, just give them some food, breakfast, whatever. I shouldn't be too long. Alright?'

Kate puts her mobile back in her bag. Well, 'not too long' can be a broad concept. She merges into traffic and continues on her way. She's quietly hoping David doesn't have his son staying, she'd rather be alone with him. The hunger she feels in her stomach is not just for food. It's past ten when she parks the truck beside David's house. No sign of him. Kate closes the door of the pick-up and walks towards the front door. Before she can ring the bell the door flies open and reveals David. Kate looks at him but somehow can't say a word. She moves closer and puts her arms around his neck. She feels his arms tight around her. 'Kate,' his soft voice sounds. David then loosens his grip and looks in her eyes. 'Everything all right?'

Kate realises she has started to cry. 'Fine. Oh, I'm such a crybaby lately,' she apologises. David takes her face in his hands and they kiss before he leads her into the house. 'Have you eaten anything yet?'

'No, I came straight here.'

'You made good time.'

No small boy on his belly in front of the television, Kate observes when they enter the kitchen.

'Kate, what do you think if we go out for an early lunch. I don't have much in the house.'

'OK, fine with me.' Kate pulls David's arm. 'David, I uh, maybe you think I reacted a bit strange this morning but … I was, or rather, have been so afraid that you were hurt … '

'Hurt?'

'Haven't you heard about the plane crash?'

'Yeah, there was something on the news about that.' He looks at her.

'It was the plane I thought you were on, the one from New York,' Kate explains.

'Really? So – '

'I was so frightened, David,' Kate says.

David wraps his arms around Kate's waist. 'I'm sorry. We were very busy, running from one gig to the next. You have to believe me, I wanted to be with *you*.' Kate averts her eyes. 'OK, I should've called you,' David admits. He pulls her closer and kisses her. 'I'm sorry,' he apologises once more. Kate knows he means it, she also knows he loves her. She only wishes he would be more communicative when he leaves her behind.

'Can we now go for some food?' Kate asks.

David smiles at her. He pulls her close as they walk towards the door with arms around each other's waist.

'Here y'are,' Earlene tells the customer and hands him the takeaway breakfast, wrapped in recyclable carton and paper. 'Have a nice day.' The customer takes his order and makes his way to the door.

After the breakfast crowds have dispersed, the mornings are generally quieter, with people beginning to pour in anew around lunchtime. With a contented face, Earlene tidies up the counter, refills the napkin holder and wipes the surface. Her workplace here is much more preferable than at her uncle's where she was always surrounded by the carcasses of dead animals, *so* distressing, all that deadness.

A few customers are sitting at the tables, others are entering. They might be 'takeaways', Earlene guesses as they walk towards her counter. One of them wears a T-shirt with Elvis on it underneath her open jacket. The other has her jacket zipped up to her chin and wears a shawl.

'What can I do for you?'

The women let their eyes glide over the menu board that is displayed above Earlene's head. 'What're you having?' the one asks the other.

'Uhm, yes, I think I'll go for that double veggie-burger … ' turning her attention to Earlene, 'does that come with salad?'

'Of course,' Earlene assures her, 'all our veggie-burgers and also the tofu-wraps come with salad. And we serve salad with our plates, too. All organic, mind.'

'Ah, well, then I'm having that, no. No, I'll take a wrap. No burger.'

'Fine,' Earlene says. 'To have here or take away?'

The woman turns around. 'What do you think?' she asks her friend. 'Are we staying here?'

The other woman, who just decided on a veggie-burger, also turns around. 'It looks nice here,' she says. 'Let's stay here.'

'Good choice,' Earlene approves as she arranges the ordered food on the two different plates. 'It's so cold out, doncha think?'

'My, winter's around the corner, I'm telling ya,' the women with the shawl replies.

'Freezing,' the other confirms.

'Anything to drink with that?' Earlene asks.

'Oh, yes. We'll have a hot coffee.'

Earlene adds up the amount at the cash register. 'That's 17.48, please.' She tells the women they can take a seat as she hands them the change and the receipt. 'I'll bring it to you.'

'Oh, that's nice.' The women find seats next to the

window. It doesn't take Earlene long before she places their order down on their table.

The door of the restaurant opens again as Earlene walks back to the counter. She recognises the woman who was here the day before with her little daughter. Today, too, she carries the suitcase with her. She smiles at the woman. 'Please, sit down,' Earlene offers. 'Miss Jennings is delayed. She told us to give you something to eat until she gets here.'

Lynn looks at Earlene with eyes that give away mistrust and she pulls Ashley closer to her.

'Don't worry,' Earlene reassures her. 'Miss Jennings *will* be here. Now, what can I get you?' Earlene smiles at the little girl, and she notices that Lynn now wears the stockings miss Jennings gave her yesterday.

Lynn turns to her little girl. 'Are you hungry?' Shyly Ashley nods her head. 'OK, then,' Lynn agrees.

'Fine, then I'll make you up a few plates. Tea? Or Coffee. Or does the little one want some soya hot chocolate?' Earlene looks at Ashley who utters a quiet 'hot chocolate'.

'OK. Just sit wherever you want, I'll bring it to you.' Earlene looks at the clock above the door that leads to the kitchen, 12.03. She wonders when her boss *will* be here. She's usually never that late. At the thought, she hears the phone in the office ring, but as Marianna is there Earlene doesn't make an effort to answer it.

When she takes the food and the drinks to Lynn and Ashley, who have found seats at the same table as yesterday, Marianna exits the office. She is carrying a few pencils and a notepad.

'May I?' she asks Lynn when she reaches their table. Lynn looks at her and wants to stand up, but Marianna motions her to remain where she is. She pulls up another chair and sits down opposite Lynn. 'Miss Jennings asked me to get your details. She can't really get here before two pm.' She shoves a form towards Lynn and gives her a pen. 'If you could fill this out, that would be very helpful.'

Lynn looks at the paper and reaches for the pen. 'We don't really have a permanent address,' she says when she has filled out her name.

'Doesn't matter, just write down where you are now.'

Marianna gives Ashley a few sheets of paper and pencils. 'Here, this is for you. Miss Jennings was wondering if you wouldn't want to make a nice drawing.'

Ashley just looks at her in a bashful way.

Marianna gets up. 'Whenever you're ready with that, just give it to Earlene. Thanks.'


Kate drives a rental car along the Interstate in the direction of Memphis. She hasn't felt so exhilarated in a long time. Her hands rest on the steering wheel, her fingers caress the ring she's wearing now. Fine smooth gold with a small diamond in the middle of it.

After they'd had their lunch, David and she had driven to his mother's house. David had hoped to find her home. Throughout he'd been rather quiet but Kate had put that down to his feeling tired. Then, after they had entered the kitchen at his mother's house, David had turned and looked at her. 'Kate, I can no longer keep this to myself.' His hand had moved to the breast pocket of his shirt -she remembers it well- 'I need to know.' He'd hesitated, held the small, blue velvet box in his hand. 'Kate, what would you say if we get married.'

She hadn't been able to find the words. She had moved closer to him and put her arms around his neck, her forehead resting against his shoulder. She had heard the small box opening, and when she stepped back to see his face, he had held the ring in front of her.

'I take it, that's a yes?' He had shown the same guiltless charm as on that day when they first met. It had made her weak at the knees and instead of crying out 'Yes! I want to! I want to be your wife!' she had David put the ring on her finger and they kissed.

Kate feels the smoothness of the ring, his token of his love for her. She will buy him something beautiful as well, as soon as she gets back to Memphis. But first, she needs to share her happiness with someone. She hopes Emmy will still be at the house that in the distance comes into view. The green Plymouth is still parked there. Kate briefly waits for the oncoming car to pass and then makes a left turn and drives on towards the house.

Emmy is just exiting through the kitchen door when Kate stops the car by the stables. When Emmy sees Kate has arrived she goes back into the house. Kate takes her bag from under the seat next to her and walks to the kitchen door.

'Hello Emmy,' she gaily addresses her aunt, who stands by the counter, one hand resting on its surface. Emmy looks at Kate, and unlike her, she doesn't seem to be her normal energetic self.

'I have great news!' Kate exclaims. She holds up her hand with the gleaming ring on her finger. 'We're engaged!'

'Oh, my sweet Katy.' Emmy's face softens, she approaches Kate and kisses her on both cheeks, 'congratulations!' before she resumes her former serious composure that now has Kate concerned. This is not how Emmy normally conducts herself.

'Is something the matter?' Kate asks.

Emmy takes a deep breath. 'Well. I don't really know how to explain this. You have to understand, I'm not crazy – '

'Of course you're not!' Kate affirms.

Emmy moves closer until her face is only a few inches away from Kate's, as if afraid that someone other than Kate might listen to the confidentiality of her account.

'After I'd done your upstairs,' she begins, 'I had a coffee and sat down, there … ' she makes a vague gesture in the direction of the lounge. 'I must have dozed off, when I heard a voice.' Emmy shrinks back. 'You wouldn't believe! It sounded as clear as daylight!' Realising the loudness in which she has just expressed herself, her voice goes down to a mere whisper. 'Jon Baker was murdered.'

Emmy's face shows a meaningful expression. 'I jumped up! I thought someone had come in! All I could say was, Who's there?'

After Emmy mentioned the sentence that she herself had heard so clearly this morning, Kate can only stare at Emmy's face.

'I'm telling you,' Emmy goes on, 'that voice, that voice was as clear as anyone's. But the worse thing was, there was no one there!' Emmy lets out a long breath. 'It gave me the creeps. I mean, I *know*, I've heard these stories, but I mean, here, in your house. You don't expect it when someone like *you* has moved into the house, Kate. *Your* house.'

Emmy suddenly becomes aware that Kate hasn't said a word and has only looked at her. *Stared* at her. 'Kate? Katy?'

Kate takes Emmy by her arm. 'Emmy, come here. Let's sit down.' She begins to lead Emmy to the lounge room. 'Kate, please. I'm not crazy.'

'I know. I need to know something, Em,' Kate says, 'for I had the same thing happening to me, this morning.'

'You did?' They sit down on the couch, next to each

other. 'You really did?' Emmy asks once more as she looks Kate in her eyes.

Kate takes Emmy's hand. 'Em, I've heard those stories about Jon Baker. Him committing suicide, found dead here on the property, but what do you know about all this? Was there a police inquiry? Has there ever been even a shred of evidence that he *might*'ve been murdered?'

Emmy withdraws her hand, and she shakes her head. 'Oh no, Kate. Don't you get yourself involved with that.'

'We are already involved, Emmy. And I don't feel like waking up every morning by someone yelling "Jon Baker was murdered" in my ear. I'd prefer my alarm any time.'

Emmy nods. 'Yeah, you've got a point. You know, I sometimes watch those TV-shows. You know, the ones where they go ghost hunting? Some of it is really true, you know. Then they find that some long dead relative comes a-haunting because of some unsolved family problem. Sometimes gives me the creeps … '

'Emmy, we need to find out what has really happened here. What do you remember about the Bakers? Is there anything that wasn't in the papers about his death, where you think, strange that they never investigated this, or that?'

Emmy shakes her head. 'Look, I was only, what, nineteen? In love. I was planning for a wedding. This Jon Baker stuff was the last thing that had me worried. Of course, there were rumours. I mean, his wife wasn't your average sweet old stand-by-your-man type of southern housewife, living in a golden cage. She had lovers. It was a well-known fact in the area.' Emmy moves her face closer to Kate's, lowering her voice. 'But then, he … he had his share of mistresses, too.' She straightens her back. 'Or so they said.'

When she was a child growing up in this area, Kate was oblivious of issues that occupied the grown-ups, other than the domesticities that occurred in her direct environment. Like the heater that never worked when it had to, or the pick-up, the only one Daddy ever owned, that didn't want to start when it needed to. She remembers too well, her daddy bent over under the hood trying things with wires in order to get the vehicle going. She only knew Mrs Baker because her daddy took her there. Mr Baker was never present. Always working, her daddy once said. She can't think of a single instant that she actually saw Mr Baker.

Kate looks down at her hands where the smooth gold of the ring reminds her of her present situation. The little diamond sparkles as it catches the daylight that falls into the room through the large French doors.

'You'd better start making plans yourself,' Emmy quietly suggests as she observes Kate. 'Anything planned yet? Where the wedding is going to be?'

There is delight in Kate's face when she looks at Emmy. 'We still have to discuss that,' she says. 'Now, I'd better go to the city, I almost forgot that this is a working day.'

Emmy waves that aside as she gets up off the couch. 'You're your own boss, you can take time off whenever you want to.'

'I'm afraid it doesn't work like that, Emmy,' Kate replies as she follows her aunt into the kitchen. 'Also a boss has obligations.'

By the kitchen door, Emmy rests her hands on Kate's shoulders. 'Don't worry anymore about this Jon Baker stuff,' she urges. 'You've got other things to worry about now.' She strokes Kate's cheek and kisses her on both cheeks. 'I'll lock up,' she reassures her. 'You'd better get to work.'

Kate feels relieved, happy. Her aunt is like a mother to her, even after all these years. She squeezes Emmy's hand before she walks across to the car.

'Oh, Kate! I almost forgot.' Emmy comes rushing after her. 'There was a man here this morning, claimed to know you, came to see you. A downright highfalutin snob, if you ask me! You know what he said?' Emmy sounds offended as Kate feels a chill. She has a hunch. 'Tell your *mistress John* came to see her. Your mistress! I ask you!? He came in a taxicab. Must be loaded to be travelling like that.'

'He is,' Kate replies resignedly as she opens the door of the car. 'Don't worry, he won't show his face here again.'

Emmy closes the car door when Kate sits behind the wheel. 'Now, you take care!' she says before Kate drives off.

In the empty space over the restaurant Kate slowly wanders through the two rooms. Initially, she had intended to use it as storage space, contemplated using one of the rooms as her office. The office space downstairs was already getting too small with the extra filing-cabinets she had installed there.

She observes the space she has up here, it must be at least 100 square metres, as it spreads all over the surface of the restaurant below. She is sure that it would do, both as storage and a temporary apartment. There is even a well-equipped bathroom, cleverly planned by Jacob in case staff would want to have a shower after work during the hot Memphian summers. It would do well for Lynn and Ashley. There was no need for them to keep living in that place.

When Kate came to the restaurant this afternoon, it was almost 4 pm. Lynn had left, had taken her little girl and had gone back to the shelter. With the information Lynn had provided, Kate could easily locate the homeless shelter. Once inside she'd become aware that the people who run it were doing their best for the poor souls to whom they were giving their undivided attention and care, but it had distressed Kate. For even though drugs and alcohol weren't allowed inside, it apparently didn't deter the addicts from satisfying their addictions before coming back to the shelter.

It was no place for a child.

She briefly spoke to Lynn who, fortunately, was given a tiny room that barely could hold the single bed. It looked more like a closet than a room, but at least it was separate from the dormitories where others were housed. Lynn promised she'd be back the next day for Kate to take them shopping for some clothes. Kate also learned that Ashley was almost six years old, but has hardly had schooling. Kate is determined to change that, too.

After she left the shelter she'd gone to a large home-furniture store and selected a complete set of furnishings to house in this space. Two beds, mattresses, a table with chairs, a sofa and a lazy chair, wardrobes and a desk for Ashley to do her homework at. And she has bought linen. It will all be delivered tomorrow.

Kate takes the storybooks she has purchased for Ashley from its bag and places them on a box that is situated in a corner of one of the rooms. She gives the space one more look, then switches off the light and goes downstairs where the last customers are about to leave. Alejandra is wiping the tables and tidying up and even though Marianna had an early shift today, she too is still here. She made sure everything ran smoothly as Kate was not there for most of the day. The kitchen staff has cleaned the kitchen and has gone home.

'Marianna,' Kate addresses her employee, 'we are going to have another member of staff.'

Marianna lends Kate a listening ear as she is zipping up her jacket and wraps a warm shawl around her neck. 'She will need quite a bit of training,' Kate explains, 'but I'm positive that she'll be a good asset to our team.'

'No worries,' Marianna replies. 'Serving or in the kitchen?'

'Well, I'm not really certain yet, but we'll soon see what her qualities are.'

When Alejandra has finished her tasks, she joins Marianna and Kate. 'Her name is Lynn,' Kate continues, 'she'll be here tomorrow.'

Now that Kate has finally dealt with the important matters of the day, and with the sounds of 'goodnight miss Jennings' lingering in her ears, she goes into her office. She should not wait any longer informing her brother about her engagement to David. She also needs to call her grandmother, who will be so pleased. Grandmother always hoped for her granddaughter to be happily married, just as her daughter once was. Kate looks at the clock. It's must be 3 am in London. Kate decides to send her brother an email, recalling the late phone calls she placed to Jacob before, and it will be more appropriate to call her grandmother in the morning.

The early morning light has awakened Kate, and with a refreshed feeling, she turns over on her side. Daybreak has sent its first rays through the drapes and now shines a playful long light on the peach-coloured walls. Thank God she wasn't woken by the words she so clearly heard the morning before. Instead, David's handsome features are facing her; he is fast asleep. Kate watches his steady breathing slightly lifting the duvet, moving down as he exhales. She shouldn't wake him. He's had a few very gruelling days: late-night TV-shows, tiring flights, arriving back at dead of night. She gently touches a strand of his hair that rests on his shoulder and places a soft kiss on his wrist. Then she silently slides her feet from under the duvet until they touch the carpeted floor. The rest of her body follows and she gets up. Kate whisks her negligée from the chair and, silently, she leaves the bedroom. She walks down the stairs, feeling the warmth of the house surrounding her. In the kitchen, she starts preparing breakfast, when the phone interrupts the quietness. It startles Kate and she is quick to grab it; she wouldn't want David to wake up now that he is having a lie-in. 'Hello,' she softly says into the receiver.

'*Katy?*'

'Gran, how are you? Is everything all right?' Her grandmother hardly ever phones her at this hour.

'*No, darling, I'm fine. I just call to congratulate you. Jacob just told me, you are to be married!*'

'Yes, Gran. Isn't it wonderful?' Kate tries to keep her voice low in her excitement.

'*I am so pleased, Kate. We will have to celebrate. When are you coming home? You will have to come home for Christmas.*'

'I will, Gran, I will. I shall have to convince David – '

'*That's right, David. Jacob mentioned his name is David. Nice name, David, very nice name.*'

'You will love him, Gran. I'm sure you will. Listen, I was just making some breakfast. Can I call you tonight?'

'*Of course, darling, don't be silly! You call me whenever you want. Enjoy your day!*'

'You too. Bye now!' Kate puts the phone down and

glances up the stairs; she hopes she hasn't woken him. When she has the coffee percolating, the bread and other necessities for breakfast laid out, Kate pours a glass of juice from the jug and makes her way to the office at the back of the hall. She switches her computer on and looks out the window to see the morning light spreading over the fields around the house. She sits down at her desk to start searching for courses Management. She's quite sure that colleges in Memphis offer adult education courses. She wonders about Lynn's schooling, for she will need some basics before she can start any course, but Kate's involvement with Lynn has given her the impression that she must have had a normal education until her life took a different turn. Kate checks the information a few colleges provide about the course she has in mind and sends it to the printer. She takes the sheets of paper and inspects them briefly before leaving her office.

Carrying the information she has just gathered, she enters the kitchen. David is standing in the lounge looking out the large windows of the French doors. He only wears his T-shirt and a pair of track-pants that Kate recognises as belonging to Jacob. She puts her papers down and goes towards him. David turns his head when he hears her approach.

'Mornin' hon',' he softly says as he slides an arm around her back. She rests her head against his chest, and they watch as the bleak sun briefly peeks from behind a cloud and sends hazy rays across the hill beyond. 'Are you ready for some breakfast?' Kate says. David kisses her forehead before they walk back to the kitchen. 'Dying for some coffee,' he replies and pours them both a cup before he sits down. 'Eggs?' Kate asks.

'Sure, you can wake me up for bacon and eggs any

time,' David replies.

Kate looks at him. 'Sorry, David, but you won't ever find the flesh of a dead animal in this house.'

'I'm sorry, it had slipped my mind,' David apologises. 'Eggs will be fine.'

'You can have veggie sausages,' Kate suggests, and breaks a few eggs in the frying pan. 'Sunny side up OK? David gets up and walks towards her. 'I might just become a vegetarian now,' he says and takes the spatula from her. 'Here, let me. You know, there is a bush that's called eggs-and-bacon.'

Kate looks at him, smiling unbelievingly.

'It's true, I'm not kidding you. It's an Australian bush-plant. They call it that because of the shape, and colour of the flowers.'

He turns off the heat underneath the pan. 'Let's eat,' he says and slides the eggs onto their plates. Kate takes her cup and starts sipping her coffee.

'Grandmother phoned me this morning. She wants me home for Christmas.'

'Then you should go,' David says. 'Don't let your eggs get cold.'

'David, I was more or less hoping you'd be able to come with me.'

David looks at her with eyes that tell her that it might be a problem. 'I will have to see, Kate.' He takes another bite from his food. 'I mean, I don't think we have any commitments around that time, but it can still change.'

Kate's looks disappointed and shows a hint of frustration.

'And then there's my boy. I promised him he could spend time with me at Christmas.'

'Can't he come with you? I'm sure he'd love it,' Kate endeavours. 'Going on an aeroplane, boys love

161

aeroplanes.'

David takes his coffee cup. 'His mom won't let him. He's never far from her.'

Kate is at a loss for reasons that could convince David to come with her to England.

'And we should also plan for our wedding,' Kate reminds David. 'Where will we get married?'

David glances up at Kate as taken by surprise. That never crossed his mind, *where* they should get married. Good old USA would suit him fine. 'I hope you weren't thinking of a big do,' David says. 'Let's keep it small. OK?'

'My thoughts exactly,' Kate agrees.

'Just family,' David says. 'Maybe a few friends, no more.'

Kate can't agree more. She remembers the elaborate wedding parties of friends she has been to, where not a Pound was spared. More than half of those who were wedded on those costly wedding days have now separated or are divorced. Kate has no intention of becoming part of that league.

David drives his pick-up onto the parking lot that is within walking distance from Kate's restaurant. He prefers driving into town in his own car that he now sees as his *disguise*. People down on their luck drive pick-ups battered as his, they wouldn't associate it with a country singer who has just reached the top spot in the country charts. David searches under the dashboard for his sunglasses and puts them on before he and Kate get out of the car. Kate, keeping in line with David's attire, wears jeans and trainers and an inconspicuous jacket. David puts an arm around Kate's shoulders as she threads an arm around his waist. They don't have a problem blending in with others that stroll along. Most of them preoccupied with their daily mundanities, and without interruptions, they reach Kate's restaurant. Upon entering the establishment, David removes his sunglasses and playfully holds them in his hand. One or two customers in the restaurant turn their heads and look with faces that betray recognition. Earlene, who is just putting an order in front of a customer, turns her head too and looks at the man who accompanies her boss, with inquisitive eyes.

'Mornin', miss Jennings.'

'Morning, Earlene,' Kate replies as David behind her tips his hat. Kate and David go to the back where Marianna is just filing some documents.

'How are you this morning, Marianna?' Kate enquires.

'Fine, ma'am.'

'Has she come in yet?' Kate asks.

Marianna's eyes have wandered to the man behind her. 'Has *who* come in, ma'am?'

'The new lady. Lynn … Oh, this is David,' Kate introduces. Marianna nods in greeting and briefly smiles.

'No, ain't seen her yet,' she says, slowly. 'But a load of furnishings has arrived. I had them put it upstairs, in the storage.'

'Excellent,' Kate says. 'Look, I have some things to take care of in town. Can you take charge until I'm back?'

Marianna's eyes once more drift to the man who escorts her boss as she answers: 'I already have, miss Jennings. Taken care of things.'

'Thank you, Marianna,' Kate says, and she and David retreat from the office. They walk through the restaurant to go outside when the person entering the establishment stops Kate in her tracks. She feels David bump against her back. 'What is it?' he asks, surprised.

Kate stares the person who just entered, straight in the face.

'Kate!' John exclaims. 'There you are, darling!' He wants to give her a peck on the cheek but Kate turns her face away from him.

'Darling?' David utters. In a protective stance, he moves between Kate and John. 'Hey, buster, don't you go calling my fiancée *darling*. Who are you anyway?'

John looks alarmed. His face turns to horror when he has a look at the man in a cowboy hat from under which long sand-coloured locks fall onto broad shoulders. Kate places her hand on David's arm. 'It's all right, David. John, this is David. We're going to be married.'

John's mouth falls open. For a moment, the capability to utter words leaves him. 'I … I … Kate, you can't be serious … '

'Congratulations would be nice,' David observes and he leads Kate to the door for them to leave. As David shepherds her away from the intruding man, Kate glances over her shoulder. 'I'll send you a wedding invitation! Bye John!'

4

*T*he taxi Kate has taken to the Public Library east of the
city centre drops her off on Poplar Avenue, in front of a
building that doesn't exactly resemble a library. 'It's right
behind there,' the cab driver says. 'Just cross the parking
lot.'

Kate hands the man his fee and steps out of the taxi.
She gives the area a brief look and then continues walking
across the square. The library is a pleasant looking
structure, Kate observes, modern with large windows that
allow plenty of daylight in. She walks up the few steps
and the moment she enters, the calm quietness of the place
envelops her as she makes her way to the information
desk. People are silently moving alongside the shelves,
their eyes fixed on the spines of books, occasionally
taking one off the shelf and thumbing through it. Others
sit at tables, reading or relaying information in whispering
tones to the person next to them.

'Yes, please,' the soft voice of the lady at the
information desk sounds.

Kate turns to face her. 'Oh, uh, do you have any old
newspaper articles?' Kate has adjusted her speech to the
level of the quiet voices she hears around her. 'I'm
looking for information, something that happened here
twenty-two years ago.'

'Sure, ma'am. You need to go to the fourth floor,' the
lady replies. 'You can take the elevator over there,' she
points out. 'If you're having trouble finding it, just ask my
colleague up there.'

'Thank you.' Kate makes her way towards the lifts.
On the fourth floor, she sees another library attendant and

she repeats her query. In the History section, Kate is shown drawers with small boxes that contain microfilms. The man assists in showing her the procedure. 'Twenty-two years ago, you said.' He pulls out a few boxes and hands them to Kate. He then points out the computer screens and shows her how to put the microfilm in the device.

'Oh, that's great,' Kate says.

'With this switch you can change the pages.'

'Thank you,' Kate whispers.

'If you like you can print things, too, with this one here.'

'Thank you,' Kate says once more and as the man disappears she sits down on the chair behind the computer screen. She looks for dates on the old newspaper pages, she guesses, are near Jon Baker's demise. Kate focuses her eyes on the screen, reading headlines, situations that occurred in the area when she was just eight years old, but before this time she and Jacob had lived with Grandmother and Grandfather for almost a year. It had taken some time before Jacob had not woken up screaming. He relived the car crash almost every night. On those nights Kate went over to her brother's bed and held his hand until he was calm again, comforted him, telling him that Tennessee was far, far away and that they were living in a castle now with Gran and Grandpa. That there was nothing to be afraid of anymore.

Kate's eyes catch a name: Jon Baker. *Landowner Jon Baker was found shot dead on his land yesterday. His body was lying in a ditch not far from the house, where he lived with his two sons and his wife, a native of Kentucky. Mr Baker's gun lay beside him. The police investigation is ongoing but the death is being treated as a suicide.* A photo showing Jon Baker's face was printed beside the article. Kate looks at it and a faint recollection of having seen that face before emerges, the robust features, the bushy eyebrows. Somewhere deep down in her memory is a mental image of this face. But where had she seen it before? Had she seen him walking on his land? Had he come to their village? Or was it on one of the occurrences Daddy took them all to Memphis?

Kate slowly moves the microfilm further and finds another article. The day after Mr Baker was found dead, the police tracked down a man who was seen *with the deceased*. Kate strains her eyes as she reads the news article. *A business acquaintance was seen with Jon Baker earlier on the day he was found dead. After interrogation, however, he was set free.* 'Mm,' Kate utters. *The man had a sound alibi but was able to reveal that Mr Baker by no means seemed suicidal. The suspect, whose name was not disclosed, stated Mr Baker had been quite 'jolly'.* Kate moves on to another day of the news relays about the death and finds that even Mrs Baker had been among the suspects, but that too was later dismissed, as a friend had come forward who claimed to have had lunch with Mrs Baker. It was Mrs Baker who had found her husband later that day and had called the police.

Kate skips some pages and reads about a new development in the case. A leading police officer had resigned after he had, seemingly, inherited a large amount of money and had moved to Nevada. *Mr Canelli was the police officer in charge of the Jon Baker case. Mr Baker was a well-known landowner from Memphis who was found dead near his house last month.* Found dead. That's all this article says. There's no mention about a supposed suicide, but neither about murder. Kate reruns the articles she just looked at and sends them to the printer. She wonders if anybody here in this room knows where to obtain information to do with police investigations of some twenty-odd years ago. She looks at the young man next to her, he must be a student, Kate assumes. He wouldn't even have been born at the time of the death of Mr Baker. He gives her a brief smile when he notices Kate looking at him. Kate smiles back. She decides to ask him.

'Try the records office,' he proposes. 'Or the Courts. Sometimes they let you read up on old court cases.'

Kate thanks him but as far as she knows there has never been a court case. She takes her printed copies from the machine and walks out of the room.

Sitting down near the entrance of the library, she takes her mobile from her bag. After having called for a taxi, it occurs to her that she has a cousin here in Memphis who studies law. She resolves to ask Emmy for the address or phone number. She also decides to give Earl Jones a call.

Kate has the taxi take her back to the restaurant where Lynn and Ashley have now set up home above the restaurant. It had taken little persuasion and Kate is certain that Lynn was mainly taking her small daughter into account when she took the offered space. Lynn has agreed, too, that doing a course at college was the best option for a way ahead. Ashley has been enrolled in a school not too far from home. Both mother and daughter will start their education when the Christmas holidays are over, and Lynn will work her hours at the restaurant after she's through for the day at college. Kate feels gratified as she gazes out of the car window. The Christmas decorations strung up along the streets and shops remind her that Christmas has crawled imperceptibly closer; she should organise her sojourn in England. It has been a tradition for years for the whole family to gather at Grandmother's for Christmas.

Gran will not want it any other way.

Kate is still not certain if David will come with her, he hasn't agreed but he hasn't declined either. He has been in Nashville this past week, recording for a new CD and he and his band are booked for 'a few gigs locally', by which David means they don't have to leave the state for their performances. Mildly comforting to Kate. David has promised to send for her when they give a show in Memphis, but that is not the only thing Kate wants to look forward to. While looking at the Christmas decorated shops that pass by the cab window, she changes her mind and has the driver drop her off in the city centre.

She walks past eateries and shops adorned with Christmas lights. In lit bulbs, Santa and his reindeer fly over the shoppers. Stars, Christmas trees and crescent moons make the surroundings look even more attractive. She finds a jeweller where, after some consideration, she buys her grandmother a necklace. She's not certain what to buy David but then sees something she is positive he will treasure. Musical notes engraved on a golden heart, musical notes that communicate *Love me tender*.

Kate flags down another taxi that takes her back to her workplace. The establishment has gradually become very popular with the locals. On entering the restaurant she sees there's hardly a free place left in the seating area and more people are queuing at the counter to be served.

Kate spots Earl sitting at one of the tables near a window, sipping a coffee.

'Well,' Kate approaches him, 'that was quick!' Earl shakes her hand. 'Hello, Kate. Good to see you.'

'Glad you could make it.' Kate slides her coat off her shoulders and pulls up a chair.

'Anything important?' Earl asks. 'You sounded somewhat serious.'

Kate looks at him. 'Earl, I know that I once told you that ghosts don't scare me. Don't get me wrong, they still don't but, I was hoping that you could tell me a bit more about this Jon Baker ... '

'Has he come a-hauntin'?' Earl chortles. 'I told ya.' He points a finger at her, jocularly. Kate smiles at his lack of seriousness about the situation.

'I just would like to find out if he indeed committed suicide or, whether he ... was murdered,' Kate explains. Earl's face loses its mirth. 'Murdered!' he exclaims. Kate makes a gesture for him to keep his voice down as a few customers have turned their heads. 'You're not serious,' Earl resumes in a confidential tone.

'Do you recall anything about what happened back then, that points in that direction?' Kate enquires. 'I would love to know.'

'Kate, I don't think it's a good idea for you to go poking around. Besides, the police had come to the conclusion – '

'That's just the thing,' Kate interjects. 'Apparently the police have never come up with any hard facts. They've just taken for granted that – '

Earl shakes his head. 'Just leave the crimes to the crime stoppers, Kate.'

Kate looks Earl in the eyes. 'How come I have the impression you know something?'

Earl lets out a sigh. 'OK. There were rumours going around at the time. Mind you, I usually don't listen to rumours ... Rumours are just, well, rumours ... '

'What kind of rumours?'

'It was rumoured ... ' Earl quietly states as he bends over to Kate, 'that she *had* him killed. Police just never found proof.'

His confession astounds Kate. At the time, she never

had the impression that Mrs Baker was any other than a kind lady.

'Why would she do that?' Kate probes. Earl shrugs his shoulders. 'It was well-known that she had lovers, but otherwise they were private people. God knows what went on behind their closed doors.'

The knowledge makes Kate feel uneasy. Her home had been the scene of such viciousness? It just wasn't in accordance with what she feels and has always felt about the property.

'I was at the library this morning and looked up old newspaper articles … '

Earl gives her a languid glance.

'… About a month after the mu … uh … death of Mr Baker the police officer in charge suddenly seemed to have enough money to resign and moved to another state.'

'Yes,' Earl confirms, 'that was something else that had the tongues wagging. But he claimed to have inherited money from a relative in Nevada. That's where he went, Nevada.'

'And the police? Did they not find that odd?'

'Odd?'

'Strange,' Kate defines. 'Didn't they think it was – '

'No,' Earl says, 'but then again, colleagues, among themselves. In the end the whole situation was more or less forgotten. Mrs B had moved away. Claimed she couldn't live at that house anymore. Took her boys and moved back east.'

Kate starts to feel agitated; she has a suspicion that there's a lot more to this story.

'Thanks, Earl. That was very enlightening.'

'Don't mention it. Just, well, I think you shouldn't pursue anything. Just let it rest.'

Kate would like to, she has enough on her mind, but

she feels she needs to know what really happened, if she is to be rid of the *ghosts*.

'Can I get you another coffee?' she offers. 'Something to eat maybe?'

'Well, as you're offering, your lunches look really nice,' he says with a smile, 'and everybody else seems to enjoy them.'

'One lunch coming up,' Kate says and goes to prepare the food herself, with her staff busy tending to a steady flow of customers.

The surroundings look dim as Kate is on her way back. She left work early and now drives along the darkening road that leads to the village of her youth. Then, she remembers, the road wasn't lit once darkness had fallen. One depended on the beams of light that the car sent forth until reaching the Interstate, or at the other end, the sparsely lit streets in the village.

She parks the car in front of Emmy's house, gets out and takes the few steps to the front door.

'Come on in!' Kate hears after she has knocked. She enters the living-room and recognises the young woman, who lies sprawled out on the couch, wearing a multi-coloured skirt that drapes onto the floor. 'Hello, Anna-May.'

'Hello,' her cousin says. She takes on a more proper pose and pulls her dark hair back into a ponytail.

Emmy comes rushing in from the kitchen. 'Kate, how are ya? Come, sit. I'll get you some tea.'

'Thanks, Emmy.' Kate sits down next to Anna-May. 'How's your sister, how's Daisy-Lou?' Kate enquires.

'Oh, she's fine. She's finally made up her mind,' Anna-May says, 'about what she wants, I mean.' She leans over to Kate. 'She wants to study *theatre*.'

'Oh, that sounds fun!' Kate declares. 'Here, in Memphis?'

'God no, she's always wanted to see the *world*,' Anna-May says, making a wide gesture with one arm. 'No, she wants to go to New York.'

'New York. Good for her,' Kate states.

Emmy comes in with a tray with cups of tea. 'Bit late for coffee,' she says as she puts the cups down on the coffee table. 'Now, what was it you wanted to ask Anna-May?'

'Well, Emmy, after your experience, and mine, at my house … You know, the other day?'

'… Ye'es,' Emmy reluctantly replies.

'I went and did some research. There are a few things that have me wondering.' She turns to Anna-May. 'And I thought, maybe, if you like, Anna-May, maybe you would want to use this material for your studies, as a kind of training material.' Kate reaches into her bag and removes the folder with her findings that she printed out at the library. Emmy looks on with genuine interest.

Anna-May opens the folder on her lap and takes out the newspaper articles. 'What should I do with these?' she asks.

'They might be useful, it might give you an inkling –'

'An inkling? Of what?'

Kate leafs through the sheets of paper and takes out one on which she, chronologically, typed her discoveries. 'Here, this is what I've come up with so far.'

Anna-May starts reading through it as Emmy squeezes in between them and reads along with her daughter.

'See!' Emmy reacts. 'See! That's exactly what everybody was always saying.'

It surprises Kate that such a public secret has never

been investigated further.

'Wouldn't you think it interesting for you to incorporate that into your law-studies?' Kate proposes.

A worried expression arises on Emmy's face. 'But this is quite serious, Kate,' she expresses, perturbed. 'You can't have Anna-May go poking around – '

'Momma,' Anna-May interjects, 'what can happen? Nothing can happen. This will be an interesting case to work on.'

Emmy looks from one to the other, facing Anna-May and then Kate. 'It never came to a case,' she says. 'The police concluded it was a suicide. Mrs Baker sold the house and all the land and moved away.'

'But what about the voices then?' Kate asks. 'And what you said just – '

'What voices?' Anna-May demands. Emmy looks as if she does not want certain knowledge revealed but at the same time is curious to know.

'Uhm,' Kate starts, 'well, I was woken one day, last week, by a voice that said, Jon Baker was murdered … quite loudly, in my ear. And then, later on Emmy'd heard the same – '

'Yes! Out of the blue!' Emmy shrieks. 'Now, Anna-May, don't go thinking we've gone crazy here,' she says, 'but rumours were flying around that the house *was* haunted.'

'My, the ghosts ain't found peace yet,' Anna-May guys.

'Now, don't make fun of us, Anna-May,' Emmy says. 'It wasn't anything to laugh about, scared me right out of my socks!'

'I think that there is just something in the house that won't rest until justice is done,' Kate says.

Anna-May looks at her cousin with an unbelieving

eye. 'Do y'all get that in England? Those spirit-ghosts, I mean?'

'Now, Anna-May, this ain't something to be taken lightly,' Emmy retorts. 'You were too small to know, but since the Bakers left there have been stories about spooky goings-on in that house. And you've seen these TV-shows where they go a-chasing after them ghosts.'

Anna-May nods. 'Mm,' she reacts with a certain disinterest.

'So, what do you think?' Kate asks. 'Can you maybe find out more about this? Then, if it is true that Jon Baker *was* murdered … there must be someone out there … '

Emmy takes a gasp of breath and raises her hands to the heavens. 'God forbid!'

Beneath the cloudy skies over Jackson, David steers his pick-up through the streets and turns off into the road where his mother lives. A cold wind blows a scatter of raindrops against his windscreen. David sees the large plastic Santa in front of his mother's house and the Christmas lights strung around the front door. He parks in the driveway as the back door opens and Sammy comes running out. 'Daddy!'

David shuts the door of his pick-up and Sammy lets himself be lifted off the ground into his father's arms. 'How's my boy?' is David's cheerful reaction. 'Have you been good?'

'Am always good boy,' Sammy says. David brushes his free hand through Sammy's hair. 'Let's get you inside,' he says. They enter the warm kitchen where David's mother Valerie is preparing lunch.

'Hi Ma,' and he gives his mother a kiss. The kitchen, too, is abundantly decked in Christmas ornaments. Greens, reds and gold are adorning the walls and the window-posts. His mother loves Christmas, and she expects her family to be home for Christmas.

'Good to see you, son. Sit down, lunch is ready.' David puts Sammy in a chair next to his and sits down too.

'Gwanny, Daddy is staying with us now,' Sammy happily states and wraps his little hand around his father's arm. David's mother smiles at her grandson. 'It's good to have Daddy home, ain't it. Now eat your sandwich, sweetheart.'

Sammy takes a big bite from his peanut butter and banana sandwich, happy that his father is among them again. David has a sip from his coffee and looks at his boy.

'How long will Mel be away for?' he asks his mother who shrugs her shoulders. 'Dunno, she just came by yesterday and asked if I could take Sammy for a few days. Good thing I've got a few days off!' She places a hand on David's arm. 'And good thing you're here, if you like you can take Sam home with you.'

David looks at his mother. 'Kate wants to plan some things for the wedding,' he says, 'and tomorrow afternoon we're doing the show in Memphis. Why don't you come?'

Val turns to Sammy. 'Do you hear that, Sam? Daddy is going to sing in Memphis! Do you want to go and see him?'

Sammy's blue eyes light up. 'Yes!' he says with his mouth full.

'It'll be all right,' Val says. 'I'll watch him when you're up there.'

David takes a sandwich from the platter and looks at his mother. 'She wants to have the wedding in England.'

'Son, I'm so happy you're gonna get married, I don't care *where* it is.'

Anxiously, Sammy looks up at the grown-ups. 'Is Daddy going away again?'

'Of course not,' Val soothes, 'we're going to see your daddy in Memphis. Tomorrow.'

David has thought it better not to explain the situation to Sammy at this stage, he doesn't want to confuse the little one even more. 'Have you told Mel?'

Valerie shakes her head. 'No, she'll know soon enough. I hope she's fine though, she looked a bit stressed yesterday.'

David glances at his mother who makes an indistinct gesture. 'Don" ask,' she says. David turns to Sammy. 'Sam, is Mummy OK? Is Mummy happy?' Sammy looks up a bit shyly and kicks his little legs under the table. He unwillingly nods his head. 'Not when she cwies,' he then contradicts.

'Does Mummy cry?' David asks. Sammy nods once more and he puts the remainder of his sandwich on his plate. David glances at his little boy to then face his mother with a concerned look in his eyes.

'She's a grown woman,' Val appeases. 'I mean, they do love each other, but … Maybe they're going through a phase. I don't know.'

David sighs. 'Yeah, but she's got Sam.'

Valerie rests a hand on David's arm. 'I'm sorry, I shouldn't have said. I didn't mean to worry you. I'm sure things are OK.'

Sammy circles both his little hands around his father's arm. 'Can we go play? I wanna go with *you*.'

'Sure Sam,' David says and he pulls Sam onto his lap. 'Can Grandma come too?'

Sam nods. Valerie gets up from the table. 'Well! Then we better go get our coats, Sam. And we all go out!'

The parking lot at the FedEx building in downtown Memphis is covered in all shades of metallic with only a few free spaces left. No doubt the parking garage is almost full, too. The big Country Show has drawn many away from their Christmas shopping this afternoon. Around the venue, people of all ages have lined up and are waiting to enter the building. As soon as the doors open, the crowds stream through and make their way to the stalls along the sides. Before long, the open spaces around the entrance hall are teeming with people, all trying to get souvenirs of their favourite country singers.

By this time, Valerie and her small grandson Sam have joined David in the busy dressing rooms. Sam holds on to his father's hand and looks up at the people that surround him as David chats with his band members and discusses some details about a few new songs they plan to perform. He turns to his mother when they're through. 'Better take your seats now, Ma,' he says. 'Sam you go with Grandma, Daddy needs to go sing a little bit.'

Sammy holds out his arms for his father to lift him up for a cuddle. David gives Sam a kiss and puts him down again. 'You be a good boy and go with Grandma, OK?' David smiles and watches his boy walk out of the dressing room accompanied by his mother. 'Oh, Ma. Have you seen Kate?' he hollers after them. Val shakes her head. 'No. But I'm sure she'll show up.'

David turns when one of his band members hands him something to drink and he takes a swallow from the bottle. His nervousness is usually at its worst before he has to go and perform. It's the waiting until the previous acts have finished that still makes him fret.

'Don't worry,' Gene assures him with a grin, 'we're right behind you.' The band members begin to walk out and onwards to the stage where David will join them straight after their intro. When the others leave and the dressing room is empty it's David's time to focus on what's ahead of him, and he takes a few deep breaths.

'David.'

As he exhales he wonders if he has heard correctly. He turns and sees Melanie in the doorway.

'Mel? What is it *you* want?' She catches him by surprise. 'I mean, Sam's with Val, they've come to see the show.'

Melanie looks at him with a face that tells him that she is closer to crying than laughing. 'It's you I came to see,' she merely says. Her pale complexion is enhanced by her hair that is dyed jet-black. David can't say it suits her. Neither do the piercings in her nose and all along the rim of her right ear. 'I don't have time now, Mel. I'm about to go on stage.'

'David, I do need to talk to you, I … ' She lets out a sigh, 'I think we have made a big mistake. Splitting up, I mean.'

'Don't be ridiculous, Mel!'

It's not uncommon for Melanie to evoke annoyance in him. 'You split. Remember? And when Sam was born you didn't even want me to know my own son!'

Melanie moves closer to him and looks him in his eyes. 'David … I know I've made mistakes. And as for marrying Stuart … Well, let's say, I was just trying to make you jealous.'

David shakes his head. 'Don't even go there, Mel. And I've got news for you, I'm not the jealous type.'

Her eyes are moist as she turns away from him. 'Oh hell!' she cries. 'It's just this damned Stuart! He – '

'What?' David demands. 'What Mel! Is he nasty to Sam?' Melanie remains standing with her hands covering her face. David grabs her by her arm. 'What! Tell me.'

179

Melanie's face is covered in tears when she faces him. 'He's nasty to both of us,' she then says. 'He's so selfish! So, self-centred! I never thought he'd be like that! Please, David,' she implores. More tears stream down her face when she pleads with him. 'Why can't we try again?'

David takes the tissue box and pulls out a few tissues. 'Wipe your face,' he says, handing her the tissues. Melanie unwillingly does as she's told, and she fiddles with the tissue paper.

'Don't forget you *chose* to marry him,' he says.

'Yes! I have a son to raise, remember?' Melanie says and she blows her nose.

'Well, I have noticed Sam's not happy living with you and that Stuart guy,' David admits. 'Why don't you divorce him? I'm sure there're nicer guys out there.'

Melanie moves closer to him, and looks up at him. As her green eyes rest in his, she slides her arms around his neck. 'I think, I let the best one go,' she says. Before David realises, she is kissing him and for a moment he can't help himself but kiss her back. Then he pushes her off.

'Mel, I just got engaged.'

Melanie looks at him with a knowing expression in her eyes. 'I've heard about that,' she merely states. David's attention is drawn by a slight rustle in the passage outside the dressing room. It reminds him of his responsibilities. 'Mel, just get a divorce if you're not happy with this guy. I need to go. I have a show to do.' He starts to rush out and go to the stage where his band is, no doubt, waiting for him, but he stops by the door. 'We will talk about this later, Mel. I won't have my son being unhappy living with that guy.'

Marianna turns her head as her boss barges through

the door of the restaurant and walks straight to her office at the back. Kate sits down at her desk and dials a number on the phone. As soon as she has an airline attendant answering at the other end of the line, she gives the person her details. 'Yes, a flight to London. First class. For today.' Within a few minutes, Kate gets the confirmation, there's a flight out of Memphis to London just after 7 pm. She takes her credit card from her handbag and tells them the number. 'Thank you,' Kate says. 'And can you cancel my other flight? Here's my booking reference.' Kate gives the airline-desk her final details and then calls Marianna into her office.

'Marianna. Can you take over from me? I'm flying out to London in a few hours.' Marianna looks at her with confusion on her face. 'I thought you were going next week?'

'Something has come up. I'm flying out now. Are you sure you can handle the situation here? Like I taught you?'

Marianna nods. 'And you gave me your contact details in London in case there're things I don't know about.'

Kate stands up and grabs her bag. 'OK, then. I wish you all a good Christmas.' Her voice sounds distant when she says it.

Marianna and Alejandra watch as Kate rushes out of the door.

'What was that all about?' Alejandra asks.

Marianna shrugs her shoulders. 'I've no idea.'

Kate hasn't even allowed herself to feel sad after she saw David passionately kissing that woman, who, in her opinion didn't look like an average fan.

When she witnessed David kissing that black-haired creature she had felt she wanted to grab a stick and beat the woman off. Instead, she ran out of the building and drove straight back to her office. She needed to be with people she could trust, and instantly her grandmother and Jacob had come to mind.

In a haze, she rushes through a few shops to get some things she might need on the way and then has a taxi drive her to the airport. She arrives at check-in with ample time to spare and without luggage to check through she's on air-side within minutes. Her feelings are still in turmoil as she is absorbed by other passengers that clutter the hall. When Kate spots a coffee shop she walks towards it and stands in line until it is her turn to order. Kate buys a tea and walks to a seating area in the departure lounge, where she sits down. As her gaze drops down to her hand, it is only then she notices the ring that still adorns her finger. She glares at it and as she feels tears well up in her eyes, she slowly takes the ring off her finger and slides that, what she so treasured, in her handbag. Tears drop down from her face and fall onto her lap, making small wet marks on her jeans. Somehow she's not inclined to hide her feelings, but she wipes her face with her hand when she hears a child's voice saying: 'Mum, that lady is crying.'

There's no need for her to make herself believe that what she'd witnessed this afternoon wasn't what it seemed. Not that pathetic cliché. The woman obviously means more to David than just a mere fan would do. Has he been seeing her all the time when she was not with him? Kate remembers the days she spent with David, the days his time allowed him and she went over to see him, be with him, and the nights they shared each other's bed. Kate doesn't want to surrender to the notion that she might be overreacting: perhaps the woman was only a remote acquaintance. How often has he shared his bed with that woman? The pains in her chest intensify when Kate is reminded of the days she thought David was working and therefore could not be with her. It all seems to fall painfully into place now. She blots her cheeks and walks over to the rest-rooms. As she stands in front of the mirror and lifts up her swollen eyes, she gets a fright. This pale face with red-rimmed eyes where no trace of eye make-up remains, was not the face she saw in the mirror only this morning when the prospect of seeing David later on in the day had enhanced her cheerful feelings. She wets a slip of paper towel and washes her face with it. Anguish prevents her from re-applying her make-up. Feeling discarded and used, looking pretty is the last thing she wants to worry about. Her head feels numb when she walks out of the rest-room to find the way to her gate. A glance at one of the clocks in the large hall tells her it's almost boarding time and she hastens her pace, at the same time fumbling through her handbag for her passport and boarding pass.

A peculiar feeling of relief overcomes her when she walks through the gate and on to the plane. Soon all will be better. Once she's back in the UK she can look upon the events of the past months as a nice romantic adventure, but as the plane taxies onto the runway, Kate has to acknowledge that a broken heart will not vanish by a mere flight across the Atlantic.

When Valerie enters the dressing rooms holding Sammy in her arms, she is surprised to find her son with a disenchanted look on his face but equally surprised to see Melanie there, chatting to the band members and musicians. Sammy instantly recognises his mother, yet writhes in his grandma's arms to go and join his father.

'What's with you?' Val is eager to know. 'And why's she here?'

David pulls Sammy onto his lap and casts her a

disinterested look. He shrugs his shoulders. 'Marriage problems,' he says.

Valerie takes a seat next to David. 'Well? Are you going to tell me?' she asks. David puts Sammy on the floor and tells him to go and say hello to his mother. 'She now realizes she's made a mistake … '

'That's not what I mean, son. I know all that. What's with you? Why this look? You did a great show out there. You should be very pleased with yourself!'

David looks his mother straight in her eyes. 'Have you seen Kate?'

'Kate?' The question surprises Valerie. 'I thought she was with you.' She senses her son's annoyance.

'Would I ask if I knew where she was?' David states.

'David, she *was* here. We met her before the show, when we went to our seats.'

'Are you sure.' David's voice sounds sharp.

'Son, I do know who Kate is by now,' Val assures him. 'I told her to come sit with us, but she wanted to see you first. Wish you luck.'

David feels the blood drain from his face as he remains focused on his mother's eyes. 'No,' he utters.

'What do you mean? No,' Val warily enquires. She starts to feel uneasy as she sees her son's demeanour change from disappointment to utter distress.

'I never saw her.' David's voice sounds hoarse. 'God help me.' He jumps up and rushes to the door. 'Take care of Sam for me!' he calls out before he's gone.

David runs out of the hall so fast that even a few fans who have lingered to catch him leave the building don't realise until he's well by his truck and jumping in. Dusk has gathered as David starts the engine and switches on his headlights, sending beams in front of him, blinding a daring fan who is just in time to jump out of the way. He merges with the inner-city traffic and into the direction of Elvis Presley Boulevard, where he moves in the southern direction. 'I'm such a darn fool,' he mutters under his breath. Why did Kate have to be there for only that one single second? 'Damn!' She'll never believe his reasoning.

When he has reached the shopping area where Kate's restaurant is situated he turns off. He jumps on his brakes in a parking space and gets out, slamming the door of his pick-up. He makes for the door of the eatery and storms in. The quiet peacefulness of the place, where Christmas music plays in the background as people are having their meals, brings David back to his senses. He slows his pace as he walks towards the counter to ask one of the ladies who is serving if they can tell him if their boss is around. From the corners of his eyes, David has a look at the place. A small girl that sits quietly at a table, drawing pictures, catches his eye. She gives him a smile, which David is inclined to return.

'Yes, sir. What can I do you for?'

David looks up. 'I'm here to see Kate. Miss Jennings.'

'I'm sorry, can't help you there. Would you like anything to eat?' Alejandra asks.

David gives her a penetrating look. 'No. I'm here to see your boss. Is she here?'

Alejandra is taken aback. 'No sir. I just told you.'

The reluctant behaviour of the girl starts to irritate David. 'Did she go home?'

'Excuse me? Sir, we do not reveal private information about staff here,' Alejandra plainly states.

'I'm her fiancé,' David says with annoyance in his voice. 'Would that make a difference?'

Alejandra looks at him. 'If you are miss Jennings's fiancé, I find it a bit strange that you don't know where she is.'

David glares at the woman behind the counter. Then, without saying another word he turns and strides out of the establishment. The girl is right, his own stupidity is the cause of his ignorance. He jumps back into his truck, searches under the dashboard, and between some maps he finds his cellphone. He looks for Kate's number and dials it but there's no answer. Her cellphone number 'cannot be reached at the moment. Please leave a message after the tone.'

'Kate, it's me. Wherever you are, we need to talk. I … I think you've misunderstood. I mean, I'm positive you've misunderstood. Please call. I love you.'

David throws his phone back under the dashboard, then starts the engine and drives off. When he makes his way back on Elvis Presley Boulevard he hesitates, but instead of returning to the gig, he takes a right turn and drives in the direction of Interstate 40.

Staring at the tail lights of a car preceding him, he thinks about how Kate would have felt when she saw him embracing Mel, her kissing him. That darn girl always had lousy timing, but if Mel thinks she can win him back with her antics she's wrong. Suddenly another possibility enters his mind. What if Kate never made it to his dressing room? What if her phone had rung with an emergency and she had to go? The idea gives David a sense of consolation, but he knows it's not a realistic notion. He has to see Kate now. He has to explain the situation to her clear and plain.

After some miles on the Interstate he sees Kate's house in the distance. The night lights brighten the surroundings. David turns off and drives on along the deserted road leading to the property. He slows down as he reaches the stables across the yard. No lights are burning inside the house. He stops and slowly gets out of the pick-up to have a look at the house as it lies there, forsaken in all its loneliness. Kate's car is not where it's usually parked either. He feels in his pockets for the keys he has to her house, then remembers he left them at home. He lets his eyes glide over the abandoned property once more. It feels desolate without anyone there. As desolate and meaningless as his life would be without Kate, and with a dull feeling in his chest he gets back into his truck to continue on to Jackson.

Valerie parks her Chevrolet behind David's pick-up in his driveway and unbuckles Sammy before they get out of the car and walk towards the door. On entering, Val calls out David's name while Sammy runs in to find his father in the dimly lit living-room. 'Daddy,' Sammy merely says and jumps on his lap. David looks in the direction of his mother who enters a moment later.

'Sam, it's your bedtime,' Valerie says and waits for the boy to follow her. 'Or do you want to take him?' she asks David but he shakes his head. 'Go with Grandma, Sam.' Sammy is reluctant but obeys. While the two leave the living-room, David pushes himself out of the chair. He has tried to reach Kate several times and left an equal amount of messages on her phones but to no avail. He refuses to believe she might have left the country. She isn't going to see her English kin until next week. Even the possibility that she might have checked herself into a hotel in Memphis has crossed his mind, but a few calls later, that thread also ran dead. He pulls the door of the refrigerator and takes out a beer, then slowly sits down on the bench by the table in the kitchen when Sammy runs in wearing his kiddy's pyjamas. 'Am goin' to bed now, Daddy,' he says and slides his little arm around his father's neck to give him a kiss. 'Goodnight, son. You let Grandma read you a story. OK?'

Sammy shakes his head. 'No, no stowy.'

'No story?'

'Only you wead stowy.'

'Better go to sleep now, Sam. Tomorrow I'll read you a story again.' He kisses Sam on his forehead and the little one runs off to his bedroom.

Not long after Val enters the kitchen and puts the kettle to boil. 'Ain't you talked to Kate yet,' she asks, trying to sound pragmatic if it weren't for the concern that rings through in her voice.

'Did you know that Mel was going to be there?' David demands of his mother. Val looks at him. 'No. And you know it. I was surprised to see her there. And her displaying herself around those musicians ... ' Val pours the boiled water over her freeze-dried coffee in a mug. 'She completely forgot herself.'

'She would,' David allows with indifference. Val sits down at the table too and looks at David's face. 'Come, out with it. What happened?'

David sighs, 'she saw us,' and takes another swallow from his beer. Val raises her eyebrows. 'Who saw who? Son, you could be a bit more specific.'

David finishes his beer and puts the bottle down. 'I was just about to go and follow the guys to the stage when Mel appeared, full of pathetic stories about her pathetic marriage to Stuart ... '

'Yes, I've heard those too,' Val says.

'And then, she leapt on me, and kissed me ...'

An unpleasant feeling overcomes Valerie.

'And ... I kissed her back – '

'David. You didn't.'

'Ma, it was a matter of a split second ... '

'Yes, I know those matter-of-split-seconds from you.

God help us.'

'Then Kate must have shown up. Just then, that one split second. I never even knew she was there until you told – '

'Oh no, son. She's gone, I'm telling you.' Valerie shakes her head.

David's face clouds over. 'Don't say that, Ma.' He looks distraught. 'I've been trying to reach her, talk to her!' His fist hits the table. 'I went to her restaurant, I went to her house! She doesn't answer her phones … '

Valerie rests her hand on David's arm. 'I'm sorry, son. I know you're crazy about her.'

'I love her,' David states, 'and I want to talk to her. Explain what happened.'

'She'll come round,' his mother tries to ease the situation. 'Mind my words. She will have to answer her messages sometime.' Valerie tries to sound convincing but David looks at her with eyes that tell her the opposite. He gets up from the table and paces towards the window where only a street light sheds some glow into his tiny back garden.

'David, it's her initial reaction … ' Valerie tries to placate the situation her son finds himself in. 'She'll be sitting somewhere right now, just like you, pondering. And tomorrow, in the light of the morning, she will realize, that … that she's probably overreacted the whole thing.'

In Nashville, too, the streets are fully decorated in Christmas lights and ornaments. Large Christmas trees adorn streets and many houses are covered in lights and serve as additional brightness in these short, dark days before year's end. It's late in the evening at the recording studio where David and his band are recording songs for their next CD. Manager Fred sits in a chair beside the sound engineer; he wants to make sure that David doesn't leave the premises before he has talked to him. The singer has been rather a bit too elusive of late. David has noticed the plump man sitting and watching them with his beady eyes for a while now, and realises the pointlessness of trying to make a quiet escape. Moreover, he isn't inclined to give Fred that pleasure. After the final song, David walks straight towards the sound mixer's booth and appeases Fred by asking him how he likes things so far.

'Very good, David,' says the manager, simultaneously drawing out a large envelope from which a few sheets of paper emerge. 'Maybe you should ask the boys to come in too. For what I've got here,' and he waves it with gratification on his face, 'are the details for a tour I organized for you … in Australia!' Fred shows a broad smile while exclaiming the last words. David doesn't hold the same ecstasy and calls his band members in. He hardly wants to leave the state, let alone travel halfway around the globe to do a tour. Even though he knows that they've gathered quite a following down-under and their CD persists on the charts there. He looks at his band members who don't show a high amount of excitement when they hear that the tour will take them a long way from home straight after the holidays, especially Gene who has only recently become a father. 'You might have to count me out,' he says. 'You might have to replace me, just this once.'

Fred isn't too troubled, bass players are replaceable, but his glare rests on David. 'As long as you don't bale out,' he says. 'You'd better don't pull any funny business.'

David looks at him with indignation and without saying a word he leaves the booth, grabs his things and walks out of the studio. He has no intention of going anywhere until he has seen Kate. He has given up on trying to reach her by phone. She hasn't shown her face at the restaurant and the times he passed by her house he only once found her aunt there who claimed to have no idea where Kate was, but somehow David sensed that wasn't the entire truth.

Outside the building, David is instantly wreathed by icy rain billowing through the streets around Music Row. He pulls the collar of his jacket up to his ears and crosses the street where he has spotted an available cab to take him to the hotel where he stays while they are recording. He beats the moisture from his jacket before he gets in, and puts his guitar next to him on the back seat.

Cruel rain beating against the cab's windshields gives the lights, that are strung up everywhere in the most extraordinary colours, curious shifting shapes as the water runs off the cab's exterior. With one hand resting on his guitar case, David stares past the peculiar colourful display into the sheets of darkness beyond as he recollects that evening he and Kate were caught in rain hardly comparable with that what presently thunders from the skies. Their warm intimate dinner and their first night together afterwards. The memory doesn't do a great deal to abate the aching feeling in his chest, rather it makes him feel even more despondent. He also recalls Fred, unceremoniously entering, and that he was forced to leave Kate by herself.

'Did I tell you what hotel?' is David's sudden request of the driver. The man glances at him through his rear-view mirror. 'Yessa, you did,' he replies. 'One more block. Weather makes for tricky drivin', sir,' he informs David.

At the hotel David hands the taxi-driver a generous banknote. 'That's fine,' he says, takes his guitar and gets out. The driver rolls his window down as David walks the few steps to the entrance. 'Thank you, sir!' he calls after him.

David collects his key from Reception and takes an elevator to his floor. When entering the room he lowers his guitar onto the chest and throws his jacket off, before he falls down on his bed. He lets out a weary sigh and turns his head. His eyes rest on the telephone by the bed. There's tentativeness in his demeanour, but then he straightens and swings his legs over the side of the bed before he picks up the phone.

After Kate had arrived at Heathrow, that had felt even more forlorn than when she left from there months before, she made for her apartment in Kensington to have a good rest and clear her head. Her good rest had come to nothing with her mind constantly interfered with by the man she had left to his own vices in Memphis. A long walk through windy Kensington Gardens, ignoring the spitting rain, and all through Hyde Park had given her some distraction, but once home she felt more lonely than ever. She then decided to take a train and be at her grandmother's before all the relatives would arrive and the manor would be teeming with family members, all spreading their individual holiday happiness. Something Kate wasn't in the mood for one bit. She had met Jacob, who'd been very surprised to see her back in London, at his office. She had explained the situation, and that the restaurant in Memphis was in good hands before she had made her way to Waterloo Station and taken the train in the direction of Basingstoke to stay with Grandmother, whose property lay nestled in the Hampshire Downs. Riding on the train and viewing the British landscape again after so many months away had given her the comforting feeling of familiarity. She hoped that her stay here would make her forget the recent months by and by. Months during which she thought she found the love of her life. When she took a cab from the railway station to her grandmother's house in the country she realised she never called her gran to let her know she was coming. The surprise was therefore considerable. Grandmother had missed her tremendously, and it had not taken her long to detect that the upcoming holiday events were not the reason for her early arrival.

Kate stares out of her window on the first floor of the 12-bedroom country house. Her cousin Kelly is expected today together with her uncle and aunt, the first in a line of relatives that will gradually appear at the house. Apart from Grandmother, Uncle Henry lives here, he is a widower and his daughter Petunia sometimes still stays in the house as well, when her work doesn't take her elsewhere. Servants have decorated the Christmas tree that still stands proudly, outside by the entrance to the house. Gran has always wanted it that way for as long as Kate can remember. Kate now and again thinks that the old Spruce must feel rather special around this time of year with its decorations either glistening in the sun or covered in rain, sleet or snow, depending on what the weather brings each year. Inside, not much fuss is made about decorations, apart from seasonal plants that brighten up the hall and several rooms on the ground floor to then disappear to the hothouse once the New Year has begun. Grandmother enjoys candles, and they are placed or hung all over the house. In a distance, Kate sees a car approach that speeds onto the cobblestoned drive, and halts by the mansion's front wall that, on one side, is draped in ivy. Kate slowly moves away from the window. She inspects her appearance in the mirror, her hair hangs loose, she hasn't felt in the mood for putting on make-up, jeans and jumper will do fine. She closes the door behind her and walks across the red-carpeted landing before reaching the equally red-carpeted staircase and goes down.

'Ka-ate!' Grandmother's high-pitched voice sounds as she comes walking out of the drawing-room. 'Oh, there you are. They're here, darling.' Grandmother looks elegant as ever, wearing a dark-blue silk dress, her wavy silver hair carefully raised into a bun.

The front door bursts open and Kate's cousin Kelly thunders in. Kate sees the fright emerging on Gran's face. 'Darling! Please! And what have you done to yourself?' Grandmother looks on in horror at the blue-haired teenager, wearing a gloomy outfit that appears more pinned together than sewn.

Kate's aunt Clementine enters right behind her. 'It's her Gothic look. Don't pay attention. How are you, Mother?' With a kiss, she greets her mother and hands her coat and felt hat to one of the servants.

'Kate!' Kelly calls out. 'My fav cousin.' She brushes her cheeks against Kate's. 'How are you,' Kate says in a tired voice.

'Weren't you supposed to be in America!' Kelly demands, and, as she lowers her voice, 'I hear you got rid of John. Thank God. He's such a mollycoddle!' She storms into the dining room as Uncle Leo rests his hand on Kate's back for a brief moment. 'How's America?'

Kate looks at him. 'Fine.'

'You do look a bit peaky,' Clementine allows. 'Are you all right, darling?'

'Fine,' Kate reiterates and follows her grandmother into the dining room who invites: 'Shall we go in? Lunch is laid out.'

'Don't you think Kate looks peaky?' Clementine asks of her husband as the latter drapes his long winter coat over a seat in the hall and puts his woollen cap on top; the items are soon removed by a servant.

Kelly has taken a seat at the long table in the spacious dining room and nibbles on a carrot stick when the others sit down too. 'Manners, Kelly,' Grandmother says. 'Haven't you eaten today?'

One by one the party fill their plates with the light lunch of salads and different kinds of bread, cakes and sandwiches. Grandmother bids Leo to pass the coffee-pot.

'Allow me,' Leo offers and pours out in the cups. Kate holds her hand over hers. 'I'll just have water,' she says.

'Please, Kate,' Grandmother implores. 'Please have something decent.'

Kate glances at her grandmother. 'Sorry Gran, I ... It's my stomach. I just can't eat or – '

'Poor darling!' Clementine exclaims so sudden it makes Kelly forget to chew. 'Have you seen a doctor? You should see a doctor, Kate, if you – '

'Clementine,' Grandmother soothes. 'That's not what's ailing Kate. Please.'

Uncle Leo looks across the table at Kate's face as Kelly returns to her plate and eagerly proceeds with her lunch. 'Maybe it's John,' the latter says with her mouth half full.

'What's with John?' her father requires.

'Haven't you heard? Kate dumped him!' Kelly obliges.

Clementine rests her hands beside her plate, holding her utensils. Leo does the same and they both look in Kate's direction with a certain contentedness on their faces.

'Well, Kate,' Uncle Leo says. 'You're much better off without him. It needs to be said.'

Kate takes a sip of water from her glass and places a

slice of dry bread on her plate.

'Kate, darling,' her aunt says. 'If there's *any*thing, you know you can always talk to me about it.'

A barely noticeable uneasiness slides across Grandmother's face while Kelly changes the subject by asking after her cousin Jacob. 'I saw him in London, you know, only last week! I do hope he'll come over soon. Things get *so* tediously boring when Jake's not here.'

Her parents both look her way with faces that demand elucidation. Kelly shrugs her shoulders. 'Well, without Jacob *and* Grand-mama of course,' she argues, casting an innocent look in her grandmother's direction who merely raises her eyebrows. Kelly sighs. 'OK, I'm sorry. But that's just the way it is – '

'*You* think it is,' her father clarifies.

'Yes,' Kelly agrees, 'and I think that Jacob is the most fun of all of my cousins. Sorry, Kate … But, hey! Maybe now that whatshisface isn't going to be here, Kate, you might be just as much fun!'

Faces turn to Kelly with disapproval until resting on Kate's visage with compassion. The latter jumps up and rushes out of the dining room. Clementine casts an angry look at her daughter. 'Satisfied?' she belts out. Kelly draws in her horns and looks at the empty chair across the table. 'You should be ashamed, Kelly!' Clementine says. 'Upsetting Kate that way.'

Leo doesn't say anything, nor does Grandmother but their faces speak volumes. Kelly jumps up off the table and hurries after Kate.

Grandmother sighs a tiresome sigh. 'More coffee anyone?'

'I'm sorry, Mother. I'll speak to her later.'

Kelly runs through the hall and up the stairs calling out Kate's name. On the landing, she draws level with

Kate and stands before her to make her stop.

'I'm sorry Kate,' she says despairingly. 'I really am! I didn't know that you cared so much about … John?' She looks at Kate's face that's wet with tears. 'Gosh Kate, I didn't even know you could cry that much.' She reaches out with both her hands as if to try and make Kate's tears stop from falling. Through those tears, Kate manages a faint smile and she looks at the thirteen-year-old girl. What does she know, so much innocence still.

'Oh, Kelly, I'm not crying for John. Please, don't make things hard on yourself.' Kate wipes her face with her sleeve. Kelly's eyes reflect disquietude. 'Well,' she mutters, 'why are you crying then? Maybe you are ill! Maybe you *should* see a doctor.'

Kate shakes her head. 'It's all right, Kelly. Don't worry your mind over this. One day you'll understand.' Kelly doesn't make an attempt to move and just stares at her older cousin.

'Better finish your lunch,' Kate says. 'And Jacob will be here tomorrow,' she adds before she goes into her room.

Kelly hangs her head and walks down the stairs and into the hall, where she takes her coat from the hall wardrobe and walks outside onto the grounds.

Even though more aunts and uncles with more children in tow appear in the course of the following day, it is Jacob, who has driven down from London in his four-wheel-drive, who receives Kelly's undivided attention. One of the youngest of all cousins, Kelly has always thought of Jacob as the older brother she never really had. Clementine and Leo's firstborn is a boy but he came into the world with a severe handicap and demanded so much care that once Kelly was born she was left to the devices of a nanny. That only changed when a nurse was hired to care for Kelly's brother.

Presently, the house is full of family members, three aunts and four uncles with eight children between them and single mum Aunt Meg with her son Adam. Kate loves having the family around, but her mind wanders and she thinks about her aunt and cousins on the other side of the Atlantic, in Memphis. And the one who is still plaguing her mind and heart.

Now that lunch is over, and most of the cousins have gone outside and have scattered around the grounds, Kate decides to follow them. She dresses in her warm winter jacket and boots and strolls across the lawn that is still covered in white frost, especially there where trees cast shade and keep the meagre winter sun from thawing the frosty surfaces. Kate looks over and sees some of her cousins being chased by Gran's dogs, two Great Danes. Her cousins' laughter as they playfully avoid the high-spirited dogs, echoes across the fields intermixed with the joyful deep barks of the Danes. Kate leaves the scene behind to seek the more quiet areas on her grandmother's property. She loves to wander over its 650 acres. Her walk takes her through the wooded area, along the meadows where, on a spring morning many years ago, Grandfather had taken them, carrying buckets full of seeds. As they walked, they had scattered the meadow-flower seeds all over the area. Since then, the fields display colourful carpets through a variety of flowers when spring and summer return every year. Now, their withered, faded colour emanates chill. In the distance, Kate sees the horses that live on the property blowing out warm breath that evaporates in the cold air. She climbs the stile and, in thought, she continues her walk across the bleak wintery landscape.

The pale sun has entirely disappeared, and Kate wonders how long she has been walking. Maybe she should return, it might be close to teatime. When she has crossed another field to walk down a slope in the direction of the house, she notices a car stationary on the path below. As she walks closer, she sees it is Jacob's four-wheel-drive. She must be late then if Jacob has taken the trouble to come and look for her. She does feel tired and is glad that she now doesn't have to *walk* the entire way back, and she picks up her pace. She is about to call out Jacob's name when an unpleasant swell pangs through her body as the driver emerges from the car. She stops in her tracks and her stomach tightens.

Even wrapped in a thick jacket with the collar pulled up to his ears she would recognise him anywhere. Kate feels as if she is nailed to the frozen soil, she can't seem to move and just glares at the man who is standing there, his hand resting on the car door, the cold air vaporising his breath into tiny clouds. He doesn't speak, he just looks at her. Kate starts to feel uneasy but is aware it would be futile to run. Slowly, she walks closer until she is within hearing distance. David's face looks different from what she is used to. He is pale and his jaw shows the shade of a two-day-old beard.

'How'd you find me,' she hears herself say, with unintentional alleviation ringing through in her voice.

David rests his eyes on hers. 'It's not the first time Jacob filled me in on your whereabouts.' He doesn't move and remains standing by the car. 'I need to explain something to you, Kate. But first, why haven't you answered any of my messages? Am I such a lesser being to you that I don't deserve a fair answer?'

Kate shakes her head. '… No, no, it's not that … '

'What is it then, Kate? I thought we knew each other

well enough not to allow such *indignities*, shall we say?'

Kate feels exasperation building up inside of her, and she can't help for that emotion to show in her eyes. Who is he to talk of indignities? David makes a slight move towards her. 'I know what you saw, Kate. And if you'd only let me explain – '

'Explain?' Kate calls out. 'David, it didn't look like a friendly peck on the cheek when you kissed that woman. I thought we had something very special but then, I … I was rudely awakened – '

'You were never rudely awakened, Kate. You only saw a split-second of something that wasn't even genuine … ' David holds up one hand for Kate not to interrupt. 'No. Hear me out. If you wouldn't be so impulsive and if you'd waited another second you would've seen me pushing her off … And,' David continues to avoid Kate's chastisement, 'I would have bumped into you and you would've known how glad I would have been to see you.' He sighs and looks at her with imploring eyes. 'I was really disappointed when you weren't there, Kate.'

Kate drops her glance towards the hard frosted ground. 'Who is she?'

'Mel. Sam's mother. She was – '

'Mel?' Kate's voice sounds sarcastic but surprised at the same time. Kate has heard David's mother Valerie speak of her once.

'Yes,' David replies. 'She's uh, she came to see me. She was a bit down, and then she leapt on me all of a sudden.'

'And so you decided to kiss her.'

'Please, Kate, can we stop this now?' David entreats. 'The woman's not fit to hold a candle to you.'

Kate deports herself in an austere manner in an attempt to hide her true feelings.

'It's pointless, Kate. What's done is done,' David assures her. 'Look, I've been totally miserable, and from what I've heard, you haven't done much better.' He gives her a penetrating look. 'You can't fight this, Kate. We belong together, and you know it.'

There's no change in Kate's countenance, and she remains on the spot where she stopped some minutes before. 'Hell, Kate, don't be so stuck-up,' David says annoyed for her persistent aloofness. 'I flew half-way 'round the world, risking losing my contract, and having to drive on the damn wrong side of the road! Hell, I could've been killed!'

A twinkle arises in Kate's eyes, and a subtle smile appears on her face. She moves towards David and slides her hands around his waist. 'I'm sorry,' she whispers. 'Damn, how I've missed you … ' and places her lips on his.

David takes her face in his hands as his eyes look into hers, eyes that tell her that she was mistaken running off the way she had, that she has been wrong about this man not loving her. He gently strokes a strand of hair from her face and kisses her back.

When David parks the four-wheel-drive beside the other cars by the ivy-draped wall of the mansion, Kate feels an entirely different person than the woman who ran away and hid at her grandmother's property to escape a miserable reality. She places a hand on David's leg. 'Please, let's stay here a bit longer,' she softly says, 'just the two of us.'

David looks at her sideways. 'Are you kiddin'? I want to meet all those highfalutin relatives of yours!' He jumps out and grabs Kate's hand. 'Come on woman. No dawdling,' and pulls Kate, who lets out a surprised cry,

into his arms. 'And your grandma. I wanna meet her too.'
He slides an arm over her shoulder and Kate holds his
hand. They walk past the dressed Spruce tree and through
the front door into the house. A cacophony of voices and
noises meet them in the hall where Jacob just walks across
to the dining room, followed by the two Great Danes.
'Hello you two. Had a nice walk Kate?' he enquires as he
gives David a knowing look.

'Hi Jake,' the latter greets him.

'Come, I'll introduce you to all those dreadful
cousins of ours,' Jacob says as he inspects Kate's hair and
pulls a bit of dry grass from it. 'Went for a roll in the hay?'
Jacob questions. Kate gives him a look. 'No, for a roll in
the back of your four-wheel-drive,' she answers back, 'and
I didn't know you hauled hay in your spare time.'

'Side-line,' Jacob quips, and they enter the dining
room. 'Everybody! Quiet please!' One by one, the
relatives turn their heads, and the noise lessens somewhat.

'This is David, he's from America. He's come to
spend Christmas with us.' A murmur of approval waves
through the room. 'Oh, and uh,' Jacob adds. 'He's Kate's
fiancé.' Jacob smiles and looks at the two, as aunts and
uncles and to a lesser extend cousins gather around the
pair.

'Her fiancé?' Clementine looks at her husband. 'Well.
She got over John very quickly.'

'John's a dope, be glad that's over,' Leo replies.

'Oh Kate! Congratulations,' Aunt Meg calls out just
as Grandmother enters the room. 'Have I missed
something?' she asks. Jacob takes his grandmother's arm
and leads her to the pair. 'Gran, this is David.'

Grandmother beams at David's face. 'Oh, so you're
David, welcome. So nice to meet you.'

'Pleasure's all mine, ma'am,' David says and takes

Gran's hand with both his.

'Ooh, and so well mannered,' Grandmother coos.
'Kate, you've done well.' Gran's hand briefly rests on
David's unshaven cheek. 'And so handsome.'

She takes David by his hand and walks to the table.
'Come, all sit! Dinner will be served in a moment.'
Grandmother takes her place at the head of the table.
'David, come. You sit next to me, and Kate there,' she
directs.

David gives Kate an amusing glance as he follows
Gran's instructions. Chairs shuffle and voices sound as all
the relatives find their seat. Kelly plop's down in a chair
next to Jacob as the twins Pete and Josh sit across from
them next to their parents James and Anne. Uncle Adrian
and Aunt Lillian with their four children Kim, William,
Stacy and Albert. Uncle Henry, who has arrived back from
work and his daughter, Petunia.

Kate addresses Jacob for she wonders why Maria is
not with him. 'She'll be here on Boxing Day,' Jacob
replies. 'Family obligations.'

A trolley is rolled in with the soup and one by one the
bowls are filled.

Gran rests a hand on David's arm. 'Maria is Jacob's
girlfriend,' she clarifies. 'So, tell me, how did you meet
my dear Kate?' Aunts and uncles and cousins turn their
heads expectantly in David's direction. 'Uh, well,' David
begins, 'my pick-up broke down and Kate came and
rescued me.'

The family members nod and smile approvingly.

'Oh, that's sweet,' Aunt Anne swoons. 'So romantic.'
Her husband James looks at her but refrains from
commenting. The others know too well the *un*romantic
situation their marriage is plagued by currently.
Grandmother straightens her back. 'Let's eat, shall we?'

Streaks of daylight stream through the drapes and onto the walls of Kate's room and she hears thundering footsteps on the landing. Not all her cousins sleep in the cottage behind the house. She pulls the cover a bit tighter over her shoulder, turns her head and looks directly into David's eyes.

'Good morning,' she mumbles.

'Mmm,' is the answer and his eyes close once more.

'Are they always so noisy?' David mutters.

'Yeah,' Kate moans, 'I'm afraid so.' David turns onto his back and tries to catch another wink of sleep. Underneath the cover, Kate slides her arm over his chest and rests her head against his shoulder.

'You know, Kate,' David mumbles with his eyes closed, 'why don't we just get married here … '

Kate glances up at the sleepy face beside her.

'… I mean, all your relatives are here, I'll fly in mine, we'll get a pastor … What do you say?'

Kate pushes herself up a bit and places a kiss on David's face. 'I think it's a good idea,' she agrees. 'But what about documents?'

David attempts to ignore that semblance of procedures. '… And that way we'll avoid the press.' David slides an arm underneath Kate's shoulder and looks at her, 'OK?' He pulls her a little closer. Her eyes tell him it's unanimous. He rolls back and closes his eyes, a subtle contented smile playing around his lips.

'David?' Kate's says, dulcetly, after a while.

'Mm.'

'How was your drive from London to get here?' David opens one eye. 'Drive?' he mumbles. 'I didn't drive. I rode, on a train. And then I took a cab.'

Kate directs a beguiling glance at the face beside her.

'And you said you had to drive on the wrong side of the road.'

David turns his head her way. 'I did. Here, when I was looking for you.'

'David, this is a private property. No public roads.' She nudges him and starts laughing. 'Silly man!' David gives her an incredulous look, then his arms appear from under the covers and he pulls her over. They roll across the bed until the bed is no more, and they fall on the floor entangled in the duvet, laughing loudly. Laughing until their laughter diminishes to giggling and Kate eventually suggests having a shower and going for breakfast. Grandmother will be wondering what keeps them so long.

Outside, some family members are braving the frosty weather and are strolling around the grounds, warmly dressed and accompanied by the two Great Danes. Inside the house, Aunt Anne and Uncle James can be heard squabbling in their room until Grandmother's voice intervenes and Aunt Anne exits the room to follow her mother down the stairs.

Kate has placed David's ring back on her finger and is joined by Jacob, Aunt Meg, Aunt Clementine and Kelly, as they are sitting around the open fire in the drawing-room, sipping coffee with nearby a tray filled with Christmas cakes. Kelly rests her feet on a log near the fire when Grandmother enters. 'Take your feet away from there, dear. You'll get burnt.' Kelly looks up and at the distance between her feet and the fire, then puts her feet down on the floor.

'I can get you some slippers, darling, if your feet are cold,' Gran tells Kelly who looks at her with indignation. 'Gran, slippers are for old people.'

Clementine is astounded at her daughter's behaviour.

Didn't she have a long talk with her the evening previous?

'Kelly! Manners!' Clementine calls out.

Kelly looks at her mother. 'What?' and sits down next to her grandmother. 'I don't mean Grand-mama.' She snuggles up against the elderly relation. 'Gran's not old.' Jacob glances at the scene with his eyes glinting amusement as Grandmother affectionately strokes Kelly's blue hair.

'Has David gone with the others, Kate?' Grandmother wonders.

'No, he's on the phone,' Kate replies, 'should be down in a moment.'

'He seems such a kind man,' Aunt Anne says, who took a seat on the sofa next to Clementine.

'Kind? I think he's adorable,' Aunt Meg states. 'Kate, between you and me, that John was a – '

'Oh, for heaven's sake, Meg,' Clementine interrupts. 'We all know what *he* was like. No need to be secretive.'

A door slams in the hall, and from the window, Uncle James is seen walking towards one of the cars, and before long he drives off. Aunt Anne's eyelashes flutter briefly and she takes another bite of her third piece of cake.

'Mind your figure, Anne,' Clementine meddles. Meg sighs at her older sister's interference.

When it comes to scenes like these between her aunts, Kate sometimes wonders what the circumstances were in the family when these four sisters and two brothers were growing up in this very same house. Before her mum formed a liking for travelling and ended up in the arms of her daddy. More footsteps approach and David enters the room. Everyone turns their head his way, and several greetings welcome him.

'Morning, morning,' David says.

'Have you had breakfast?' Grandmother asks. 'I don't

think you have.'

David waves it aside, 'I'm fine, ma'am. I'll have some coffee.' David pours himself a cup and sits down next to Kate. 'They'll be here, day after tomorrow,' he tells her in a quiet voice.

With Kate at the wheel of Jacob's four-wheel-drive, she and David are driving to the nearest town to see if the vicar or maybe a pastor would be available on these busy days before Christmas. David's arm rests on the back of Kate's car seat as he looks out over the bleak winter landscape. The cold frost still hangs heavy in the air but the faint sun remains tenacious in the steel-grey sky, keeping snow clouds at bay. In the distance, the town appears in their view and it doesn't take Kate long to find its church. 'What religion are you anyway?' Kate begs David who looks at her with a certain objectivity. 'Does it matter?' he says. 'My mother is Baptist and I went to that church, but in the end, doesn't everybody believe in the same God?'

Kate has to agree. She was raised by her grandparents in the belief of the Anglican Church. 'As long as we're not moving into irreconcilable *religious* differences,' Kate jokes.

'Don't you worry about that,' David replies. 'Ain't we all the same in God's eyes? As long as the man in charge of this church doesn't make a point of it, we should be fine.'

'It's a woman, actually,' Kate says as she turns off the engine.

'Even better!' David responds and he jumps out of the car. He looks up at the quaint stone church and takes Kate's hand as they walk towards the adjacent little stone structure where they have their appointment with the vicar. After a knock on the door, a middle-aged lady opens up. Only her white collar that peeks out of her jumper gives away her being of the cloth.

'Hello,' she cheerfully says. 'You must be Kate, and this your soon-to-be husband?'

David looks at the woman and nods.

'Come in, quick, it's become so cold.'

Kate and David follow the lady vicar inside the vicarage. 'You have come at a time when it is indeed very hectic in my small congregation,' the vicar informs them. 'When were you planning your church wedding?'

David looks at Kate as he places their documents on the table. 'Well, as soon as you're available,' he says. 'We don't want a big do, just small, simple.'

Kate nods in agreement.

'We don't really do big do's,' the vicar confides in him. 'Small community, you see.'

She takes out her agenda. For the upcoming weeks, it doesn't show any favourable dates that coincide with David and Kate's plans. Kate takes David's arm, seeking assurance.

'Oh, but ma'am, I'm sure you can squeeze us in somewhere,' David tries to convince the vicar. 'It won't take long to marry us. There's only two of us.'

The vicar looks at him. 'Yes, that's usually the case,' she says, 'and then there's the matter of your nationality,' waving David's passport in her hand. 'And the matter of you having lived in the area for a minimum of seven days.'

'Pardon me?' David questions. 'I only got here, what, three days ago.' The vicar looks at him to then turn her attention to Kate. 'What about you? I know you moved to the United States.'

'Oh, but I'm still an official resident here,' Kate is

quick to inform the vicar. 'I have permanent residency for America. I was born there, you see.' The lady vicar glances from Kate to David, then back to Kate. 'I can offer you a licence, but it will be at least three weeks before we can proceed with the wedding ceremony.'

'Three weeks!' David is astounded. 'But, I'll be in Australia then. We want to get married this coming week!'

The vicar gives him a didactic look. 'I'm sorry, sir, but this is not Las Vegas.'

Kate feels her expectancy of a quick wedding, becoming a rather dismal prospect whereas David is nothing less than frustrated for all the bureaucracy.

'Is there nothing you can do?' Kate pleads with the vicar who looks at her with compassionate eyes, then shakes her head. 'Well, that is to say, we could have a *ceremony*,' she then offers, 'but it won't be legal. You'd have to have another one to make it legal.'

Kate's eyes light up but David is more reserved. 'What's the point in having a ceremony when that won't make us legally married?'

'I'm sorry, sir, but banns need to be up three weeks. That's the law in this country.'

David looks at Kate and she sees his disappointment. 'Unless,' the vicar continues, 'unless you apply for a *special* licence.'

'A special licence?' David asks.

'Yes, but I can't help you there. You need to apply at the Registrar's office,' the vicar concludes. She casts a glance at the clock. 'The one in Basingstoke should still be open. But don't forget, tomorrow's Christmas Eve.'

The vicar walks them to the door. 'That's all I can offer, I'm afraid.'

'Thank you, ma'am,' David says. Kate shakes the vicar's hand. 'Thank you for your help.'

David takes Kate's arm as they walk out of the vicarage and into the street. Kate senses David's discontentment that he tries to conceal by asking if this town has a jewellers store. Kate wreathes her arm around his. 'There was when I last looked. Come with me.'

'Let's get some rings,' he says.

They enter the main street of the town where locals are patronising the shops to get everything in order in the final days before Christmas. For Kate, the sight brings back fond memories of a time past; she spent most of her adult life in London. She points to an old fashioned sign above one of the shops. 'There, Crown's, it's still here. They've been here for as long as I can remember.'

David hastens his pace with Kate holding his arm when she sees a familiar face in the street.

'Look,' she points towards the balding man who comes their way. 'There's Uncle James.' Kate can't help but feel surprised at seeing him here. James now spots his niece as he too stops in front of the family business.

'Oh, hello Kate. David. Getting some last minute gifts, are we?' he assumes. 'Always such a drag, Christmas shopping.'

'Well,' Kate begins and looks up at David. 'We're just getting a few wedding rings,' David explains. Uncle James marvels over that revelation. 'Well, you've come to the right place,' he then says, nodding towards the shop they find themselves in front of. He smiles at his niece as he and David simultaneously grab the doorknob to the jeweller's shop. 'After you,' James says, and the three of them enter. 'Was just getting the wife a small trinket,' James elaborates.

As they drive back home from Basingstoke, where Kate and David had no problem obtaining their special marriage licence, David pulls Kate close.

'Please, not while I'm driving.'

'Then I'll drive.'

Kate looks at him. 'You must be joking. And get us killed?'

David smiles broadly. 'No, you drive. Say, where are we going on our honeymoon?'

Kate steers the car into a road leading to her grandmother's property. 'What about Australia?' she suggests. When there's no answer, Kate briefly looks his way. David's face has lost its former glee. 'Australia means work, Kate. And it was planned without my knowledge.'

Kate releases the accelerator somewhat and adjusts her speed to the local limit. 'Sorry,' she says. She doesn't want their recent happiness disrupted by David's recollection of his escape from America, for he had left without letting anybody know.

'Your mother is coming tomorrow,' she tries to cheer him up. 'And little Sam, he should be coming with her.'

David nods. 'Yeah, he's coming too.'

'As long as she hasn't gone through the trouble of booking a hotel,' Kate hopes. 'There's still space at Gran's.' Having his little boy near would make David feel much more at ease, but the latter is still in thought about the situations he left behind in Nashville and Jackson. Kate reaches out and places her hand on his arm, keeping the other hand on the wheel.

'Please, David. You did the right thing. By coming here, I mean.' She slows down and stops the car in a drive-by. 'David, don't worry about that manager. He's not *you*. The people, your fans, will still be there, for *you*. They will come to see you and your band.'

David glances in the other direction. 'I know,' he

merely says.

'What's bothering you, then?' Kate wants to know. 'David, just do that tour and when you're back we can plan the honeymoon.'

He turns his head her way. 'Let's go,' he says. Kate looks at him and then steers the car back onto the road. 'You know, there's no harm in letting me know what's bothering you, David.'

'A wedding?!' Grandmother can't say she's surprised, she just wasn't expecting Kate and David to marry so soon. She gives them both heartfelt hugs and kisses. They are soon interrupted by the stumbling footsteps that sound through from the hall. Footsteps accompanied by excited voices, and before long family members file into the room. Faces beaming the fresh pink glow of a frosty afternoon outside, appear before them. Some of them walk straight to the fire while others find a seat on chairs and the sofa. Kelly fights for a spot on the *chaise longue* with cousin Josh. In the corner of the room, a pile of Christmas presents has now appeared, Kate notices. It reminds her of her failing to purchase gifts for her relatives. It also reminds her of the present she bought David in Memphis, and that is still in her house in Tennessee, wrapped and ready to be presented. Kate sees Uncle James, who has shown his solicitous side only this afternoon, now not even acknowledging Aunt Anne, who has come in with the others.

She feels David's arm around her waist. 'Maybe we could drive to London tonight,' he whispers close to her ear, 'and pick up my mother and Sam in the morning.'

Kate glances at him. 'Things getting a bit too crowded for you now?' she guys. 'I thought you liked my relatives.'

David pulls her closer to him. 'I do, but there are so many of them.'

'You'll get used to it,' Kate smiles. 'We can go upstairs, if you like. I need to check my emails anyway.' David pulls Kate away from the throng of relatives and they move to the door where they are met by the dogs, with Jacob in their wake. 'Hello Jacob,' Kate says. 'Hi, Jake,' David says.

Jacob glances at the two rushing up the stairs, wondering what the jolly undertone in David's voice could've meant.

In her room, Kate switches on her laptop that is on the small escritoire near the window. David spreads out on the bed and grabs a book from the nightstand. 'My kind o'life,' he says, as he flicks through a few pages. 'No worries, no commitments.'

Kate looks his way. 'You'd soon get bored,' she says and sits down in front of her laptop. After she has logged on, she notices her email box containing many mails she has neglected. She reads some subject lines until her eyes rest on the words 'Memphis murder'. It's from her cousin Anna-May and Kate clicks her mouse to open it.

*Hi Kate*, she reads. *I don't know where you hang out at the mo, but I found out some very interesting tails to that murder. I went to the PD here in Memphis and they actually let me see the <u>original</u> file! They never bothered to digitize it so I sat there surrounded by all that paper for hours! Here's what I've discovered: The file is not complete (if you ask me) with pages missing. There were major inconsistencies (you were right!). What's more, there were photos taken near the body of footprints in the mud. These photos were tucked away at the back of* *the file. Kate, these prints were definitely women's shoes! I'm chasing it up right now, also some more hooks and ends that in my opinion don't match up. Have to go now! Anna-May x*

Kate can't help but feel delight at her cousin's efforts. 'Something the matter?' she hears David ask. Kate shakes her head, but that doesn't deter David from getting up from the bed and standing behind her, leaning on her shoulders as he looks on while Kate replies to the email. 'Memphis murder!' David reads. 'Who was murdered?'

Kate focuses, she was sure she told Anna-May that Jon Baker's wife found the body so there shouldn't be any reason to feel dubious about the female shoe prints.

'What?' she asks. 'Oh, this happened a long time ago.' She doesn't want David to become suspicious about her unearthing a murder that happened at her house all those years ago, or worry him. David returns to the bed and continues his previous occupation as Kate finishes the email. She checks a few more but then becomes weary, most of it can wait. Outside, dusk has wrapped the countryside in a dark blanket where here and there lights have emerged. In the distance, she sees headlights of cars sweeping over the fields and nearby, the light inside the house falls onto the forecourt creating oblong, pale-yellow forms. She turns away from the window and walks towards the bed, where David has fallen asleep; the book he was reading rests on his chest. Instead of waking him for dinner, Kate lowers herself on the bed and lies down beside him, facing David, who is in a deep sleep.

Sammy's small stature doesn't rise above the two Danes, and he hides behind David's leg, shying away from something he has never encountered in his brief life before. With encouraging words David reassures Sam of the gentleness of the giant dogs. Sam remains apprehensive as he eyes the large heads of the dogs from behind the safety of his father, uttering anxious giggles. One of the dogs then sniffs the hand of the boy, who jumps aside with nervous excitement. 'See?' Kate can hear David say, as she looks at the scene from behind the window of the conservatory. 'See how nice they are? He wants to be friends with you.' Sammy slowly puts out his little hand, and when the dog's licks it, Sam shows a bashful smile.

'He worries about Sam, you know,' Kate hears Valerie say behind her. 'He won't admit it, but he hates going off to Australia and then having to leave Sam with his mother.'

Kate turns to face her. 'Why don't you take him?' Kate asks.

Val sighs, 'I wish I could have him, but I've got my work too, 'sides, Mel wants the boy with her. Understandable. She's his mother.'

Kate casts another look outside and sees Sammy taking a liking to Grandmother's dogs. He and David walk off along the path with Sam's arm raised and his little hand resting on the back of one of the dogs. Val and Kate move away from the window and sit down at the small table that has the tray with tea on it in this winter garden.

'Mel should get her life in order,' Valerie says with a criticising tone in her voice as Kate pours them both a cup of tea.

After David and she had collected Valerie and Sam from the airport, Kate had gone out with Val to buy some final Christmas presents before the shops closed.

Footsteps announce a family member entering the conservatory and Uncle James shows his face around a banana tree. 'Oh, hello, ladies. Seeking some quiet time before the major family event, are we?'

'Join us, Uncle James,' Kate offers, and she pulls a chair aside for him to sit on. 'Tea?'

'Wouldn't mind a cuppa,' he says as he sits down. 'Don't think we've met,' he addresses Valerie.

'I'm Valerie, David's mother,' she replies.

'Pleased to meet you,' James says. 'Here for the wedding, I assume?'

'Of course,' Valerie says. 'Who'd want to miss a son's wedding?'

James nods appreciatively. Voices sound and Aunt Clementine and Aunt Meg appear from behind the banana tree. 'Ooh, we're not alone,' Meg establishes. 'Also seeking a quiet space, folks?'

'Please, come join us,' Kate offers and pours two more cups of tea. Clementine and Meg sit down on the wicker two-seater. 'James, you really should pay better attention to your wife,' Clementine says. 'She's been sobbing in her room all afternoon.'

James refrains from facing his sister-in-law and casts an unwilling look towards his teacup.

'It's insufferable, you know,' Clementine continues, 'with you two squabbling all the time.'

Meg puts her cup down on the saucer. 'Don't meddle, Clem,' she says, 'for *that*'s insufferable too.'

Clementine glares at Meg with slight indignation but refrains from commenting. 'Well, shouldn't Christmas be a time of peace? And love?' Clementine amends, which evokes a tiresome sigh from Meg.

The ticking of the dogs' nails on the stone conservatory floor announces more company entering. Meg shrinks back when one of the dogs lifts his large head to sniff what she's holding in her hand. In the dogs' wake,

Adam and Kelly enter, which has Kate ask herself what's keeping her fiancé and his son.

'Mum, when's dinner?' Adam asks his mother in a breaking adolescent's voice. The fifteen-year-old wears frayed jeans that are too big for his lanky teenage body, and the crotch is hanging halfway down his thighs, his shabby shirt droops from his bony shoulders.

'Dinner?' Meg replies. 'Usual time, Adam. Why?'

'Kelly and I want to look for the horses,' Adam says in a deep voice that doesn't really suit his outer appearance.

'The horses? What on earth for?' Meg questions. 'You never want to look for the horses.'

Clementine scrutinises Kelly. 'Nor do you, Kelly. You've never shown any interest in the horses.'

'We just want to see where they are,' Kelly justifies.

'The horses are fine,' Meg says. 'They look after themselves.'

With hanging shoulders, Adam shambles out of the conservatory. 'Why did we have to come here anyway?' he protests.

'We came to spend Christmas with your grandmother,' Meg states. 'Like we always do,' but those last words are left lingering in the air, unheard. Kelly, realising there isn't much sympathy to be gained from her mother or the other relatives, hurries after her cousin. The Great Danes have found a spot on the floor and lie there as if guarding the small group of relations that remain.

When Kelly and Adam had finally come back from their adventurous wander over the fields to see what the horses were up to, the family had at long last been able to start the festive dinner. Not in the least to celebrate Christmas but also the upcoming wedding.

After dinner, most of Kate and Jacob's cousins were unanimous in that it was time to unwrap the gifts that so enticingly had been on display in the drawing-room for the last few days.

Grandmother has taken a seat on the sofa and Kate admits to her gran that the present she bought her is still in her house in Tennessee. Grandmother isn't worried about that and she currently enjoys having her family around her. Sammy is sitting next to her, his newly acquired toys piled up on his other side, his eyelids heavy, but he refuses to let sleep come between this exciting event and being taken to bed. Kate and Valerie mingle with the rest of the family when Kate observes her aunt Anne's crestfallen face. She places a hand on her aunt's arm, looking at her sympathetically. David has spotted Uncle James, who has retired from the whole party and now stands alone in the bay by one of the windows, looking through it with a bland glance.

'How're you doin'?' David enquires. James turns his face briefly. 'Oh, hello. Fine, fine,' is his only reply before casting his eyes into the darkness outside once more.

'Uh, sorry,' David begins, 'but, uh, your wife doesn't seem too happy … I noticed you haven't given her the *small trinket* you got the other day.' James remains focussed on the nothingness outside. 'You know, I'm not one to interfere with other people's business,' David continues, 'but, I found your wife in a sobbing mess this afternoon.'

'I don't blame her,' James says without batting an eyelid. 'And actually, I lied, about the trinket, I mean. I didn't buy it for the wife.'

David gathered as much. 'We all make mistakes,' he says. 'But I'm sure she'll forgive you your liaison with that other woman.'

James sighs. 'It's a man, actually.' He turns to face David whose eyes freeze into James's.

'That … that can be a problem,' David utters, nodding thoughtfully.

'She knows. Anne, I mean,' James confides in David. 'She found me in *flagrante delicto*, shall we say?'

'Oh man,' is all David can answer.

'That's why she's so unhappy. Hard to live with, you see.'

'You guys need counselling,' David says.

James nods, 'maybe, maybe not. I think it's mostly Anne who'd need that.'

'And what about your boys?'

James appears troubled. 'I can't really say how they will feel about it,' he says. 'They don't know, you see. They're usually away at boarding school and know nothing about our domesticities.'

David gives James a friendly slap against his arm. 'You've got a load on your shoulders, man. I wish you luck. You're gonna need it.' He walks back to the others as James turns to face the blackness beyond the bay-window.

'I will.' Those two words, a few letters only, sound a bit trite to Kate's ears. She has heard them said often, spoken by people in her family and friends' circles. Sometimes they sounded sincere, at other times on hearing those two words mentioned it was clear the 'happy couple' wouldn't stay happy. When Kate utters those words she is sincere. The words come straight from her heart and when David slides the ring on her finger, and she looks into his eyes, she knows that he, too, is undeniably serious about his love for her.

David's brother Pete was unable to make it to the UK on time, so he had requested Jacob to be his witness, and

Kate had asked Aunt Meg to fulfil this post as well. Little Sam was, without hesitation, appointed page boy and Kelly was over the moon when she was asked to be a bridesmaid. She set her Gothic phase aside for this occasion and washed the blue dye from her hair, leaving it a peculiar shade of pale green. She hadn't even objected when Kate suggested she wear a pale blue lace dress, albeit Kelly wore ripped stockings underneath.

All aunts agree that Kate is the most beautiful bride they've ever seen as she slowly walks there, wearing a simple yet sophisticated cream coloured gown trailing slightly on the floor, showing white shoes underneath. Her blonde hair raised with a few strands falling loosely over her shoulders. All aunts agree too, that David is the most handsome groom they've ever seen. David not once thought of bringing a suit with him when he was rushing to fly out of Nashville, but here Jacob has been obliging and lent him one of his.

Currently, Valerie is in the first row and holds a tissue to her eyes to dash away a tear. Sammy, wearing an immaculate white shirt with bow tie and dark blue velvet trousers, is seated between her and Grandmother, leaning his head against her arm as if wondering what the commotion is all about. Grandmother has been beaming at the couple ever since the 'I wills' sounded, and as the necessary papers are signed by the respective parties, her eyes show a watery glow. Next to her and in the second row, her grandchildren are becoming restless. Gran looks beside her and notices that Josh, Pete and Adam have disappeared. Adrian and Lillian's four are still sitting patiently, watching the proceedings. Her son-in-law James is the only one absent. He left the house on Boxing Day. Apart from Maria, only family is here today. Kate has decided to hold a party for her London friends at a later date as most of them would be away during the Christmas period. When the official part of the ceremony ends, Kelly gently directs Sammy in front of the buoyant couple, holding their baskets with rose petals, and while Kate and David walk towards the door Sammy and Kelly add more rose petals to those that are on the carpeted floor.

The whole party stands up to follow Kate and David out of the room. At the door, Kelly directs Sammy across from her and they throw the last petals over the married couple's heads. David and Kate hold their hands in a protective gesture not to become too overwhelmed.

In the hall, the whole family gathers around the newly-weds to express their joy and wish them well, when around the corner the three absent cousins appear.

'See? I told you they'd come out of that door,' Pete says, holding a bowl with rice and confetti. The three look somewhat lost as they observe the others.

'Yeah,' Adam expresses his annoyance and nudges Josh in his side. 'Who's blaming who?' the latter objects. The three move towards the rest of the family that is now making their way to the exit to go home where a wedding reception awaits them.

5

*K*ate frowns when on a cold but sunny Tennessee morning, she looks down from her bedroom window and sees a man standing in the field some 150 meters away from the house. With him is a woman. Kate puts on a final piece of clothing and, as behind the bathroom door the shower still runs, walks out of the room. Before going outside, she grabs her jacket from the stand and a glance at the clock tells her it's past 10 am. What are those people doing on her land? And what were they staring at? When she proceeds into the field the woman turns and waves at her. A young lady Kate now recognises as her cousin Anna-May. On closer view, she identifies the man as Earl Jones. Kate can't recall having introduced those two to each other.

'Morning!' she calls out when she nears the pair.

'Hi Kate!' Anna-May replies. 'When'd y'all get back?'

'Hi Kate,' Earl says. 'Had a good time in England?'

'Marvellous,' Kate replies with a smile but is curious to know what the two are doing, standing here in the middle of the field.

'Didn't you read my last email?' Anna-May questions. She hands Kate a copy of a photograph with, in its corner, a file number. 'This is where he fell when the bullet hit him,' Anna-May clarifies.

'Oh? How can you be so sure it was here?' Kate wants to know; she refrains from looking at the photo. 'There are acres of land around the house.'

Anna-May nods in Earl's direction. 'I ran into Earl one time when I was digging up more proof.'

Kate looks at Earl. Had not *he* told her to let the whole situation rest?

'Sorry Kate, but you made me curious too, and when I met your cousin here, I said I'd help her.'

The situation starts to dawn on Kate. 'Yes, but, Earl, don't tell me you were here when they found the body.'

'Oh, there's nothing strange about that,' Earl replies. 'The road was lined with people standing behind the police cordon. Anna-May and I just figured out from what I could remember that it was about here where he fell.'

Anna-May reaches for the photo in Kate's hand. It only shows part of the body with the focus on the shoe prints nearby. 'Look,' she says as Earl, too, bends over her shoulder, 'these were identified as hers, Mrs Baker's, and as you said, she found the body. But these,' and Anna-May's finger circles around the larger footprints in the photo, 'are a man's footprints.'

Kate assumes they must be his, Mr Baker's. 'No, that's just the thing,' her cousin says, 'these prints never matched those of Mr Baker, completely different size.'

Earl agrees. 'Those were never identified as belonging to anybody. Now, that's weird, too, if you ask me.'

'Have you told the police about it?' Kate asks her cousin whose face drops.

'They don't want to know,' she says. 'For them the case is closed. One of them even told me they should've burned that file ages ago.'

'But,' Earl adds, 'they can re-open the case when new evidence is found, so … I'm just saying. I just don't think the PD wants to be reminded.'

Kate agrees as she turns to walk back. 'Let's go inside,' she suggests. 'Tell me everything, Anna-May.'

Earl and Anna-May walk abreast of Kate as they

make their way to the house and Anna-May continues: 'Now my theory is, that this police officer, Canelli, knew a lot more and twenty-two years ago he tried to cover up facts. Either that or he was involved … '

'That's what was said at the time, too,' Earl states.

'… And I tell you why,' Anna-May resumes. Kate listens attentively. 'Canelli did go to Nevada, but he never moved there, or lived there,' Anna-May says. 'He actually went to Kansas where he has been living happily ever since, as the husband of Mrs Baker.'

'No!' Kate exclaims. 'Really? He *married* the *grieving widow*?!'

'You'd better believe it. I've searched on the Internet, made enquiries and it all matches. Birth dates, marriage certificates, career. Would you believe Mr Canelli has been in the same profession there, too?'

They walk across the yard to the kitchen door. 'Good heavens,' Kate says. 'So, it is a possibility that Mrs Baker actually … bribed him, I mean, she was loaded then.'

'Yep,' Anna-May says. 'After the death of the husband.'

Kate opens the door but stops before continuing. 'Wait a minute … ' It suddenly dawns on her where she has seen the face, the man with the bushy eyebrows. 'Now I remember!'

'What?' Her cousin is eager to know what epiphany Kate just had. In Earl's face, an anticipating expression arises as well. They follow Kate into the kitchen. 'The man with the bushy eyebrows,' Kate continues, 'I once went with my daddy, he had to go to the police department in Memphis, and I sat there on a bench when this man … '

'Mr Baker,' Earl declares in a decided tone.

'Yes, and he was arguing with one of the policemen at the desk. He was very angry, demanded to see someone.

But then my daddy came out of a room and we went.'

'Wow ... ' is Anna-May's reaction. 'So ... so, you've seen Jon Baker ... '

They turn their heads when a person is heard coming down from upstairs and David appears in their view, wearing jeans and a chequered shirt, his long, still damp hair falling over his shoulders. Kate walks up to him and kisses him endearingly. 'Good morning, darling.'

Anna-May stares at the man who has just come in while Earl seems to recollect having seen this man before somewhere.

'May I introduce my husband? David,' Kate says and addressing David, 'my cousin Anna-May, and Earl, an old friend of the family.'

'Your ... your ... David Nelson, *your* husband?' Anna-May is awestruck but shocked at the same time. 'Mum did say you were seeing someone, but she never said that it was ... it was ... Oh my God!'

Earl now, too, remembers. The TV-show. That's where he has seen this man, singing country songs. David shows the visitors a lazy smile and shakes Anna-May's trembling hand. 'Please to meet you,' he says. Anna-May can't help but stare at the face of the man in front of her. 'Kate,' her quivering voice sounds. 'Kate, I mean, David Nelson in *our* family ... '

Kate nods. 'Right,' she says sensibly, 'shall we have some breakfast? We're a bit late, you see,' as she motions the others to take a seat at the table, and David starts preparing a fresh pot of coffee.

'Well, don't mind if I do,' Earl says.

Anna-May slowly sits down at the table as well, all too aware that she is in the same room as her all-time favourite country singer. David is not bothered by the attention. He makes them a pot of coffee and puts toast and jam on the table. For Anna-May, it is all too unreal.

The following morning David has to travel to Australia with his band for a two-week tour. The fourth of January is the date they have been dreading, for it was the day they would be separated again. David had tried to convince Kate to accompany him but Kate owed her time to the restaurant. Her recent absence was longer than intended. Neither is happy to be separated, even if it is only for two weeks and once again they find themselves in an airport, a place of goodbyes and farewells. David holds Kate close, embraces and kisses her with such tenderness tears were beginning to well in Kate's eyes.

When the last passengers have walked through Customs and passed from sight, David releases Kate and is the last passenger to walk through and on to his gate. Kate wipes a tear from her cheek and smiles an unconvincing smile when David briefly turns his head. He waves at her before he vanishes from sight.

Kate makes her way through the throngs of people that either gaze at screens or, puzzled, look for the right gate. She takes an escalator to an upper floor and finds a bench where she has a view of the gate where David's plane is waiting for take-off. She watches the uploading of the luggage and the refreshments and dinners the food trolleys bring. Then, slowly, the first passengers appear behind the small windows of the walkway before they enter the plane. From this distance, she can barely distinguish one person from the next.

After a while, the plane moves away from the terminal and taxis to the runway. When the plane has disappeared behind the airport buildings she stands up and walks towards the escalators that will take her down to ground floor level.

In the parking lot, she finds her car and drives back to the city. Since their return, Kate has only had contact with her staff via telephone but now reality has sunk in and it is time to go back to work. Driving along Elvis Presley Boulevard she realises it is Elvis Birthday week in Memphis. They must have some Elvis music playing in the restaurant.

When she enters The Veg and the Vegan, she concludes her previous reflection was unfounded as the sound of The King's voice streams her way. Lynn is engaged in wiping tables, while Ashley is at the table she seems to have adopted, drawing pictures. The little one is slowly becoming quite an artist. Alejandra lingers behind the counter with another person Kate doesn't recognise. There aren't many customers at this hour. 'Hello all. Happy new year,' Kate greets them and then walks behind the counter to see who the new employee might be.

'Hello, I'm Mrs Nelson.' The young man takes her hand and introduces himself as Colin. 'Pleased to meet you.'

Kate looks at the tidiness of the displays and then walks to the back where she gives the kitchen staff her best wishes for the year to come, before entering the office where she finds Marianna at her desk. 'Hello, Marianna. Happy new year.'

'Miss Jennings!' Marianna exclaims. 'Good to see you.'

'It's Mrs, actually. We were married over the Christmas period.'

Marianna comes from behind the desk. 'Congratulations,' she says and shakes her boss's hand.

'Thank you … Who's the young man?' Kate asks.

'He's a temp. We were so busy over the holidays and then Earlene got the flu, we had to juggle so much. So I hope you don't mind we got a few temps in,' Marianne explains. 'They don't work full-time,' she adds as if justifying her actions. 'How was England?'

Kate's face lights up with such happiness that her uttering *wonderful!* is almost superfluous. 'How is Lynn managing upstairs?' she then says, returning to the affairs of the day.

'Mrs Jennings, I've never seen such an assiduous person. You know, she's already studying in her books, too? Even though her classes don't start until next week.'

'Excellent,' Kate says.

'And Ashley. ma'am, now there's a sweetheart if I ever saw one,' Marianna adds.

'She's a lovely girl,' Kate asserts as she goes to the desk and sits down behind the computer. 'Now, let's see.' Kate opens files with orders and starts the tedious process of checking the administrative part of her business.

The last customers have left when Kate logs off and gathers her belongings. David called her from LAX, where he had met his band. He enlightened her about the scorn he had received from his manager Fred for just 'disappearing off the face of the earth' and resurfacing in a wedded state. He is increasingly dissatisfied with his manager's antics, he told her.

Faint stumbling above her head indicates Lynn and Ashley have made their home upstairs. Kate checks the doors and sets the alarm before leaving the restaurant through its front door. She locks it behind her and wanders off to the parking lot where she has parked her car on the outer ring as many spaces were already taken when she arrived earlier on in the day. When walking towards her car, she initially thinks she has received a parking ticket when she sees a piece of paper under her windshield wiper. When she takes the piece of paper and opens it, all it says is 'LEAVE IT ALONE'. Kate looks up and around the parking lot. Leave what alone? She starts to feel uncomfortable. Her eyes scan the street where still quite a few people are ambling along. She turns to the bushes behind her, but through the dark foliage can't distinguish someone hiding there. Kate nervously opens the door of her car and swiftly gets in, puts her handbag underneath the chair and the key in the ignition. She glances in her rear-view mirror and starts pulling back when there's a loud thud on the hood of her car. In a reflex, she applies the brakes when all of a sudden a man stands by the driver's side of her car. He bangs on her windshield. 'Leave it alone!' he yells. Kate's eyes are wide open with fright, and for a few seconds, she sits as if frozen before gathering the presence of mind to pull her car back and turn the wheel. Another slap on her windshield reverberates through her body. 'Leave it alone, miss Jennings!' the man calls out. Kate trembles as she speeds off, almost hitting a pedestrian when she turns from the parking lot onto the road, at the same time realising he knows her name! Who *is* he?

She speeds along Elvis Presley Boulevard when her warning system reminds her of the speed limit. She glances in her rear-view mirror but only sees headlights of cars following her.

Kate takes a few deep breaths. He didn't seem out to rob her, it crosses her mind. Trembling, her eyes search for a sign that will direct her to a police station. Kate scans the broad street and gradually starts to feel annoyed by the absence of a police station. Finally, she sees a sign that points to the presence of a police station. She indicates and waits impatiently for oncoming traffic to pass, her eyes shooting on and off to her rear-view mirror, and then she turns off into the street. Her eyes study the buildings until she sees the bureau, a rather small, local department. She grabs her bag, jumps out and hurriedly walks to the main entrance. Unwelcoming neon-lighting hits her when she enters, *that* and a frosted glass door, showing large cracks in one corner, covered up with duck-tape. There's a small counter behind glass to her left and she rings the bell. A puffy looking lady in her fifties appears in front of the window, wiping crumbs from her mouth. 'Can I help you?' she asks.

'Yes,' Kate replies. 'Yes, you can help me. I was attacked, while I was in my car. Just now, and … ' The crumb-eating lady slides a sheet of paper underneath the window in her direction. 'Complete this, please,' she says. Kate takes the sheet of paper and looks at it. Name, address, d.o.b..

'Excuse me,' Kate says. 'I just need to report something.'

The lady looks at her with tired eyes. 'Fill that in please,' she says. 'You need to fill in the form before we can help you.'

Kate sighs and sits down on the only chair that is present in this small reception area. Kate is expeditious in filling in her details but takes more effort writing down the event in the parking lot near her restaurant. She digs up the crumpled note that was under her windshield wiper and slides it all under the window. Kate peers through to see if the lady is still there, and suddenly she appears again, this time chewing. 'Thank you,' she mumbles with her mouth full.

'Can I speak to someone now?' Kate asks. Without a word being said, the glass door opens and Kate enters into a corridor. The lady from the window enters through another door and beckons her to follow. She opens a door where, in a small room, a desk and a few chairs are visible. The lady places the completed sheet of paper on the desk. 'Someone'll be here in a moment. Take a seat.'

Kate sits down in front of the desk to wait. As she waits she looks around at the 'Wanted' photos on the wall and leaflets with information in a rack beside those. It's peculiarly quiet in this police station, she seems to be the only client, but it would be naive to think that that is an indication of a low crime rate in Memphis.

Suddenly, a door is swept open and an officer in uniform enters. Or is he just an office clerk dressed in a police uniform? Kate asks herself. He sits down while breathing out a 'good evening'. He takes the sheet of paper and starts reading. 'Did you get a good look at him?' he then asks.

'Yes,' Kate replies. 'Dark hair, bit long. I'd say in his mid-thirties. Caucasian.'

'Mm. Well, that doesn't leave us much to go on,' he concludes. 'There's millions of men out there fitting that description.'

Kate reaches for the piece of paper with the warning scribbled on it in capital letters. 'What about this? This, he must have shoved under my windshield wiper. Can't your forensics do anything with this?'

The police officer gives her a tiresome glance. 'Lady, what're you thinking? We have much more pressing matters that need investigating. Look, the man didn't touch you. You weren't harmed – '

'Yes! But what if he comes back?'

The police officer gives her another look. Kate can't help but think it's one of contempt. 'Look,' he says. 'What I can do is file your complaint, but that's all.'

Kate has not intended bringing up the subject. She sighs. 'There's also another matter. A murder that happened on my land … '

'Lady … ' the police officer utters soporifically.

'Why do we pay taxes in this country?' Kate calls out. 'To at least get some police protection when needed!' She lets out a sigh. 'Twenty two years ago something happened, on what is now my property,' she resumes. 'A man supposedly killed himself. We have now found out, he was *actually* murdered – '

'Who's we?' the police officer asks.

' … and now this man comes along and screams at me to leave it alone? Now, what do you say to that, sir?'

The police officer scratches himself behind his ear. He looks at Kate and then stares at the piece of paper. 'Twenty two years ago,' he says. 'OK, I'll look into it for you. Write down what you know.'

With a certain wariness, Kate gets up, takes the piece of paper and puts it in her bag. 'I'll send you copies,' she says sharply. 'Thank you for your time.'

Kate walks towards the door, but that appears locked when she tries to open it. She turns to address the police officer. 'Excuse me,' Kate says.

The police officer reaches for a button under his desk and the door opens so Kate can leave. In the corridor, the frosted doors slide open, and when Kate passes the window, the chewing lady has made herself invisible again.

Kate opens her car doors gets in. Once in her seat, she locks all the doors and takes her mobile from her bag. It's almost eleven and she hesitates before calling her cousin Anna-May, but she soon finds Anna-May is at home in her flat here in Memphis. Kate turns the key in the ignition and starts her car to drive there.

Anna-May's small but cosy apartment is a welcome

change from the chilly reception Kate experienced at the police station. The first thing Kate hears when she enters is her husband David's voice streaming through the room. To Kate, it feels almost eerie with him being miles away but still his voice is so close. 'You *are* a fan, aren't you,' Kate ascertains.

'Kate, you really took me by surprise yesterday. I mean … Here we are, cousins, practically only just met. And then you're marrying my favourite singer! It's too much, Kate!' Anna-May cries out.

'I'm glad you like him,' Kate says with a smile. 'And I'm glad to hear his voice here. I miss him already, you know.'

Anna-May pours them both a glass of wine. 'I can imagine,' she says. 'Now, what's this disturbing thing that happened to you?'

Kate elaborates on what she already told Anna-May over the phone. 'But I don't think there's much the police will do about this case,' she infers. 'And they'll just file my complaint.'

Anna-May is not so certain. 'I've befriended a police officer and he's digging back into the case. So, Kate, we could say, it's been re-opened.' She raises her glass. 'Bottoms up.'

Kate raises her glass as well, but she remains doubtful, for if that means they are to look forward to threats like the one that occurred this evening, Kate might just become a bit more discriminating. 'And I actually won't feel safe in my own house at this stage,' she says. 'What if someone waits for me there? I mean, I'm all alone there in that big house with no one around.'

'Oh, but you can stay here, if you like,' is Anna-May's immediate reaction. 'Daisy-Lou's room is still vacant.'

'That's kind of you, Anna-May, but I can't impose on you – '

'Don't be so standoffish!' Anna-May calls out. 'It must be your Britishness. Of course you can stay.'

Kate has to admit that it would be wiser for her to take the offer, at least for this night. 'OK, and maybe we can rotate a bit, you staying with me, until this whole thing has blown over.'

Anna-May agrees. 'Great! We'll stay at yours this weekend and then we can go horse riding!' She takes the bottle to top-up the glasses but Kate declines. 'Not for me, thanks. I've to be careful with that.'

The following morning Kate makes sure to park her car near her restaurant. She looks around the area where quite a few cars are parked, but can't distinguish anything that could pose a threat. She enters The Veg and the Vegan and finds staff has already been rather busy with the breakfast crowd that is presently dispersing to make way for the lunch crowd. Kate pours herself a coffee and instead of going to her office, she sits down at the small table that is generally occupied by Ashley. Not for long, Lynn and Ashley come down and Kate invites them to sit at the table with her. Lynn has shown her devoted ability to the business and her persistence to improve her situation, but she still seems to be suffering from incertitude as she sits down in a chair across from Kate.

'Lynn, we hardly spoke since you moved in upstairs. I just wanted to know how you're doing. Are you OK with the rooms?'

It's obvious that Lynn hasn't expected this question and her eyes light up. 'But … miss Jennings … Kate, it's the best place. We'd never dreamt of living in such a nice, clean apartment. How could you have doubted … '

'I'm glad,' Kate says. 'It's sometimes hard to tell, if a person likes something or not.' What Kate is also interested in is what situation led Lynn and Ashley to become homeless, but she's not sure how to approach that subject without being intrusive. Ashley slowly unrolls one of her drawings and places it in front of Kate. 'I made this for you, miss Jennings,' Ashley says.

'It's a present,' Lynn says, 'for your wedding.'

Kate is enchanted. 'Oh, that's beautiful Ashley.' Kate studies the drawing with great affection. 'You're a real artist, sweetheart,' she says as she looks at the cottage style house in the drawing surrounded by trees and animals. Where did this little girl gain such artistry?

'It's lovely, Ashley. Thank you,' Kate says as she strokes the girl on her cheek. 'I will frame it and hang it up in our house.'

'She always liked to draw,' Lynn informs Kate. 'But then … after the fire … well, you know the rest.'

Kate glances over to Lynn. 'What actually did happen, Lynn? If you don't mind me asking.'

Lynn hesitates as she looks at Kate. 'I lived with this guy,' she then says. 'Not Ashley's father, no idea what's become of him … We'd been roughing it, me and Ashley, and then I met this guy and we went to live with him. It was OK at first, but then he started bringing friends home. Well, then, one evening, when they were all drunk, all of a sudden the house was on fire. We barely escaped with our lives. So, we ran … I left those drunks for what they were and we ran … '

Ashley's face has turned gloomy as she listens to her mother's account of a situation they don't like to be reminded of.

' … I didn't want Ashley to be in there, in that environment. I had just enough money to get us as far as

Memphis, where everything started all over again.'

Lynn casts a serious look at Kate. 'So, don't for a moment think we don't appreciate what you've done for us.' Lynn reaches and takes Kate's hand. 'And I will pay you back,' she says. 'We're honest folk. I will pay you rent an' everything.'

A feeling of gratefulness overcomes Kate, but she feels sad at the same time when she remembers her own situation as a child and that not much has changed. There are still so many like Lynn and Ashley who have to live the way they had to.

'Well, I'm just glad I was able to help,' she says. 'And don't worry about rent just yet. The rooms would be empty otherwise. Now they come to good use.'

Lynn shows her an appreciative smile. 'Well, I'd better get to work,' she says and stands up.

'Me too,' Kate says. 'No point in idling one's time away.' She gives Ashley a wink who looks up at Kate with her former cheerfulness.

Kate turns to walk to her office, but she stops dead and feels a chill running through her body, when the man who gave her such a fright the night before, is standing right in front of her. 'Hello, miss Jennings.'

Kate tries to distance herself from the unwanted customer who looks at her with eyes that send a shiver down her spine.

'What do you want from me,' Kate demands while trying to suppress the trembling in her voice.

'You can read,' he tells her menacingly. 'And I take it, you're not deaf.' His glaring disturbs Kate. 'You don't know who I am, do you,' he says.

'No, and I can't say I regret that,' Kate replies. She instantly feels sorry for that remark when the man takes a step in her direction and she finds his face only a few inches away from hers. Kate's hands search the edge of the table and grab it for balance. She hears Ashley behind her, moving her chair.

'Stop prying,' he hisses in her face. Kate feels spittle hitting her cheek but gathers the presence of mind to push him off. 'Leave this minute!' she hisses back. 'Or you'll have the police to deal with.'

The man takes a step back. 'I just wanted to show you,' he warns, 'how easy it is to get to you. So, *you*'d better be careful.' He backs away from her. 'Don't forget what I've just said.' He looks at Ashley, and then his threatening eyes rest on Kate's face before he turns and walks out of the restaurant, leaving Kate trembling, holding on to the table. She feels as if all the blood has drained from her face when she watches the man pacing away along the sidewalk. For a brief moment, she closes her eyes, then loosens her grip on the table and starts walking towards her office. 'Call the police,' she instructs Lynn who has followed the scene from behind the counter. 'Now!'

Lynn motions Ashley to come to her before she grabs the phone off the charger on the counter to call the emergency number.

Kate paces past the kitchen and enters her office where she sits down at her desk. She swallows some water from a glass when Marianna enters. Kate dials a number on her mobile. It goes to voice-mail. She then sends a text message and hopes her cousin will pick it up soon.

'Is something the matter?' Marianna asks when she sees her boss's troubled face.

'No ... and yes,' Kate says; she now has found some calmness in herself. 'No, it doesn't really concern you, or the others. And yes ... the police will be here soon. Hopefully.'

'Were we mugged?!'

'Please, Marianna, don't make a big thing out of … something.' Kate doesn't really know *what* to tell her staff. It does concern them too when that dreadful man starts showing up here and threatening everybody.

Around lunchtime, Anna-May received her cousin's text message and she currently walks through the door while two policemen leave the establishment. She looks at them as they walk back to the police car, then walks through the restaurant and into Kate's office. 'Hi Kate,' she says with some inquisitiveness in her voice.

'Anna-May, thank heavens you could come.' Kate stands up from her desk and grabs her coat and bag. 'Marianna, please take over.'

Anna-May follows Kate outside. 'Let's go somewhere downtown,' Kate suggests. 'Have some lunch and we'll talk.'

'OK. I've got my car right there,' Anna-May says.

They get in and Anna-May steers her car in the northern direction.

'Have you spoken to your police officer friend?' Kate asks. 'I would like to talk to him.' She glances at her cousin sideways. 'I mean, Anna-May, we're entering dangerous ground here. If the police still think what happened twenty-two years ago was suicide, they should really think again.'

Anna-May glances in the rear-view mirror and looks over her shoulder to move in the left lane. 'Look in my bag,' she tells Kate. 'There's some more stuff I've printed off the Internet.'

Kate takes Anna-May's bag from the back seat and heaves it across onto her lap. 'Gosh, woman, what do you carry in here,' Kate says with amazement. She starts rummaging through the bag until she sees a pile of paper and pulls it out. Anna-May reaches with her right hand to indicate what she should look at. 'Those top ten sheets,' she says. 'There are a few photos there of the Baker family.'

Kate scrutinises the papers and then finds the ones Anna-May refers to.

'Now, that man with the bushy eyebrows is Jon Baker, that's the one you saw when you were with your dad. That lady in the other photo, I copied that from an old newspaper article, that's Mrs Baker.'

Kate looks at the picture. She doesn't really recognise the woman she sees in the photo.

'Are you sure?' Kate wonders, although, there is some familiarity.

'Well, don't forget, she has aged a bit there. This one was taken about seven years ago. She won some prize in some local baking contest.' Anna-May's hand moves sideways once more. 'Now look at those two men in the background. The older one is Canelli, but the – '

'That's him!' Kate calls out. 'That's the guy!'

'Canelli?'

'No, the younger one! That's the guy who's been threatening me!'

Anna-May briefly glances at Kate. 'That's the son, one of the Baker sons,' she confirms. She pulls up and drives the car into a small parking space a few streets away from the centre.

'Good heavens!' Kate exclaims. 'We should take that to the police right away.'

'I gave copies to my police officer friend,' Anna-May says as they get out of the car. 'I'll give him a call.'

Even though the women find that the case is now becoming quite clear, it doesn't suffice to put Kate's mind at ease. It is obvious that there is someone who does not want to be found out and that is something that worries Kate.

'Thank God the police have promised to patrol more often around the restaurant,' she says as they both walk to one of Anna-May's favourite eateries.

'I hope you ain't thinking of staying at *your* house tonight,' Anna-May says. 'It's too unsafe for you to go anywhere on your own.'

Kate has to agree. 'I'll stay with you another night, and then tomorrow evening we can go to my place for the weekend.' She opens her bag when her mobile is ringing its tune. A warm feeling engulfs her when she sees David's number on the display. 'It's David,' she informs her cousin.

'*Hon' how are ya ...? I tried calling you at home but no one answers ...* '

'Sorry, David. I'm staying with my cousin for a few days. How are you?'

'*Fine. We just did this TV-show, breakfast show and tonight we're giving a concert –* '

'I miss you,' Kate interrupts him. 'I wish I'd come with you.' Anna-May looks at Kate and raises her eyebrows.

'*I miss you too, hon'. Say, why don't you just get on a plane and –* '

'No, I shouldn't,' Kate realises, 'you'll be home soon, won't you.'

'*You know, Kate, you know when I'll be home. What's the matter? Something wrong?*'

' ... No, no, everything's fine. What time is it where you are?'

'*Well, it's tomorrow here, it's just after seven. AM.*'

'Isn't that funny,' Kate says, trying to avoid telling

him the truth.

'*Oh, Kate, I think my credit is low. I'll call you tonight. OK?*'

'Can't wait, David. I love you.'

'*I love you too, Kate. You don't even know how much.*' Kate hears the yearning in his voice.

'I do, David. I do,' her voice has gone down to a whisper. 'I'll text you Anna-May's land-line number.' She smooches a kiss in the receiver. 'Talk to you soon.'

Anna-May looks at Kate as the latter puts her phone back. 'Wow, you two,' she says, 'proper lovebirds.'

It is a bright winter morning, and the sky is crystal blue with a milky sun shimmering above. The horses are out in the frosted field and stand almost motionless, with their heads bowed down to the ground as their noses nuzzle the surface in search of something edible, creating minute clouds of vapour. Some birds that hold out during the Tennessean winter can be heard in the distance, trying to survive in the frozen branches of trees on the sloping knoll. Through those trees, a shadow moves along under their protection until it has reached the edge of the field. Briefly, the figure stands between two trees, then moves further and disappears over the rim of the slope. Down below, two figures emerge from the house and walk towards the fence that surrounds the fields. A whistling sound brings the horses in motion, and they amble towards the two people by the fence.

'Come on, Chief!' Kate calls. 'Is the cold making you slow?'

Anna-May lets out another shrill whistle. 'C'mon guys! Come on.' The horses hasten their pace and soon allow Kate and Anna-May to stroke them on their necks. Kate opens the fence and takes Chief by his halter. 'Let's get you two saddled up,' she says. They walk towards the stable and Kate goes inside to come out with Chief's gear. Anna-May follows her example and puts a saddle on the brown mare's back. 'There you go, Maxi.'

The ladies, dressed in jeans and short winter jackets, throw their legs over the horses' backs and trot towards the field and onward. 'Be careful not to slip,' Kate warns her cousin. 'The soil is rather frozen here and there.' At a steady pace, they gallop across the fields around Kate's house, up the sloping hill and on its rim. Kate slows down and strokes Chief's neck that has developed its thick winter coat. She moves up beside Anna-May. 'Down there,' she says as she points to the path below. 'Down there's where David and I first met.'

Anna-May looks down on the dividing dirt road with its grey muddy surface, now hard with frost. 'Wow, Kate. So romantic,' she responds with some awe in her voice.

'Yes, it was rather special,' Kate replies. 'I liked him instantly, you know. But, well ... ' Kate doesn't want to go into the John-chapter. 'I do think it was meant to be, that we should meet.' Her eyes drift to some tracks in the frosted grass on the side, going up the slope.

'OK, let's go on,' she says and steers Chief back over the rim. 'Let's go to the other side of the house. I actually hardly ride in that direction.' They give the horses free reins and gallop along the tree line. The hooves clatter on the hard soil while manes fly for speed of the run. Anna-May cheers with pleasure. Kate is more subdued but enjoys the ride no less. At the other end, they ride down the knoll and back towards the house.

'We'd better put them inside now, dry them off,' Kate says as they dismount in the yard, taking the reins and leading Chief and Maxi inside the stables.

'I really enjoyed that, Kate,' Anna-May says. 'I love

riding, but I have to depend on people like you, people that own a few horses and have the space.'

'You can come and ride any time you want, Anna-May,' Kate assures her cousin as she rubs Chief's back with his towel. After they have finished caring for the horses, Kate pours some feed in the horses' trough and refreshes the water. 'OK, that's done. What about some lunch,' Kate suggests. The bleak sun shines at its brightest when they leave the stables and make their way to the kitchen door to enter the house.

'I think we forgot to close it properly,' Anna-May says as they see the door just barely in the lock. On entering, they take off their jackets and Kate fills the kettle with water. She enjoys having people around and hopes that having her family stay with her will become a regular occurrence rather than a sporadic one. Anna-May inspects the fridge. 'What'll we have, cuz'?'

'I don't think you'll be hungry once I'm done with you,' a deep man's voice sounds.

Kate turns around with such abruptness she almost drops the kettle. Anna-May shrieks and slams the refrigerator door with fright on her face.

In the doorway to the hall is the man, the Bakers' son, a shotgun loosely dangling in his hands. He looks at Kate as he slowly comes near. 'I warned you, didn't I,' he says in a menacing tone.

He moves closer to Kate and suddenly points the gun at her face. Anna-May cries out. Kate freezes as she looks into the cold eyes of the intruder. 'What … do you want,' she manages to say. The point of the barrel inches towards her chin.

'I told you to leave it alone,' his icy voice spells out. Kate now feels the cold metal of the barrel against her chin, she doesn't dare move, and she doesn't dare speak.

'LEAVE IT ALONE!' the man yells close to her face. 'Or do you have a problem understanding!'

Anna-May holds her breath as Kate's eyes are fixed on the face in front of her. She's trying to be calm, think about what she has learnt in college, her self-defence classes race through her mind. But she can't move. 'I ... I ... ' The words won't come. Anna-May takes a hesitant step towards the table.

'Stay where you are!' the man yells.

' ... Uh, sir,' Anna-May endeavours.

'What!' pointing his gun at Kate's face.

'It ... i it was me.'

'What are you talking about?!' he screams without leaving Kate out of his vision.

'It was me ... who ... dug up the case.'

Kate sees the man's face relax somewhat from a savage glare to a condescending one.

'Oh, you are the culprit now, are you,' his head turning slightly away from Kate. Within a second Kate has grabbed the barrel and gives it a hard push upwards.

'KATE!' Anna-May screams but sees her chance and runs towards her struggling cousin. A shot thunders through the kitchen as Anna-May jumps on the man's back and starts hammering on his head with her fist. Kate holds on to the barrel of the gun and pulls it, twists it, digging her nails into the man's wrist until he has to let go. He roars like a madman as he tries to throw Anna-May from his back who then falls on the floor with a hard thump. For a moment, she is stunned but then crawls to her feet again.

'ANNA-MAY!' Kate calls out as the man storms directly at her cousin but Anna-May seizes a chair. The man runs straight into a leg. He grabs his crotch in agony and rolls onto the floor. With trembling bodies, Kate and

Anna-May watch as he squirms. 'We have to call the police,' Anna-May pants. Kate nods. 'He'll get to his feet soon,' she says with a quivering voice. She takes the phone from the charger on the kitchen counter and dials the number. Anna-May reaches for the shotgun that Kate dropped from her hands onto the floor, and points it at the man. 'I'll guard *him*,' she says, determined but still shaking.

Kate is connected to the emergency service and gathers the clearness of mind to give them the details of the place of attack. While doing so, fright emerges in her face as she sees the man on the floor, who has recovered from the sudden blow, get to his feet.

'Anna-May!' she screams. Anna-May, too, feels the anxiety build up once more.

'Stay where you are!' she yells at the man, pointing the gun at him. With the predicament changed, he looks along the barrel at Anna-May's face, less savagely than he did before.

'Be quick! Please!' Kate calls into the phone before she drops it. She stands behind her cousin and wonders why Jon Baker's son is so adamant about keeping them from learning more about the person who murdered his father all those years ago.

'Why do you want us to stop searching?' Kate dares ask the man. 'Don't you want the killer of your father found?'

The man slams both his fists on the floor. 'He was not murdered! You stupid bitches. He killed himself!' The man glares at Kate who won't allow his behaviour to intimidate her.

'But, proof shows, otherwise,' she carefully utters.

The gimlet eyes of the man move from Kate to Anna-May before focusing on Kate again. 'I remember your father.' His voice sounds hoarse. 'Nice man. It would be a shame if something happened to his nice daughter.' While uttering those last words, his eyes turn cold. Kate feels her skin crawl.

'Hey!' Anna-May calls out. 'Don't forget who's holding the gun now!' She cocks the gun when, at the same time, the man shoots to his knees and grabs the barrel.

The action causes a bullet to release from the gun and hit him on the head. He falls back. Kate screams. Anna-May drops the gun and shrinks back, her hand over her mouth.

For moments they stand there looking at the man on the floor. Blood is streaming from the wound on his head.

It is Kate who gathers the presence of mind to move closer, as Anna-May carefully follows her cousin's actions. Kate bends over the man and circumspectly tries to determine the man's state when, slowly, the kitchen door opens, and an elderly woman enters.

Anna-May is the first to spot her. She reaches out with her hand to make her cousin aware. The woman looks around the kitchen with a distant glance in her eyes, and she perceives Kate standing by the man on the floor.

'I must say, it has improved,' the woman says in a detached tone of voice. 'What a little decorating can do.' She moves closer to the others in the kitchen. Her face is the same but she has aged, Kate observes, lines around her eyes and her hair is dyed. She was never a brunette. It makes her fair complexion look cold. With the same indifference as the words she uttered before, the woman now looks down on the man on the floor. 'I told him it was no use. But, as always, he wouldn't listen.' She turns her eyes towards Kate. 'You're Jake's little girl, aren't you? You have fared well. Almost as good as I did, years ago.'

Anna-May glares at the woman she recognises from the photo she printed from the Internet. Kate can't believe this is the same kind woman she once met as a child. What has happened to that woman? So cold and distant as her son lies here on the kitchen floor. Kate looks at him, the bleeding seems to have stopped. A chill goes through her body.

'You really should have let the case rest, miss Jennings,' the woman says impassively as she puts her hand in her purse. 'You had no business poking around in my affairs.'

Anna-May grabs Kate's arm as Kate reaches to take her cousin's hand when they see a piece of metal appear from the woman's purse. Outside, sirens are heard nearing the house. The woman abruptly turns her head.

'Damn!' she exclaims, stamping her foot. 'Damn!'

'Run,' Kate says softly, and she seizes Anna-May's hand. While the woman takes out a handgun, they both rush towards the kitchen door and run out, across the yard, and on to the driveway towards the approaching police cars that are followed by an ambulance. Kate points to the house as the police cars come to a halt with screeching tyres. Policemen immediately jump out and grab both Kate and Anna-May. 'They're in there!' Kate yells pointing at the house. 'They have guns!'

The other police cars proceed at high speed and stop by the stables. Kate sees policemen emerge from their car with guns in hand and cautiously approach the kitchen door. Anna-May has started sobbing as she holds on to Kate, who embraces her crying cousin. The policemen look at them as they realise that the two women are the victims.

While holding each other, Kate watches as police

officers enter the kitchen, guns pointed. The paramedics stay behind until they too are seen entering the house.

Only then, when policemen are coming out of the kitchen, one holding a handcuffed Mrs Baker by her arm, Kate and Anna-May venture back towards the house, following the police officer who remained behind.

When they reach the yard, the paramedics are just leaving the house with the Bakers' son on the stretcher. His eyes are open. Anna-May turns her tearful face away while Kate addresses one of the male nurses.

'How is he?' she asks.

'Scratch wound, he'll survive.'

Kate looks at the man on the stretcher. The look in his eyes has changed from the savage coldness he displayed earlier to one of resignation.

Kate holds her cousin by her arm and they both follow the police officer into the house. One of the officers is standing in the middle of the kitchen taking in the scene. Kate spots another one on his knees near the bloodstain on the floor.

'The woman must've shot him,' the police officer says. Kate sits Anna-May down at the kitchen table. 'No,' Kate says. 'He tried to shoot *us*. She came in later.'

The officer looks at her. 'You're the one that phoned?'

Kate nods. Only now she realises the severe situation they've been in. 'Are you all right, Anna-May?' she asks. Anna-May glances up at her cousin with eyes still red from crying. The expression on Anna-May's face tells her she has been better.

'We had no idea that Mrs Baker was out there,' Kate tells the policeman. 'Her son had threatened me before, the police knows, but we had not expected him *here*.' Her voice sounds tired and she, too, is close to crying, but her reservedness keeps her from doing so. That, and the anger she now feels, someone just entering her house and terrorising her, *them,* in her own house!

'You knew the woman?' the police officer wants to know.

'She used to live here when I was a child.'

'You two have to come with us to the station,' he says. 'Give us a full report.'

'Can't we tell you now?' Kate asks. 'Here?'

'Found it!' the policeman on the floor calls out. 'Here's the bullet hole,' he says as he points to the baseboard below one of the kitchen cupboards. One of his colleagues, too, has a look at the find. 'Forensics will sort that.'

'You'll find that one's from the same gun,' Kate mentions. She points to the shotgun that still lies there where Anna-May dropped it.

'Same gun? What do you mean? Has he fired more than one shot?'

Kate looks up at the ceiling and sees the destruction the first bullet has caused, a hole marred by scorch-marks. 'There,' she points out.

The policeman follows Kate's directions and looks up, too. 'Well, he's not a great aim,' he states. 'That's for sure.'

Kate doesn't want to think what would have happened to that bullet, had she and Anna-May *not* fought off the intruder. She goes to her cousin and places an arm around her shoulder. 'It's all about a murder that happened here twenty-two years ago,' Kate explains. 'One of your colleagues has re-opened the case.'

Anna-May looks up at Kate. 'We should give my police officer friend a call,' she says. 'Could you look in my bag, please, for my cellphone?'

Kate goes to the lounge where Anna-May left her bag while the two officers look at each other.

'Well, this turns out to be more than just a case of a simple break-in,' notes the police officer, who is now back on his feet. Anna-May looks at him. 'Why did you think Mrs Baker fired that shot?' she asks.

'Well, miss, when we came in, she just stood there over the man's body, gun in hand. Didn't say a word. We just cuffed her and took her out. She was as tame as a lamb.'

'She wasn't so tame before you arrived,' Anna-May says. 'She could've shot us if you wouldn't have shown up.'

Kate hands Anna-May her phone who proceeds calling the befriended police officer.

'You two need to come with us, ma'am. This place will be cordoned off for the Forensics team. There'll be an investigation. You won't be allowed in here for a few days.'

Kate understands.

'He'll meet us at the PD in Memphis,' Anna-May says and puts her phone down.

'Anna-May,' Kate addresses her cousin. 'We're not allowed in the house for a few days … I'll just be upstairs to pack a few things.'

As she wants to go to the hall, one of the officers stops her. 'Sorry, ma'am. No going upstairs. You might disturb something. You've come far enough as it is.'

Kate gives him a surprised look but follows his advice.

'Better come with me, ladies,' one of the policemen says and he escorts Kate and Anna-May out of the house.

The doctor's office appears clean in all its modern

sterility yet not so disconcerting that one wouldn't want to wait for an appointment there. Kate is at present the only client in the waiting room. Looking around, she sees the indistinct paintings that serve as splashes of colour on the white walls, for Kate can't think of what the artist could have meant by the abstract scribbles on the canvasses. The obligatory magazines that are on the small table don't entice her to even thumb through one. Kate still tries to keep the attack at her house from tormenting her mind. She hasn't stayed at her own house now for a week, still plagued by the happenings of last Saturday. Anna-May's apartment has been a welcoming home, even though Anna-May herself has not entirely overcome their ordeal. Thankfully, her police officer friend Nigel has been a great help to her, and she is now slowly starting to become her old cheerful self again. The threat is gone, and her mind is finally coming to rest after the tribulations of the days passed. She will have to tell David about the whole dreadful affair when he returns but until that time has come, she does not want to think about Mrs Baker. She, at last, had confessed that she was indeed the person who had murdered her husband and had bribed the ones that had stood in the way of a new life she had planned with Mr Canelli. She even brainwashed her own sons into believing their father had committed suicide. The reason why the eldest son, Jon jr., had come after her and had made his threats out of some contorted conviction that a stranger was besmirching his father's legacy.

Kate recognises she had been too young to realise the true nature of Mrs Baker. That true nature that had so distressingly come to the surface. Her husband of the last twenty-one years might have suspected something but still, he chose the money and a new life with Mrs Baker instead of duly investigating the case. Mrs Baker and her son are now to look forward to an extended stay in prison. Jon jr. perhaps would be released sooner, but the fact remains that his threatening her and Anna-May could very well have ended in his murdering them.

What Kate is planning now is a party at their house when David returns. A party for their family and friends, a belated wedding reception, for their relations here. Kate resolves to go and shop for that festivity as soon as she finishes here at her gynaecologist. She looks up when a door opens and her doctor addresses her. Kate stands up and enters the office.

With a mug of tea in one hand and a sandwich in the other Kate enters her workspace at the back of the restaurant. She's been feeling restless ever since she woke in the morning, and the feeling doesn't seem to have the intention of subsiding. Instead, it has become more intense with the passage of time.

Marianna has been busy helping out behind the counter and is now standing in the doorway, attempting to draw her boss's attention.

'Oh, Marianna,' Kate says as she notices the young woman, 'I need you to take over from me this afternoon.'

'Okay. When will you be back?' Marianna asks.

Kate looks up at her. 'Oh, I won't be back today, Marianna. Nor will I be here this weekend. My husband is coming home today, you see.'

Kate observes Marianna's face changing from a hopeful expression to one of disappointment. 'Something wrong?' Kate inquires.

'Well,' she begins. 'I actually wanted to ask if I could leave a bit earlier. I know we're busy but, I wanted to go to the Nineteen Day Feast and – '

'The what?'

'The Nineteen Day Feast. I also had to miss out on the last one … '

'Well, won't there be another feast? Marianna, he is my husband. I need to collect him from the airport.'

'Mrs Jennings … uh Nelson, I understand, but … it's not like a *feast* in that sense. It's more like, well, like other people would go to their church services.'

Kate looks at Marianna with an inquisitive eye and yields. 'OK. I can't keep you from practising your faith.'

Kate is briefly in two minds. 'OK, then, Lynn will have to lock up,' she says. 'Lock up and see to it all's clean and tidy.'

Marianna is pleased by her boss's lenience. 'Thank you, ma'am,' she expresses and wants to leave the office.

'Marianna? What religion is that, you're part of?' Kate questions.

'Bahaí Faith, ma'am. I'm a Bahaí.'

Kate nods with sympathetic perception. 'Really? I've heard of that. Well, you enjoy your feast, and I'll see you after the weekend.'

Kate's nervous anxiety keeps her from staying focused on her job. She wishes the time was there for her to go to the airport where David's plane will be arriving this afternoon, but she realises it would be senseless to go there now and sit in the airport, wasting time. She forces herself to concentrate and finish that what she can still accomplish before she needs to leave. Among busy noises in the background of clattering utensils in the kitchen, incoherent voices of customers, opening and closing doors, Kate is able to finish some of the work she intended to do and breathes a sigh of relief when a glance at the clock tells her to log out and leave for the airport. This time the airport will be a welcoming one. She tidies her hair and straightens her top. She grabs her jacket and bag on exiting the office.

'Enjoy your weekend, all of you,' she cheerfully says before leaving. She enters into the January chilliness outside and walks towards her car. She feels a sense of liberation when she puts the key in the ignition before driving her car onto Elvis Presley Boulevard and driving to the airport. A push on the button of the CD player and music accompanies her there. The clock on the dashboard tells her she could be in David's arms again within the next forty-five minutes. She's certain he will be happy with the surprise she has in store for him. It has taken her quite an effort to keep it to herself this past week.

Kate parks her car in the short-stay lot and hastens to the arrival hall. She checks the monitors for the arrivals and sees David's plane is to arrive in the next twenty minutes. She walks through the airport and remains in the area where David will be arriving, to wait between neatly dressed people holding up signs with names of specific passengers. Others, more indistinctively dressed, waiting for relatives and friends. Kate astounds herself for her nervousness when the first passengers start emerging through the sliding door. She moves closer to the dividing gate to watch heavily laden trolleys being pushed forth by exiting passengers and others only holding a carry on.

Kate's eyes light up when the doors slide open, and her man is manifested, casually inspecting the surroundings, wearing jeans and a shirt, his hair tied at the back, his eyes covered by sunglasses. She utters his name as he lays eyes on her. In one step David is in front of her and slides his arms around her waist. She feels his strong embrace as she hides her face against his shoulder, her arms tight around his neck. 'Hey, hon',' he whispers close to her ear before taking her face in his hands to kiss her through the tears, their salty wetness doesn't bother him and for minutes they kiss passionately. Other passengers turn their heads at the sight, one even whistles through his teeth. 'Go for it, man.'

'Sorry, I'm such a cry baby,' Kate apologises, but this time she knows what is causing it.

David smiles at her. 'You *are* a cry baby,' he says. 'And I love you for it.' He gives her another kiss then grabs his trolley. 'Let's go home.'

Kate threads her arm around David's as they leave the arrival hall to walk towards Kate's car.

'David,' Kate says. 'David, I need to tell you something ... '

David looks at her. 'And I need to tell you something,' he says. Kate reacts surprised. 'What is it?'

'I hope you're OK with it, but I think we should have Sam live with us ... No wait,' he says when Kate wants to say something. 'I hope you're willing to adopt him. He'll be much better off with us than with his mother. What do you say?'

'I'd say ... I'd say, we will have quite a busy household then.'

'Oh, that shouldn't be a problem. We can hire someone,' David says.

Kate stops in front of David and looks into his eyes. 'David ... David, I'm pregnant.' Kate's eyes are lit with pleasure but David's show disbelief, until adopting a twinkle. 'Kate,' he softly says, shaking his head. 'Already?'

Kate nods. 'Aren't you happy?'

''Course I am!' he calls out, grabs her around her waist and lifts her off the ground. Kate lets out a surprised scream. 'Woman, you're getting heavier already,' David jokes and puts Kate down again. 'Kate, I am happy ... for us!' David exclaims. 'My. And baby makes four.'

'Well. Actually. In that case, it will be five.'

David gives her an even more incredulous look.

'Five? Kate. Twins?!'

Kate nods and kisses him. 'Twins,' she says.

'No Dan, not like that,' Daisy-Lou tells her brother. 'What?' Danny looks disgruntled as he attaches a colourful garland on the wall in the hall.

'Daisy-Lou's right, Danny,' Anna-May says. 'It looks tacky. Take it down.'

Reluctantly, Danny rips the paper chain off the wall.

'Careful there, young man,' Jacob observes as he comes walking down the stairs. 'The place has just been repainted.'

Danny looks up at him but refrains from commenting.

'You've done well,' Jacob praises his cousins. 'It looks marvellous! All ready for the party.'

'Thanks, Jake,' Anna-May says. They have been busy decorating the house that some weeks before had been the stage of a terrifying happening. No trace of that remains. After the police had finished their investigation, the bullet holes were concealed and the kitchen and hall were newly painted. The overpowering and appetising smells coming from the kitchen, cover up the weak smell of paint that lingers.

Jacob walks into the kitchen where clattering sounds of spoons in bowls come his way. Emmy and Valerie are busy baking and cooking. Maria is with them, preparing a large dish. Danny ambles into the kitchen and finds a large bowl with remnants of dough. He sits down at the kitchen table and starts scraping it clean with a spoon. 'Mind, you don't get sick, Danny,' Emmy says. 'Better have the pie when it's done.'

'I'll have that too,' is the teenager's reply and he licks

the spoon. With the women occupying the kitchen, Jacob goes to the lounge room where a warm fire crackles in Jake senior's fireplace. When Jacob lit the fire in the morning his thoughts had taken him back to their happy childhood in this region and, for a moment, he had seen his father's face in his mind's eye.

Currently, a younger generation is walking in and drops down on the couch by the fire. Daisy-Lou and Anna-May sit down on either side of little Sam, who has his eyes transfixed on the television screen where footage of his daddy's Australian tour is transmitted via DVD. Jacob joins them and takes a seat in one of the lazy chairs.

'Your daddy, Sam,' Daisy-Lou smiles, which leaves a broad grin on the boy's face as he sits snuggled between the two young women.

In the kitchen, Emmy inspects a tray with another pie before placing it in the oven. 'That's the last one, Val,' she says with a heated face.

Valerie draws Emmy's attention as she looks through the kitchen window and sees Kate and David leave the stables with their horses to go for a ride on this bright day, now when it is still allowed for Kate to ride her horse. David has a hand around Kate's shoulder, holding the rein of his horse with the other. He helps her in her saddle before he swings his legs over his own horse.

Laughter rings through from outside as Kate and David ride off and onward through the fields. On the rim of the knoll, they stop for a moment and overlook the scenery, to then  resume their ride.

If you enjoyed reading this book, then a review would be greatly appreciated, as it will help others to discover the story. Thank you!

You can join the Readers List here and get your free Ebook: https://cmuntjewerf.com

Printed in Great Britain
by Amazon

26282967R00146